Readers love
TARA LAIN

Hidden Powers

"Bravo, Tara, for a brave move to a new literary challenge. I can't wait to read what the boys get up to in the next book."

—Rainbow Book Reviews

"Take a deep breath, hold your Kindle tight and dive into this brilliant adventure. The best Tara Lain book I've read!"

—Bayou Book Junkie

The Case of the Voracious Vintner

"This book has everything – good writing, a strong story, engaging characters and some beautiful world building."

—Love Bytes

"This author knows how to write stories. With the precise amount of ingredients, temperature, and equipment she creates a delightful appealing read with just enough heat."

—Diverse Reader

Trex or Treat

"*Trex or Treat* is short, it's heartwarming, it's sexy, and I totally enjoyed it. Happy Halloween!"

—The Novel Approach

"This is a really hot, super fun story with an entirely satisfying conclusion. It is the best kind of fiction, reading purely for feel-good enjoyment."

—Mainely Stories

Published by DREAMSPINNER PRESS
www.dreamspinnerpress.com

Home IMPROVEMENT

TARA LAIN

DREAMSPINNER
PRESS

Published by

DREAMSPINNER PRESS

5032 Capital Circle SW, Suite 2, PMB# 279, Tallahassee, FL 32305-7886 USA
www.dreamspinnerpress.com

Home Improvement – A Love Story
© 2019 Tara Lain

Cover Art
© 2019 Reese Dante
http://www.reesedante.com
Cover content is for illustrative purposes only and any person depicted on the cover is a model.

Trade Paperback ISBN: 978-1-64405-542-7
Digital ISBN: 978-1-64405-541-0
Library of Congress Control Number: 2019933803
Trade Paperback published July 2019
v. 1.0

Printed in the United States of America
∞
This paper meets the requirements of
ANSI/NISO Z39.48-1992 (Permanence of Paper).

To Hal Isen, who showed us the wonders of Ashland, and Mark Dewey, who guided us through the most agonizing real-estate mess ever to find us a perfect house in a perfect town.

AUTHOR'S NOTE

THE HOUSE that plays such a central role in this book is a real place! My hubby and I almost bought it, but we couldn't justify the expense of all the renovations. As you'll see, this house needs to be owned by someone who can afford to turn it into their own love story—and we hope such a person arrives.

CHAPTER ONE

"UH, GABE, there's a lost-looking customer on aisle sixteen."

Gabe Mason glanced away from the pile of bathroom fixtures he was restocking toward Harry Johnson, a name that gave all the guys no end of chuckles. "Does he need something unusual?" Harry might not know as much about the inventory as Gabe, but he was perfectly capable of helping most customers.

Harry grimaced and shrugged his big shoulders. "I think I scared him. When I asked if I could help, he practically melted into the drawer of cabinet handles he was searching. I was afraid he might run." He shifted uneasily. Harry was such a massive guy, he could be intimidating.

Gabe nodded and waved at the stack of boxes. "You want to take this over, and I'll go check on the lost lamb?"

"Yeah, thanks."

"Aisle sixteen?"

"That's where I left him." He was already stacking. Harry definitely didn't want to deal with this customer.

Gabe walked toward sixteen. Hattie and Mary waved from the checkout stands. Mary always gave him an extra smile. She knew, as all the personnel in the store did, that "Gabe didn't exactly go for women," but she didn't really believe it. Good old regular-guy Gabe—single father of a teenage girl, most knowledgeable employee on everything having to do with hardware, lumber, and home improvement—gay? Hell no. Gay guys wore chartreuse and kept cats, right? They didn't build furniture and repair cars. He smiled tightly. As long as he didn't give them any reason to doubt his man's man image, they accepted him and, more importantly, accepted Ellie, his daughter.

Rounding the corner on the hardware aisle, he spotted a couple of customers looking like they needed help. One was a woman with two little kids tugging on her and each other, and the second was an older man in a red cap who stared at Gabe like he'd been waiting for him for two hours. With a frown, the man said, "Can you help me?"

A quick glance up the aisle revealed no lost shoppers, if you didn't count the woman, who might be looking for a cage to house her children in. She glared at the man. "I was here first."

"You left." The old man scowled.

"I chased my son, that's all. I've been waiting longer."

Gabe stepped forward. "No worries. I'll help you both. What do you need, ma'am?"

She flashed a victorious smile at the old man. "I need some screws."

Gabe glanced at the entire wall of screws behind her.

The older man stepped forward pugnaciously. "I do too."

Gabe nodded. "Excellent. What are you screwing?" He kind of wanted to say *apart from each other*, but didn't.

"Wood." They answered at the same time, then looked at each other as if the other person had stolen something from them.

"That's really good. We can look at the same options. Now, will the wood you're screwing be used indoors or outdoors?"

The woman looked at the man suspiciously. "Indoors."

The man said, "On my deck."

"Okay, here you go." Gabe waved at an array of screws. "These are all production screws. This batch"—he pointed—"is specifically deck screws." He smiled at the man, then turned to the woman. "And these are for indoor applications."

As they both pounced on their screws, Gabe looked up for his fastest escape route and caught a glimpse of a tall, thin man in a beanie peeking around the end of the aisle toward him. *Now that looks like lost lamb material.*

He glanced at the screwers. "Got what you need?"

The man held up a screw. "Is this the right size?"

"Are you screwing two-bys or plywood?"

"Redwood two-by-fours."

Gabe held up a screw. "Here ya go." He smiled again. "If you'll excuse me, there's someone trying to track me down." He started walking down the aisle, and the head of the person who'd been staring at him disappeared.

Gabe slowed his steps and tried to look as harmless as possible. While Gabe was a good-sized man, he was a shrimp next to Harry, so maybe the customer would be willing to talk to him. If not, screw it. He had plenty to keep him busy.

When he got to the end of the aisle, he looked casually to his left. Tight against a display of light fixtures, back turned to Gabe, stood the guy in the beanie. He had long legs in baggy jeans, an equally baggy sweatshirt that still stretched across really wide shoulders, all his hair covered by the cap, and still the total strangeness didn't obscure the view of one world-class ass inside the jeans.

Gabe cleared his throat but didn't get too close. "Can I help you find something, sir?"

"Wha—" He half turned, and Gabe saw he'd put on sunglasses after he'd withdrawn from peering around the corner.

"Can I help you, sir?" Gabe thought he should probably walk away, but the guy had become kind of a challenge.

The customer reached into his jeans pocket and pulled out a drawer handle. He muttered, "Need handles this size."

Gabe took it. "All right, sir. If you'll come with me, we have the drawer pulls at the end of aisle sixteen."

The guy nodded and turned but never raised his head enough to look Gabe in the eye. Still, his high cheekbones and full lips made his face striking, even when it was pointed at his shoes.

Gabe started walking, trusting from the soft scuffling of sneakers behind him that the man was following. Those footsteps slowed when they passed the woman with the kids as she gathered the last of her screws, but he sped up again after she dragged the children toward the checkout registers. In front of the rows of drawers containing handles and knobs, Gabe pointed to the samples attached to the front of each drawer. "See any you like?"

The guy's head barely moved, so through the glasses, Gabe couldn't see if he even looked. He shrugged.

"Do you like modern? Traditional?"

"Modern."

"Brushed nickel, maybe? Or are you a chrome guy?"

The slim nose wrinkled.

"So no chrome. Nickel, then." Gabe walked to the drawers and held out the sample the guy had given him to check for size and spacing center to center. He picked a couple of modern pulls he liked and took them from the drawers, then held them out to the man.

He looked at the pulls intently, cocked his head, and then ripped off the glasses somewhat impatiently, as if someone had made him wear them.

Gabe sucked in a soft breath. The guy's eyes were two different colors, one a deep blue and the other light green. Startling and very distinctive. Maybe it affected his eyesight or sensitivity to light and that's why he was wearing sunglasses in ImproveMart?

The guy reached out a long-fingered hand and tapped the handle that was Gabe's favorite—a simple wide U-shape of brushed nickel. Gabe nodded. "Yeah, that's a good one. How many do you need?"

"Uh, eight." His voice was soft to the point of nonexistence.

Gabe pulled the drawer out farther and began counting out the plastic packages that contained the handle and necessary screws, piling them on the shelf beside him. "Need anything else?"

The guy had put his glasses back on by the time Gabe turned to him. *Darn. Those eyes are something.* The man nodded his head and pointed to some simple, ball-shaped drawer pulls. "Ten."

"Oh, I hope I have enough." Gabe pulled open the drawer and started counting.

The dude stepped closer to watch the counting, which turned out to be a bad idea for Gabe's autonomic responses. *What is that smell?* Like some mix of orange and spice. Whatever it was, Gabe's lower regions came out for a sniff. He shifted his feet and pressed his elbows against his work vest to be sure it covered his crotch. *Down boy.*

He forced a smile as he scraped the last package from the drawer. "There you go. We just made ten." Gabe looked around. The guy had no cart. Not even a carry basket. What exactly was he planning on hauling stuff in?

The man seemed to realize it at the same time as Gabe. He grabbed his lip between his teeth, looked down, took hold of the hem of his giant sweatshirt, and held the bottom out like a bag.

Gabe chuckled. "Excellent save." The problem with the dude's invention was it raised the shirt from his narrow hips—and what might, just might, have been a half-mast condition thrusting out the front of his jeans. *Don't need to know that—if it's true.* Hell, just what he needed. To get turned on by weird customers.

Stalwartly, taking pretty shallow breaths, Gabe piled the handles and knobs into the guy's shirt, smiled, and gave him a short wave. "Glad you got what you needed. Have a great day."

Walking away as fast as he could without looking conspicuous, he headed for the lumber department, which was as far as he could get from where that disturbing dude was likely to show up. It wasn't officially Gabe's assignment, but since he'd commandeered Harry to do his stocking, he could go anywhere he might be useful, and not that many of the store personnel knew lumber as well as Gabe.

He ran his hand over some of the boards. He loved wood. No matter how cold it got, wood was slightly warm to the touch—kind of like skin. Not that he'd know much about that.

Gabe waited on customers and cut two-bys for an hour—*the guy had to be gone, right?*—then walked back to hardware.

Harry was checking something on the computer. "What happened? Did you have to chase that customer all over the store to get him to say what he wanted?"

"Ha. Ha." He gave Harry a toothy smile. "Thanks a bunch. Actually, I finally got out of him that he was looking for cabinet handles and pulls. He wanted a lot of them, but he hadn't brought a basket or cart. Anyway, after I got done with him, I figured I'd check on lumber since I heard they were down a man today."

"Oh yeah. And thanks for helping that customer. He kind of freaked me out."

"Yeah. Me too." *But likely not for the same reasons.*

Harry glanced around. "Not too busy. Call if you need me. I've got some work in the stock room." He started walking, then looked back. "Some of the guys are going for a beer after work. Wanna come?"

"Not tonight. Ellie's cooking. But thanks for asking. Rain check."

Harry nodded. He was a great guy and always made a point of inviting Gabe to join him for whatever he and his friends were doing. Gabe liked them all, but sometimes being with them made him feel more alone.

Harry probably wouldn't be so happy to hear that his weirdass customer gave me a boner.

Gabe sighed and went back to work.

"Honey, this is amazing." Gabe took another bite of the pot roast his sixteen-year-old kid had managed to conjure for their dinner. She often cooked when she didn't have an evening shift at her fast-food job, but tonight she'd even set his handmade table with their best dishes. Of course "best" in their house meant most of the dollar-store plates matched. "You sure you want to become such a good cook?"

She snorted. "Why, because it'll be hard to stay unmarried?" She wrinkled her cute, short nose. She'd gotten mostly Tiffany's features, with the fairer hair, brown eyes, and softly rounded face. That was good since Gabe looked all Mount Rushmore, with a sharp nose, prominent cheekbones, and a cleft in his chin. Not even a little girlie.

He sat back and patted his stomach. "Exactly. Some guy's gonna go, 'She can cook too?' and try to slip a ring on your finger while you sleep."

"Yeah. No. I'm learning to cook so I can feed myself in my perpetual single state." She took her last bite. "Just don't tell Mom that."

"I promise." He smiled at her. "But I also promise that getting married someday doesn't mean you're going to end up with the wrong guy like your mom did."

She wrinkled her nose at him. "You mean like my mom did twice? Going on three times?"

"Admittedly, she didn't do a whizbang job of choosing the second time, but the first time was on me." He gave her arm a pat, then grabbed the plates and started toward the kitchen sink.

"Oh come on, you were sixteen. Not exactly the age of enlightenment."

"Yeah." He sighed. "But I knew better." Then he grinned. "I must have known that if I kidded myself for a while, I'd get you, and trust me, honey, that was worth anything."

She kissed his cheek as she put their utensils in the sink for him to wash later. "I didn't want to get so domestic I made dessert, so want an ice cream sandwich?"

"Perfect." He returned to the table, and she followed with two paper-wrapped ice creams.

"Don't tell Mom about this either." She unwrapped an end and took a bite.

"Why?" He tried to control the frown on his face.

She shrugged.

"Is your mom on you about weight again?"

"Yeah. It's her constant refrain right after her sudden onset of Christianity."

"You're not too heavy, Ellie. And you're way more Christian in the human-kindness sense than most people I've met." She made a face, and he leaned forward and waved his ice cream. "I'm totally serious. I don't want you thinking that you need to lose weight. You have to take your mom with a grain of salt on this subject."

"You mean because she freaks over every pound she gains?"

"Yes. You can never be thin enough for your mom, so don't try. You look wonderful."

"You're biased."

"Nope. You've got to trust me on this subject." He grinned.

"Because you're a gay guy, and everyone knows gay men are experts on beauty and style, right?"

"Damn straight. Uh, damn right. There's got to be some good coming from all those stereotypes." He gave her a sidelong look as he chomped his last mouthful of ice cream.

"Um-hm. I totally trust you, your nail gun, and your flannel shirts on the subject of style." They both laughed. She returned that side-eyed look. "And on the subject of keeping an open mind with regard to men, how about you do the same?"

Uh-oh. Sore subject. "I'll focus on the same sex later. Right now I've got other priorities."

"Other priorities like me." She rocked back in her chair, crumpled the paper her ice cream had been in, and tossed it on the table. "Come on, Dad, it's a year and a half until I'm out of here and off to college. Good grief, your gonads will dry up and blow away by that time."

He tried to stifle his laugh and failed. Then he sobered. "All I care about is you, baby." It was true, though sometimes it was hard not to wish for maybe one more person in his life.

She picked up the crumpled paper and dropped it. "You're just worried she's going to try to get primary custody." The crease between her eyebrows stood out on her pretty face like a crater.

"There's no discrimination in Oregon against gay parents. You know that. There's nothing to worry about." He clasped her arm.

"That won't stop Irving, the family-first fanatic, from trying to get custody if he marries Mom." Her frown got even deeper. "Jeez, he's a freak."

"Should I talk to Mom? Is there anything about him we should know?"

She expelled a long breath. "Not really. He's just a religious pill, and I don't know why Mom's so gone on him. I think she feels like she needs to be saved, you know?" She entwined her fingers with his. "Come on, she's been married and divorced and reengaged, and you've barely had a date. I just want to see you happy."

"You make me happy, Ellie." She did. God, he loved her.

"Hell, if it weren't for me, you could have hot hookups every night and find a boyfriend."

He snorted. "A, consider the source." He waved a hand over his opposite of hotness. "B, I don't want hookups every night." Though he wouldn't mind one occasionally.

She plopped a hand on her hip like someone's mother. "If it wasn't for me, you'd focus on your furniture business instead of handing out screws at ImproveMart."

"I like ImproveMart, the world isn't ready for handmade furniture, and I'm focused on more important things." He leaned forward and stared across the table at her.

"Okay, what? What's so important?"

"The identity of the concert you've chosen for your birthday."

She made a face. "Slick way to change the topic there, Dad. But yeah, I did pick one." She gave him that sideways look again. "I'll have to go online the second the tickets go on sale because they'll sell out instantly, and they'll probably be kind of pricy."

"Money's no object. I'm willing to spend up to twenty dollars for those tickets." He tried to keep a straight face.

"Dad!" She smacked his arm. "Worst of all, we have to drive to Eugene to see it. Is that okay?"

"Not a problem. I told you to pick. Maybe we'll stay overnight, but it's only a two-and-a-half-hour drive, so we'll play it by ear."

"Actually, this guy is a big star, but he's doing this special concert at the university since he went there or his father did or something. Anyway, it's a huge deal. He usually only performs in places like New York or Vegas."

"Okay, I'll be properly impressed. Got any friends you want to take?"

"I thought about asking MaryAnn. But really, I'd just as soon go with you."

"You sure? I'm not going to squeal with you and do posts on Instagram."

"That's okay. I'll do enough for both of us." She flashed her dimples.

He laughed as he walked to the sink to wash the dishes.

Ellie said, "I'm starting my homework. Are you going to work on the coffee table tonight?" She pointed toward his workshop in the garage.

He tried not to look too discouraged. "Maybe. I don't think Mrs. McRae's going to buy it, honey. So no rush."

"But it's so beautiful."

"Yeah, but like I told you, it's hard to charge enough for all the work that goes into handmade furniture. If I sell it at a loss, she may buy it."

"Nuts to that. Keep it for a customer who appreciates your genius."

"I'll tell them you said so." He started scraping and rinsing. Ellie really wanted his business to succeed, but the fact was he needed to be someplace like southern California or New York to sell his kind of furniture, and he needed to stay in Oregon. Partly because his ex, Tiffany, had joint custody, and partly because it was a great place to raise a kid. But from Oregon, it was hard to find buyers, and shipping cost a lot.

Most daughters would have accepted Gabe's building his life around them as their due. Ellie seemed to feel guilty.

From behind him, he heard the music from the old upright piano they'd managed to squeeze into the small living room so Ellie could practice. She loved music in all its forms. She played in the high school orchestra and seemed to be pointing toward music as a possible major.

Gabe rinsed plates in time to the practice piece she was sifting through.

"Dad?"

"Hmm?"

"Just keep an open mind on finding the right guy, okay?"

He chuckled and nodded.

At least he didn't lie out loud.

CHAPTER TWO

GABE SHOVED his empty food containers back into the thermal bag, gathered his trash, and carried it to the can. He waved at Mary, Hattie, and the other people he'd been eating with as they also gathered their stuff. "Back to work."

As he strode into the department, Harry came rushing toward him, wide-eyed.

Gabe cocked his head. "What's up?"

"He's back."

"What?"

"The weirdo who was here yesterday."

Well hell.

Harry grinned. "And he's asking for you, my man. By name."

"You're not serious?"

"As a heart attack. 'Gabe, please,' he says, never looking me in the eye. That's what you get for being so charming and customer-service oriented." He slapped his own leg.

If Gabe's heart slammed hard against his ribs, it didn't have to be clear why, right? Gabe sighed loudly. "Okay, where is he?"

"Aisle eleven."

"But that's lighting."

"Yep."

"Did you tell him I don't do lighting?"

"Nope, didn't mention that. After all, didn't you teach us that the customer is always right?" Oh yes, Harry was having a good old time.

"I said *almost*. Almost always right. Lanaya can help him better in lighting than I can."

"Don't think he cares, buddy."

He had to force his lips not to turn up, which was plain stupid, but all he could think about was the mismatched eyes and that smell. Orange and cinnamon. He'd wakened in the middle of the night because his head was full of those scents. He heaved his shoulders. "Okay, I'll go see him.

Thanks, Harry. For nothing." He gave Harry a mock glower and took off at a jog toward the unfamiliar turf of the lighting department.

When he turned the corner and looked down aisle eleven, he saw the tall, lean figure who'd invaded his dreams. New beanie. Same sunglasses. As Gabe drew closer, he could see that the guy's clothes, a sweatshirt from Disneyland and black jeans, fit a little better, which for Gabe was a little worse.

He plastered on his most professional customer-service face. "Hello again. How can I help you?"

The guy swung toward him, though he didn't raise his sunglass-covered eyes to Gabe. "I need lights."

"Okay. Uh, for indoors, outdoors, walls, ceilings—"

"Yes." The guy's lips turned up, and something in Gabe's chest got warm.

"You need a lot of lights?" He had to smile back.

"Yes."

Gabe leaned against the shelves beside him and crossed his arms but tried to look casual rather than closed off. "It sounds like you might need a lighting plan."

The guy looked up, and Gabe so wanted to pull off the sunglasses and stare at those unusual eyes again. The guy said, "I do?"

"Uh, yes. I'll be honest, I'm not a lighting expert, but Lanaya, who runs this department, is and—"

The guy's eyebrows rose above the top of the glasses, and he took a step back.

Before the customer turned and ran and Lanaya lost what might be a big sale, Gabe said, "Tell you what. How about we sit down for a minute and you tell me what you need. The big picture. Then I might be more help." He pointed toward a small table and chairs at the end of the aisle. "Does that work?"

The guy glanced around but nodded.

Gabe walked to the table, and when he turned, the man was pulling out one of the chairs. Funny, Gabe thought of him as a man, but he was young. Probably in his twenties. Definitely a few years younger than Gabe's thirty-three. *Of course, on me thirty-three is the new fifty.*

Gabe sat and stuck out his hand. "I'm Gabe, by the way. I guess you know that."

The guy nodded and stared at Gabe's hand for a long second, then took it. "Je-uh, Jerry Castor."

"Pleased to meet you, Jerry." Oh man, that slim hand was warm and amazingly soft, but also strong. Gabe forced himself to let go. "So what kind of building are you lighting?"

"Kind?"

"House? Office?"

"House."

"Okay. So what rooms? Or is this outdoors?"

He chewed his lip.

"Jerry?"

"All of it."

"Oh." He leaned forward. "Are there already fixtures in place and you just want to replace bulbs, or do you want new fixtures, or—"

Jerry started to look panicked, but what the hell could he do?

"Are you wanting to add outlets?"

Jerry nodded.

"It sounds like maybe you need an electrician and a lighting designer."

Full-on panic. Jerry said, "Would—would you?"

"Would I? Oh, I'm not an electrician. I work with wood and not—"

Jerry nodded and pushed back his chair.

"Wait." *Okay, why did I say that?* He inhaled. "I could look at your plans and work out something with Lanaya."

"No plans." His brows—they were light brown—pulled together in distress.

Gabe released a sigh very quietly. "Jerry, how can I help you?"

He didn't expect an answer. He figured Jerry would get up and leave. Instead, he smiled tentatively. "Come to my house?"

Gabe opened his mouth—and closed it.

Jerry's smile faded.

"Yes." *What the hell am I saying?* "Uh, maybe I should ask where you live?" He grinned to try and make Jerry's smile come back.

"Ashland."

"Good. At least it's not Utah."

Jerry's eyebrows beetled down farther over his nose. "I'd never live in Utah."

"I'm kidding. I just mean Ashland's close. I'll have to come after my shift's over."

He nodded, looking a little less stressed. Interesting that he wasn't worried about having some strange guy show up at his house.

Gabe pulled out his phone. "Give me your address, and better include a phone number in case there's a problem."

Jerry recited a house number on South Mountain Avenue in Ashland, then peered at Gabe nervously. He cleared his throat and gave his phone number.

Gabe keyed it in. "Don't worry. I won't use it unless I have to make a change." He glanced up. "When shall I come?"

"Today?"

Jerry certainly didn't waste any time. "Okay. How about three thirty?"

For the first time in their weirdass, two-day acquaintance, Jerry smiled full-on and revealed one tooth slightly crossed over the other in the front.

The whole deal, the smile and that endearing flaw, made Gabe smile back. *What am I doing?* "I'll see you at three thirty unless somebody calls somebody."

Jerry pulled out his phone and looked at Gabe expectantly.

"Oh right, sorry." Gabe reeled off his phone number as Jerry typed it into his phone with flying thumbs. Then he turned and walked away.

Man, that is one strange dude. But that is one magnificent ass. Both facts were good reasons to not be going to Jerry's house, but he wasn't an easy guy to say no to.

Not that I tried very hard.

He reached for his phone to tell Ellie he'd be a little late getting home.

An hour and a half later, after checking his watch more times than he cared to admit, he grabbed his windbreaker from where he'd stashed it in the desk drawer.

Harry came down the aisle also wearing his jacket. "Hey, man, got time for a beer?"

He didn't really want to turn Harry down too many times. He might stop asking. But he wasn't totally crazy about admitting what he'd done. He gave Harry his best sheepish look. "I told that customer I'd come look at his lighting problems at his house."

"The strange guy?"

"Yeah." Gabe shrugged. "He couldn't seem to deal with the idea that he might need an electrician and a lighting designer. He asked me to come. I told him I'm no expert in lighting."

"Hell, man, what you're not good at is better than most of our specialties."

"Hey, thanks. But it seems like he might have a big project, and I can pass it on to Lanaya." He tried not to look embarrassed.

"You should have done it on company time, man. Or at least charge OT for it."

"I want to be sure there's something there first. Then maybe I can justify it."

Harry shook his head. "Jesus, no wonder management thinks you're so great."

"Yeah, right." Gabe glanced at his watch. "Better go. I told him three thirty, and he's in Ashland."

"Should have known."

Gabe chuckled and hurried toward the door. In semiconservative southern Oregon, Ashland stood out as a home to superprogressive liberals. *Fruits and nuts, baby. Fruits and nuts.* He never told Harry or any of the guys that he'd move there in a second if he could afford enough house for him and Ellie. Their three-bed, two-bath place with the big garage workshop had cost about half what the same property in Ashland would have. He'd rather have money left over for rock concerts and a decent teenager's wardrobe instead of opting for the more gay-friendly culture of Ashland—but a guy could wish.

Driving south on the 5 Freeway, he smiled as Ashland came into view, its houses built up the side of the mountain with trees bursting into full leaf and flower everywhere. It was a seriously pretty place.

He pulled off at exit nineteen, the main one for Ashland, since Mountain Avenue was about halfway through the town. As soon as he drove under the railroad bridge and caught sight of the sign that said Welcome to Ashland, the magic of the place took hold. He'd once heard the town described as Brigadoon. He'd looked it up and found out that was the name of a musical play about an enchanted village that only became visible to the outside world once every hundred years. He could get behind that idea.

Gabe passed Lithia Creek and the town square and then drove down Siskiyou Boulevard past the beautiful tree-lined campus of Southern Oregon University, a possible college for Ellie. He made a right on Mountain and started watching for street numbers as he climbed the hill. Clearly, he had a ways to go.

University buildings lined the road, and then they gave way to houses as he ascended. He turned right at a jog and drove higher. Still hadn't found the address. He was about ready to ask Siri for help as he reached a dead end and had to turn around. Then he saw the number written on a huge boulder beside the road. Between it and another big rock, a narrow lane climbed the hill to a house he could barely see through the trees. *Damn. That's it.*

He maneuvered a hard left into what must be the driveway, squeezed his truck between the rocks, and climbed the hill on a gravel path that made a circle around a huge tree at the top.

He parked on the drive and slid out of the truck. Ahead of him was the wall of a big house that might once have been the entrance to a garage but now had double french doors leading who knew where. It didn't appear to be the front door. Everything around him was in disrepair, with cracks in the stucco and moss growing on walls and walkways.

From the driveway, a flagstone walk led onto a lawn. He peered around the corner just as Jerry stepped out on one of several large wooden porches and waved. "Here."

Oddly, the walkway stopped, and there didn't seem to be a clear path to where Jerry was standing, so Gabe struck out across the grass, found another walkway leading down the side of the hill, and took it to the porch. "Hi. This isn't an easy place to find."

Jerry smiled. He'd taken off his glasses, but he still wore the beanie. "I'm glad you found it." His voice seemed to have dropped half an octave since earlier at the ImproveMart, and it shivered down Gabe's spine. "Please come in."

Even on the porch, it wasn't completely clear where a person was supposed to enter the house. There were doors on two different walls, but Gabe followed Jerry through the entrance on the back wall of the porch and stopped. "Whoa."

Spread out in front of him was a wide-open house with thick plaster walls, polished-wood ceilings, a huge two-story great room with floor-to-ceiling windows, and a hand-polished wooden staircase leading to a second floor. The whole thing was run-down and in need of repair, but what an amazing house.

Gabe shook his head. "This is fantastic. How did you ever find it?"

"I saw it online and called the real estate agent."

Gabe glanced at Jerry. Apparently in the comfort of his own home, the guy could actually put an entire sentence together. While you couldn't describe him as relaxed, he didn't appear to be ready to run. In fact he grinned. "Want to see the rest?"

"Sure." He could hardly wait, actually. The place was some marvelous mix of midcentury and craftsman styles with all the wood details Gabe loved.

Jerry walked to the great room first—and great it was. A huge fan in the shape of giant palm fronds was suspended from the center of the soaring ceiling. Gabe pointed. "Does it work?"

Jerry shook his head. "No. It needs fixing."

In the center of the room, in front of a giant fireplace that Gabe would bet also didn't work, sat two plastic camp chairs—all the furniture in the entire room.

Off the great room was a smaller paneled library. After Gabe looked into it, Jerry led him back across the big room and up the beautiful staircase to the second floor. A long hall illuminated by skylights stretched in front of them.

Jerry laughed, and it was a light, airy sound that bounced through Gabe's belly like a swig of champagne. "I think I must get a cat. Can't you see a cat chasing a toy down this hall?"

"How many bedrooms and baths?"

"Five of each. One bath downstairs. I'll show you when we go back down."

Each bedroom had some kind of damage—peeling drywall, water-soaked woodwork, and stained carpet. The bathrooms were a particular mess with old, rust-stained fixtures.

Finally, they got to the end of the hall and stepped into what had to be the master—a huge room with floor-to-ceiling windows on two walls. Gabe drew a breath. "This is gorgeous. The light's magical."

"Yes. It's one of my favorite rooms."

Gabe glanced at the mattress lying on the floor covered in mussed sheets directly under a skylight. Must be quite a view. He swallowed hard.

The tour went back downstairs, and Gabe saw the wreck of a kitchen. "Does the cooktop even work?"

"No."

Several pizza boxes lay on the large central island.

Finally, they walked out the dining room french doors to a huge backyard. "How big is the property?"

"Two and a half acres."

"Wow." The centerpiece of the back was an enormous pool, not quite Olympic standard, but it would have served a good-sized community. "At least it's full of water. It must not be in too bad repair."

"No, it's pretty good, but the filter equipment is total trash. It leaks like the West Wing."

Gabe snorted. Who dreamed Jerry had a sense of humor?

Jerry turned in a circle, like he was seeing the mansion for the first time. "It'd been on the market for years and people were scared off by all the work."

Gabe stared at him. Giving the tour, Jerry had put together the most words he'd spoken end to end since Gabe met him. "And you're not scared of the work?"

Jerry shook his head and grinned like a loon. Clearly, this was his baby. "No, I'm not worried." His smile lit up his face, making his unusual eyes shine. "Not since I met you."

CHAPTER THREE

"Uh, me?" Gabe's voice came out squeaky. He cleared his throat. "What does meeting me have to do with anything?"

Jerry smiled. "I heard your friend, the big man, telling someone that you're the best person in the whole store. That you know about everything and can do everything." He waved a hand around the big space. "Obviously, that's what I need."

What the hell? "Uh, Jerry, what you need is an architect and an interior decorator." He pointed toward the pool. "And a landscape architect and pool guy too."

"Okay. Good. I'll write that down." He walked into the house, and Gabe followed him to a polished-wood, built-in counter where Jerry grabbed a notebook and pencil, then jotted something in it. "So who shall we get?"

"We?"

"Um-hum. Who's your favorite architect, for example?"

This is crazy. Gabe walked over to the counter where Jerry stood. "I'm just an employee at ImproveMart. I don't have any special expertise in architecture. Or landscaping, or interiors, or much of anything else you need. If you have a call for some more cabinet handles or other miscellaneous hardware, come and see me."

Jerry grabbed Gabe's forearm with a surprisingly strong grip. "No, please. I need help. I trust your judgment. I'm—I'm not good with people."

He also had a talent for understatement. "I have a job."

Jerry released him, but his expression pleaded. "I'll pay you more."

Gabe wiped a hand over the back of his neck. "I appreciate the offer, but I have some tenure at my job. It's not flashy, but it's steady, and that's what I need. I have a family."

"Oh." He gazed at Gabe with his two-colored eyes glittering. "Of course you do." He looked down at his notebook. "But you can see that this job will go on for a long time."

"Still...." He didn't say, *I don't know you from Adam and why should I go to work for a guy with two camp chairs and a mattress?*

"Would you be open to working for me part-time? You could hire the people we need and then keep working for ImproveMart if you want to. I'll pay you anything you ask." He smiled shyly. "And you can buy all the materials from ImproveMart."

"Once you have an architect and designer, they'll have ideas as to where you should source your materials."

"But you'll make the decisions." He said it with total certainty.

Gabe's brain was going to explode. "Jerry, this house is going to cost a bundle, no matter where you get the materials. Maybe you should work out a phased plan so you don't get in over your head, you know?"

Jerry frowned and stared at his notebook seriously. "Oh. Should I? I was thinking I'd like to have the whole thing done in time for next Christmas."

Gabe counted on his fingers. "That's eight months. That would be really ambitious, to say nothing of expensive."

"But we can do it, right?" He smiled, and Gabe wanted to smile back, even if the dude was wacko. No, the wacko one was Gabe, because what he really wanted was to help Jerry. Obviously, if Jerry went around trusting people with no more evidence than a brief encounter in the hardware department, the man was going to end up in a heap of trouble. Gabe felt responsible. Maybe he could find him a couple of budget consultants to help.

"I'll tell you what. I'll ask around some and see if I can find an architect and maybe a landscape guy, because I noticed some trees that probably need to be removed from your property. First I'll talk with my, uh, family, because if I take another job, it cuts in on my time with her."

"Oh, of course. I understand." He stared at his hands and chewed his lip.

"But I'm sure we can use a little extra money since we've got some big expenses coming up."

Jerry's smile gleamed like someone turned on a lamp inside him. "Oh, I'd love to help out with the expenses."

"I'll see what she says."

"Yes, of course." He gazed at Gabe through his surprisingly long, dark lashes.

"I'll call you." Gabe walked out the same door he'd come in, even though he had to make his way around the house to get to the driveway. *If I find a landscape guy, I'll have to do something about this entrance. Maybe a torii gate to let visitors know how to walk to the front door?*

His steps paused. *What the hell am I thinking? Jerry probably can't even afford a gravel path.*

JERRY CASTOR stared at the broad back and long legs of the man he'd mysteriously put in charge of his house. *What the hell am I doing?*

Gabe's tall form disappeared around the corner of the wacko front yard that had no consistent path to the front door. It was like the people who built the house hadn't wanted anyone to find them.

Works for me.

He stepped back and closed the front door, then just stood there. *The silence. Oh man.* It was as thick as water, and he wanted to swim in it forever.

He turned and walked back to his kitchen, pulled a bottle of water from the fridge, and took a swig.

When he'd bought the house, admittedly on a wildass whim, insanity hadn't been his plan. *Call Margot and let her handle it. End of agenda.* But every time his hand reached for the phone, he yanked it back like he'd been burned. *No. No interference.* He wanted something for himself.

Then he'd turned around in that store and seen Gabe Mason.

His cell rang and he smiled. *Maybe Gabe has a question?* But his pocket wasn't vibrating.

The ring sounded again, and Jerry frowned, sighed, and opened the drawer on the far side of the island. He glanced at the screen and then clicked it on speaker. "Hi."

"What the fuck, Jer? Where the hell are you? Why hasn't anyone heard from you? Are you even checking your emails?"

He didn't say anything. Fred was a one-man conversation.

"When you said you were going on a personal retreat, we thought you meant to the ashram or the monastery. We didn't expect you to vanish from the face of the earth."

"How do you know I vanished?"

Silence.

"It's not exactly a retreat if you're spying outside the gate or the wall, now is it?"

Fred rallied. "Nobody went inside the gate or wall, now did they?"

"Uh, brother dear, how would they know I'm not there if they didn't? You don't need to know where I am every minute. Just leave me alone."

"I do need to know. Come on, Jerry, a lot of people are counting on you. You can't just walk away from your responsibilities. Just tell me an address and I'm there."

An image of Gabe flashed in Jerry's mind. "Sorry." He hung up, and when the phone rang again a minute later, he didn't answer.

GABE GLANCED at Ellie, who was bent over her laptop doing homework at the dining room table. He had his own laptop balanced on his knees while he researched architects and design-build firms in the area.

"What'cha doing?" She didn't even look up. Women had eyes in places men never got them—like the tops of their heads.

"Uh, actually this unusual thing happened today."

That got her attention. "Tell me."

"This customer came in yesterday, and Harry got me because the guy was so shy he could barely tell Harry what he wanted."

"But of course he talked to you." She smiled.

"Uh, yeah." He cocked his head at her.

"Because you're really easy to talk to. You know that, right?"

"I never quite thought of it like that, but anyway I helped the dude, and he went away. But then he came back today, and he started talking about all this work that needed doing at his house. Then he asked me to come and see it. I'm thinking maybe there's a big sale in it for ImproveMart, so I went to his place in Ashland."

"Ooh, did he try to lure you in to see his etchings or something?" She waggled her eyebrows. "You know those freethinkers from Ashland."

"Excuse me, what do you know about etchings?" He gave her a mock scowl. She'd had a few school dates, but so far no major boyfriend.

"Let's see, the birds etch the bees and then—"

"Okay, no further details required."

"So you went to his house...." She made a circular motion with her finger.

"Yeah, and it turns out to be this amazing place. A huge property with a giant swimming pool on two and a half acres."

"Wow."

"But in terrible condition. Really run-down, lots of delayed maintenance. And here's this quiet, shy guy living in this huge place with two camp chairs and a mattress on the floor."

"Oh my gosh. That's so sad. He must have spent all his money to rescue the house, and now he's all alone—"

"Yeah, that's what I think too, but he offered me a job. He says he's not good with people—I tried not to laugh because this guy makes Howard Hughes look like the life of the party—and wants me to take over finding people to work on his house. He says I can make all the decisions."

She raised one dark eyebrow. "No kidding? I mean, can he pay you to make all the decisions?"

"That's the question, isn't it? Anyway, I told him I already have a job."

Her dark eyes widened. "Really? You don't want to make all the decisions?"

"Well, when I refused, he asked if I'd work for him part-time."

"Oh."

"I was thinking, if he actually can pay, it might be a good way to earn extra money for college. I could try it, and if it's not worth it, I can easily quit without jeopardizing my real job."

"That's a lot of work, Dad. You won't get any rest."

"Well, mostly I'll get less time with you, but summer's coming, and if I'm still at it, I was thinking you could come with me and swim in his pool and stuff."

A grin spread across her face. Ellie loved to swim. "Hey, it sounds like this dude needs furniture in a big way, and I happen to know a guy who can make some for him."

He chuckled. "Let's make sure he can pay me minimum wage first." But he could sure picture his furniture in that amazing house. "So what do you think?"

"I think it sounds like a new challenge, and you need one. I'm all for it."

"How'd I get such a great kid?"

She made a snorting sound, but she smiled.

"And we don't have to care how much your concert tickets cost, right? Did you already order? Maybe you should get box seats or something."

"It's not the opera, Dad. I got really good seats."

"Three? Four?"

"Two. You and me."

"You sure?"

She nodded.

"So what days shall I book on my busy social schedule?"

"Two weeks from Friday."

"Ah, the actual birthday. Shall I book a hotel?"

"I think I'd rather be home to tell everybody about the concert on Saturday. If you don't mind driving."

"Don't mind at all." Neither of them said their budget didn't need a couple hundred dollars in hotel fees littering up the credit cards.

"So you're going to tell this guy—what's his name?"

"Uh, Jerry."

"You're going to tell Jerry you'll help him?"

"If you say I should."

She leaned back on the dining room chair. Their house might be basic, but their furniture was fantastic, thanks to a lot of hours in his workshop. "Go for it, Dad. It's not much of a risk."

He inhaled slowly. His reaction to Jerry might actually be a risk, but he was a grown-up. He didn't have to start rolling on the floor with a tongue-tied loner just because he had an amazing ass. "Okay, I'll do it."

"Who are you going to recommend?"

"Remember Jorge Alvarez who I worked for one summer?"

"He sold some of your furniture."

"Exactly." Ellie knew every person in the United States who liked his furniture.

"Yeah. He's reliable, has a good eye for design, and doesn't cost a lot."

"Sounds perfect. I'm looking forward to meeting Jerry. What's his last name?"

Gabe stopped scrolling through his contacts. "Huh. I actually don't know."

She laughed. "You sure you have a new client?"

"Nope. Not sure at all." He laughed with her, but he pulled out his phone, found Jerry's number, and texted, *Are you still interested in having me work for you?*

The little bubbles started bouncing instantly, showing an answer on its way. Jerry must have been staring at his phone. *Yes, for sure. I researched and found that $80 an hour is average for a construction supervisor, but you'll do more than that so how does $100 sound? Start right away.*

Gabe stared at the phone and forced his mouth to close.

"Dad? What?"

"Uh, Jerry wants me to start right away." *And he wants to pay a $20 an hour employee $100 an hour. Holy crap!*

"Oh, good." She went back to her homework.

Gabe madly typed, *Will start right away. That's too much money.*

We'll see. Start tomorrow?

Okay. BTW, what's your last name?

He waited several minutes, but he never got an answer.

"I REALLY appreciate you thinking of me. This is a fantastic project, and I'd love to do it." Smiling, Jorge Alvarez glanced at Gabe.

Gabe leaned against the side of the living room fireplace as Jorge walked around the huge space, trying light switches and the controls for the fan shaped like giant palm fronds. "You think you can respect the architecture without spending an arm and a leg?"

"For sure. It's all here. Our biggest problem will be electrical in these solid plaster walls. Installing wall-mount televisions will be really tough. We'll actually have to shim out the walls so we can run wires behind them. But it's all doable, and we'll work to keep costs down."

"I'll expect estimates on each phase of the project, and I want to be billed regularly so your expenses don't get ahead of the client's bookkeeping, deal?"

"Deal."

"So what would you do first?"

Jorge waggled a finger. "The kitchen, I think." He walked out of the great room into the open passageway that connected the dining room, family room, kitchen, and beyond. When they got to the open kitchen with its stack of empty takeout boxes, he said, "Seems like your client might need something besides pizza in his diet, so maybe we should redo this room first."

Gabe hopped up and sat on the edge of the island. "Am I right that this kitchen is kind of small for a house this size? By today's standards, I mean?"

Jorge nodded. "It's a nice kitchen, but yeah. In a modern house this size, the kitchen would be twice as big."

"How about making this one bigger?"

"What? How?" He looked around.

Gabe walked to the far wall of the really ugly kitchen, which was positioned almost exactly in the middle of the house. He tapped on the wall. "This wall isn't plaster."

Jorge knocked on it for himself. "So I see. What's on the other side?"

Gabe led him to the run-down laundry room that was separated from the kitchen by a pretty thin wall. "Ta-da!"

"So if we take over the laundry room for the kitchen, is there someplace to move laundry?"

"Yes. You'll have to extend the heating system beyond the mudroom door, but I think we want to do that anyway. There's a ton of room back there where we can put a laundry and other spaces as well."

Jorge grimaced. "Expensive proposition, heating all the rest of the enclosed space."

"But it'll extend the usability of the house a bunch. Get your heating and air-conditioning guy in here, and I'll show you the areas where we need to expand the ductwork."

"You'll probably need a new unit."

"Maybe, but the one that's down there looks to me like it could heat the White House, so we'll see. Bring in a designer, and I'll tell him or her what I've got in mind. We can go from there."

"Okay. Day after tomorrow works. I can schedule my designer by then. Same time?"

"Yeah. Three thirty is good for me."

"So do I get to meet the client?"

Gabe shrugged. "He wasn't here when I arrived. No idea when I'll see him again."

"Aren't you discussing plans with him?"

"To be honest, Jorge, he put me in charge, and I don't really know yet what that means. But I'm moving ahead with what seems best for my client and the property."

"Want me to see more upstairs?"

"No. Bring your appraiser tomorrow too, and we'll break down the whole job by project based on specialties."

Jorge stuck out his hand. "Honor and a privilege."

Man, Gabe sure hoped that turned out to be true.

CHAPTER FOUR

GABE WALKED to the door with Jorge, but as soon as it closed after him, Gabe glanced at his texts. No messages from Jerry. When he'd arrived earlier, there had been a blue Prius in the driveway and the front door was unlocked, but no sign of Jerry. Of course, this was Ashland. People walked places and left their doors open when they did it. Still, it was a big house....

He glanced outside. Nobody beside the pool or in the overgrown yard. Glancing again at his phone, he walked back to the kitchen where he'd left his notebook. Suddenly, he turned and took off up the stairs at a trot. He walked down the long hall softly, halfway seeing that cat playing with a ball that Jerry had conjured. The master bedroom door was partly closed.

Gabe stopped outside, took a breath, and gently pushed. The door moved a little, but it was big and heavy, so he still couldn't see in. He peered around the edge of the door. As some weird instinct had told him, there lay Jerry on his rumpled mattress, curled on his side, sound asleep.

Gabe took a step closer and stared. *Angel face.* His crazy cap had shifted slightly, and a lock of fair hair hung down the side of his cheek. His lashes were darker than his hair, and they shadowed his eyes like little fans. But the face. Dear God, when all the stress and anxiety were gone, that face fell into pure sweetness.

Not wanting to wake him, Gabe turned quietly and stepped out the door.

"Gabe?"

Gabe looked back. "Sorry. I didn't mean to bother you."

Jerry struggled to sit up cross-legged in his too-big gray sweats, wiping a hand over his eyes like a little kid. With a slap, he adjusted his beanie, then looked up with a smile that turned into a yawn. "S'cuse me. So did you make some decisions about the house?"

"I asked the design-build firm for quotes. When we get them back, you can decide if they're doable and interesting."

He sprang to his feet in one smooth move. *Wow.* "Tell me your ideas."

"Okay."

Jerry stretched, showing off an inch of hard, tan belly. Kind of surprisingly hard and tan for such a recluse. Jerry asked, "Want pizza while we talk?"

"I should probably get home."

"Oh sure. Of course." He stared at his feet as he walked out of the bedroom into the long hall.

God, the guy seemed so alone. "I could use a few bites of pizza."

Gabe was rewarded with a beaming smile. "Great. I'll order right now. They know me, so they come right away." He tapped some keys on his phone as he continued downstairs. Gabe followed.

When they hit the main floor, Gabe pointed to the left. "Let's talk in the kitchen."

Once they'd entered the dilapidated, cramped space, Gabe said, "I know you don't seem to have much use for cooking, but here's what I'm thinking. A modern house this size would have a much bigger kitchen than this, so for resale value, it would be smart to expand the kitchen." He explained about taking over the laundry room and moving the laundry to the space closer to the garage. "Of course, we need to turn the garage back into a garage."

"Oh yes, that would be wonderful. I'd love to have a place to park."

"What about the kitchen idea?"

"Oh sure, fine. It will be nice not to have to go to the Laundromat."

"Uh, we can order you a washer and dryer and have them set up in the garage space to use for now. There's no sense in you having to haul your stuff down the hill."

"That would be great. Thanks."

Gabe grinned. "You want to pick your own washer and dryer?"

"What are my choices?" He looked like a kid being told he could have one candy bar.

"Well, there are top-loading washers and front loaders."

He pulled his brows together for several seconds. "Top seems better."

"Okay. Color?"

"Red." He laughed. "I saw some red washers the other day when I was looking for you."

"Red it is. I'll order them tomorrow and have them delivered as soon as possible."

"I can't wait. I love red."

"So back to the question. What about expanding the kitchen?"

He shrugged. "Sounds great."

"I'll make the current kitchen open concept and turn the rest into more of a scullery and prep kitchen that isn't as open. That way, you can hide pots and pans from your guests."

"Oh, Mimi will love that." He nodded.

"Mimi?" He tried to sound neutral. Mimi was probably Jerry's girlfriend.

"She cooks for me sometimes." He pressed his hands together. "What else do you want to do?"

"Well. All the decks need to be reinforced, or in some cases rebuilt."

"Yes, and what'll you do with the lookout tower?"

"What's that?"

Jerry pressed his hands to his chest. "What? You missed the best part of the whole house?"

"Uh, I guess so."

"Well come with me, my deprived friend, and I—"

The front doorbell rang.

Gabe snorted. "It works!"

"Yes, one of the few things." Jerry took off toward the door. Good to know he didn't kid himself about the condition of the house.

Jerry walked back a couple minutes later with a large pizza box that smelled like cheesy, tomatoey heaven and a big handful of napkins. He set them on the island.

Gabe said, "So what about the, uh, what did you call it, lookout tower?"

"Come with me." Jerry led him back down the hall to the staircase and started up. Gabe trotted behind him. At the top of the stairs, Jerry stopped and pointed to a polished-wood ladder that spanned the stairwell and seemed to disappear through a hole in the ceiling. "Go on up and look."

"Uh, okay." Gabe frowned but took off up the ladder. It wasn't a hard climb if you didn't look down. Below was the open stairwell that fell two stories. A trapdoor blocked his way at the top of the ladder. He grasped the handle, pushed, and it rose easily. Brilliant light flooded around him. As the trapdoor fell away, he rose into a square room surrounded on all sides by windows, with a door that led out to a small deck. He stepped off the ladder onto the floor of the room and was greeted by the best view in the whole house. All around, he could see the mountains and the trees of the Oregon forest.

A big flat box slid onto the floor, and Jerry emerged through the trapdoor. "So what do you think?"

Gabe gave a little laugh. "It's amazing."

"Yeah." He nimbly sprang to his feet and stood beside Gabe. Interesting. Gabe was nearly six-three, and Jerry was only maybe an inch shorter. He just seemed so—frail. But nothing about his physical presence supported that impression. It must be his extreme shyness and awkwardness that made Gabe feel like he had to protect Jerry. Jerry turned in a circle. "It's a big reason I bought the house. I mean, where do you ever see a room like this? I want to sleep up here."

"I'll bet there's a way to create a staircase to make it easier to get up here."

Jerry shrugged. "Maybe. But I think the ladder's part of the fun."

"But will you feel that way when you're eighty?"

Jerry raised one shoulder. "I don't know how I'll feel when I'm thirty." He grinned. "Let's have pizza." He folded onto the floor as graceful as a dancer and sat cross-legged in front of the box. He flipped open the lid, closed his eyes, and inhaled deeply.

Gabe managed to get his big body to the floor and into a sitting position. He didn't match Jerry's catlike grace, but maybe didn't look like a water buffalo. "So you really like this stuff, huh? Not just a matter of convenience since your stove doesn't work?"

Jerry scooped up a big slice on a napkin and handed it to Gabe. "I'm working on proving that man can live on pizza alone."

Gabe bit into his pizza slice. It had been a while. He didn't like to suggest to Ellie that pizza was a substitute for real food, so they only had it as an occasional treat. "Have to admit it's good." He chewed. "So how long until you're thirty?"

"What?" Jerry cocked his head as he licked oil from his lips with a quick pink tongue.

Gabe dragged his eyes away from Jerry's shiny mouth. "You said you don't know how you'll feel when you're thirty. I just wondered when that is."

"Oh. July." He took another bite and chewed, then grinned. "Four years from now."

"You're a baby." Gabe smiled tightly.

"I am? Why, how old are you?"

"Thirty-three."

"That's young."

Gabe snorted. "Not the way I did it."

"What do you mean?"

Why did I bring this up? He almost never talked about himself. Still, sitting in a tree house eating pizza took him back to a childhood he'd hardly had. "I have a sixteen-year-old daughter."

Jerry stopped midbite. "You're kidding. Wait, that means you were a dad when you were—"

"Not quite seventeen. Right."

"Holy crap."

Gabe just chewed.

"Wow. That must have been so hard. I can't even imagine."

Had it been hard? Funny how he barely thought about it. "I guess. I was kind of never a kid, so when I found out I was going to be a father, I just went with it." He smiled. "Ellie's so great. It gives me the willies to think I might not have had her."

"So she… uh, Ellie's home with your wife?" Jerry grabbed another slice.

"No. No wife."

Jerry gave him that sideways glance he had. "Aren't females usually required?"

"I was married for a few years, but we knew from the beginning that it was about Ellie, not about us as a couple."

"Oh, I'm sorry."

Gabe shrugged.

"Do you and your ex get along well?"

"Yeah, although she shifts her attitudes based on who she's with at the time, which gives me whiplash." He leaned back against the wall.

"You haven't remarried, though." Jerry didn't meet his eyes as he chewed pizza.

"No. Taking care of Ellie's full-time. I started working as soon as I knew she was coming. That didn't leave much time for dating, or schooling either for that matter."

"But you know so many things."

"Glad you think so, but master of none, I guess. Anyway, I ended up with a great life."

"Thirty-three's hardly the end."

Gabe laughed. "And that brings the conversation full circle." He wiped his fingers on the paper napkins. "I better get home. Let me help maneuver the box down the ladder."

Jerry looked up through his lashes. "I usually throw the boxes off the deck and then pick them up in the yard and put them in the trash."

"Creative, but maybe we at least need to rig up some kind of dumbwaiter to your tower so you can transport stuff up here more easily."

He spread his hands. "I'm open to all modern conveniences."

"Even if the modern conveniences date from the nineteenth century?"

"Especially then."

Gabe maneuvered down the ladder and grabbed the box that Jerry handed him, then tried not to stare at Jerry's butt as he climbed down.

When Jerry was back on solid ground, Gabe said, "I haven't had a chance to assess the master bedroom closet or bathroom. Maybe I should take a quick look before I go."

"Sure. It's not much." He paced down the long hall.

Gabe followed at a fast clip. "That's a problem right off, because master baths are another one of the big selling features in a house. So unless you plan on staying here until you're eighty, we probably should focus on resale value, at least a little bit."

"Okay. How come you never remarried?"

Gabe stopped. Then he barked a laugh and kept following Jerry. "Never met the right person. I just haven't focused much on a social life since—I guess ever."

"I'd think you'd be a great catch."

"You're joking." They walked into the big bedroom with its beautiful light and view of the treetops and mountains beyond. "Wow. I mean seriously, this room deserves to have a fabulous bath and closet and the full deal."

"Yeah. I'm not joking."

"What?" Gabe went down the little narrow hall beside the sleeping area and into what might make a good dressing room if it was fixed up. He took note of the peeling drywall and the broken light fixture.

Jerry leaned against the wall. "I'm not joking about you being a great catch."

Gabe peered into what must be the master closet—a long narrow room with a couple of rods and a makeshift shelf. It was a mess compared to what it needed to be in a house like this. "We're going to need to figure this area out." He walked through the other door into a smallish bathroom with a big shower but no tub and broken tile and peeling drywall everywhere. The one interesting thing was a door leading out to a deck. Gabe threw it open and looked out. "Aha!"

"What?" Jerry stuck his head under Gabe's arm and peered onto the deck. A wave of heat and that scent like some kind of spice Gabe loved in apple cider filled his nose, fogged his brain, and dove like a spark of electricity to his balls.

He stepped back and cleared his throat. "Uh, if you wanted, we could think about expanding this bathroom out onto that deck. The roof already extends over it, so it wouldn't be too costly to do it. That could give you a big bathroom with a tub and double sinks, plus a separate room for the toilet. We could probably expand the master closet by stealing some of the next bedroom. That would really increase the home's value." He could feel himself getting excited and took a breath. "Of course, you don't necessarily want to overvalue the house for the area."

Jerry pressed his hands together. "Oh, I'd love a bathtub. A great big one."

In his current state, Gabe did not want to think about Jerry's lean, graceful body reclining nude in a big bathtub. "Okay. We'll see what it costs to make that happen." He hurried back into the bedroom and came face-to-face—uh, face-to-memory-foam—with the mattress covered in messed-up blue sheets. A light comforter—it shone like silk—had been kicked into a heap. The whole scene took his breath away.

Trying not to look at the bed, Gabe rushed through the room, hurried along the long hall and down the stairs, and was nearly at the front door before he even considered what his speed must've looked like. He turned as Jerry caught up with him. "Sorry, I just realized Ellie must be expecting me."

"Bring her with you next time."

"Oh, really?" Jerry seriously wanted someone else around? "Yeah, maybe so."

Jerry extended his hand. "Thank you, Gabe. This whole thing is fun now that you're in charge. I was dreading it before."

Gabe couldn't help the real smile. "It's fun for me too." He swallowed. "I mean, not everyone gets to work on a house like this."

Jerry glanced down at his feet. "I'm glad you like it. I couldn't stand to pass it up."

"Okay, so see you." Gabe opened the front door and trotted down the porch stairs. He'd be fine when he had a little space.

"Gabe?" Jerry's voice came from behind him, and Gabe stopped and looked back.

"Yeah?"

"I don't care what you think. You're a great catch." Jerry grinned. "Good night." He closed the door, and Gabe tried to close his mouth.

CHAPTER FIVE

BRAIN EXPLOSION imminent. As he attempted to maintain the speed limit on the way home, Gabe tried to focus on changes he wanted to make to the house, but that led him back to *how can a guy sleeping on a mattress on the floor afford a new washer and dryer, much less the enclosure of an upstairs deck,* and that made him think about that mattress, which brought him back to Jerry lying asleep on that mattress with his long body wrapped around that comforter, and that... was driving him nuts!

Just get home. Actually, he needed to think about maybe having a date like Ellie kept suggesting. Hell, if he kept popping wood every time he saw his new client, maybe finding a one-night stand would be better. Less complicated. It had been years and years since he'd had his cock sucked in an alley or fucked somebody up against a wall in a dark club. He was too worried about being recognized and having that kind of story get back to the court or to Tiffany, which was the same thing.

He pulled his truck onto his street with the close-together houses and campers parked in the driveways, and slowed because the kids loved to play and ride skateboards in the street.

As he got close to his house, he frowned. As if he'd conjured her, his ex-wife's Camaro was parked in front of the house, and where Tiffany went, Irving likely wasn't far behind. Technically, Tiffany could visit with Ellie whenever she wanted. They had joint custody, although the judge had allowed Ellie to live with Gabe because she requested it and judges gave lots of weight to kids' preferences. The fact that Ellie had made that choice didn't please Tiffany, but at the time she'd been engrossed in trying to establish her second marriage, so she hadn't objected. Now she was on relationship three, and for some reason, she'd gotten superfocused on Ellie and the entire custody issue. The whole thing gave him shivers.

He pulled into the driveway and was out of the truck practically before the engine shut off. Someone must have heard him coming because the front door opened and Tiffany and that idiot Irving walked out. Tiffany said, "Bye, dear. So good to see you." She looked at Gabe as if she hadn't known he was there. "Oh. Hello, Gabe. We were just having a lovely visit with Ellie." Her singsongy voice could have been an ad for a 1950s floor wax.

"Tif, what's with you? You don't even sound like yourself." He glanced at Irving, who stood rigid as a stick, staring into space with a smile plastered on his face.

Tiffany said, "Of course I sound like myself." She slid her arm through Irving's. "I sound like Ellie's mother." She marched down the porch stairs, dragging idiot Irving with her.

Gabe rushed into the house. "Ellie! Ellie, where are you?"

The guest bathroom door opened, and Ellie walked out. "Here, Dad."

He took her arms in his hands. "Are you okay? What was that all about?"

"She's wacked, Daddy. I know I shouldn't say that about my mother, but I swear that man's done something to her. She came in here telling me how I can't grow up in the home of an unnatural sinner and expect to go to heaven. My mother! Who used to see God in a shot of Juvederm. Jeez. And that creepo just stands there and smiles."

He wrapped his arms tightly around her. "I'm sorry I wasn't here. If she keeps this up, I'll try to get a ruling through the court."

She shook her head. "I hope you don't have to do that. If we can just hold out for a year, I'll be an adult, and she won't have any say in my life."

"Don't worry. We'll make it." He spoke more confidently than he felt. Still, Oregon was liberal on gay custody generally, and the judge wasn't likely to change the custody plan unless he had a damned good reason. Gabe needed to keep his nose cleaner than clean. And he needed to get Ellie thinking about other things. "So how was school?"

"Fine. Good." She wiped at her eyes. "How was your visit to the house?"

He walked her over to the couch and plopped on it with his arm around her. "Strange, but really amazing. This house is so cool, Ellie. It's in very bad shape, but there's so much that could be done to it."

"Can your strange client afford to do it?"

He gave a sigh. "That's the big question. I mean, seriously, I talk to him about the changes I imagine, and he seems willing and even excited. He never mentions money. But honestly, the guy lives on pizza. He's been taking his clothes to the Laundromat and seemed really thrilled when I suggested buying a washer and dryer. I mean, who wouldn't think of that themselves—if he has the money?"

"Maybe you should just ask him?"

"Yeah, I guess."

"Why not?"

Gabe shrugged. "I don't know. He's such a, like, innocent guy. I don't want to embarrass him."

She got her stern accountant's face on. After all, she balanced their checking account and kept the savings. "That's sweet, but he's taking your time. If he can't afford to pay you, you probably ought to know."

"You're right, of course." He tightened his arm and hugged her tighter. "I'll ask him."

They sat quietly for a minute in comfortable silence. That was one thing he thanked heaven for. He and Ellie had a great relationship. She actually seemed to like being around him. What sixteen-year-old girl takes her dad to her birthday concert instead of a girlfriend? She always acted straightforward with him and didn't seem shy about telling him anything. Of course, his life was probably a cautionary tale for her, but she was a damned good kid.

Ellie spoke softly. "I told Mom if she's going to keep up with her bull crap about you, she shouldn't expect to see me anymore."

Wow. "I'm sure she took that very seriously, sweetie. And I'll reinforce it, okay?"

"But I don't want to give her any reason to go back to the court and claim she's being denied her parental rights or something." She sounded nervous, and that made him mad.

"Don't worry. The judge knows you want to live with me."

She sighed. "I hope that's enough. I sure liked it better when she didn't pay any attention."

"Me too, honey. Me too."

"By the way, I work until seven tomorrow night, and I'll eat at work, so you're on your own for dinner."

"No problem." He leaned his head against hers and tried not to wish that Tiffany's third relationship would go the way of the other two.

GABE STARED at the two shiny appliances.

Isabella peered over the top of the washer at him. "What do you think?"

"They look like if I clicked them together, they'd take me back to Kansas."

"Ha!" She slapped a hand on the lid of the top-loader. "You're too funny. But yeah, they sure are red."

"That's what my client says he wants."

"Well, we've got a special on them because your client's in the minority."

"Great. I'll take them. We need them delivered as soon as possible."

She walked to her desk, and he followed. After a couple of taps on the computer keys, she said, "How's tomorrow?"

"Perfect." He gave her all the details. "Uh, I'll get my client to give you a credit card, okay?" She nodded, and Gabe called the number he had for Jerry.

"Hello?" The voice was soft and tentative.

"Hi, Jerry, it's Gabe. I picked out your washer and dryer and they can deliver tomorrow, but I need a way to pay them, and—"

"Okay, write this down, and when I see you next, I'll give you the card."

"Uh, are you sure you don't want to give the card to the store?"

"No."

"Okay." He grabbed his notebook from his pocket. "Shoot." Jerry recited all the information from an Amex card, complete with the date and code. Gabe wrote it carefully. "Thanks."

"Are you coming over today?" He sounded like he was trying to cover being anxious. The image of that slim, solitary figure wandering around that big house flashed in Gabe's mind.

"Uh, yes. I'll be over when I get off at three."

"Great. See you then." Man, he sounded happy.

As Gabe walked back toward hardware from the appliances department, Harry trotted up. He wore a funny grin. "Hey, my man, we've got a couple new guys on the floor, and we're taking them out for a beer at about five. Want to come join us?" He cleared his throat. "We'd really like you to come. These guys need a good role model."

"Yeah, right."

"No, seriously. It'd be great if you could come. The guys would like it."

Harry seemed to really want him to show up. It had been a while since he'd joined in. He should go. "Yeah, Ellie's doing her fast-food job this evening, so I think I can stop by for a beer."

"Perfect." He rubbed his hands together. "Just perfect."

Gabe gave him a quizzical smile, but Harry grinned and walked out of the department.

Gabe worked the rest of the day and tried not to notice the rising sense of excitement and anticipation as his trip to Ashland got closer. At three, he focused on gathering his stuff and walking to his truck without thinking too much. Still, when he drove up Mountain Avenue, he got flips in his stomach. Not good, but he'd said he'd do this job, and he wasn't a flake.

He slid out of the truck in front of the house—mansion—whatever. The fact was, the house was incredible, but you still couldn't find the damned door. *The place needs work. Full stop.*

As he strode across the grass and drew closer to the porch, the front door opened and Jerry bounced out. Bounced was the only word that entered Gabe's mind. Jerry waved. "Hey."

"Hey."

"Hope you're hungry. I got Chinese."

Gabe smiled as he climbed the porch stairs. "Actually, I'm starved, and I'd love some Chinese."

Gabe walked in, greeted by the smell of soy sauce. Everything else seemed pretty much the same. No added furniture, no additional hominess, nothing.

At the kitchen island that seemed to serve as the center of the house, since everywhere else was empty, Jerry had set out two paper plates, plastic utensils, and paper napkins. In the middle of the big island were some Chinese food containers. He pointed. "This is cashew chicken, these are moo shu vegetables, and this is egg fried rice." He looked up shyly. "I can ask them to bring something else."

"No. This is great." Jerry seemed to be waiting for him, so Gabe dished up some of each, spreading plum sauce on the moo shu wrapper with his plastic knife.

Jerry mimicked him, taking a big helping of each dish. *Did he wait to eat lunch for me to come over, or is this an early dinner, or both?* Jerry said, "Want to go in the living room and sit down?"

"Sure."

Gabe stared at the plastic beach chair suspiciously. Not that he was huge, but the chair was small and a long way down. He set the paper plate on the tile floor, folded himself into the chair, then managed to get the plate on his lap plus fork and napkin without getting plum sauce on his pants.

As on the mattress, Jerry gracefully settled like a cat onto a sunny windowsill. He looked around and smiled. "I just love this room, don't you?"

"Yes, actually, I do. It's the amazing light coming from all directions. And the wood ceilings are beautiful. What do you plan to do about the fireplace? It doesn't look like it works."

"I don't think it does." He scooped up some cashew chicken. "So what do you want to do with it?"

Man, when this guy surrenders control, he doesn't mess around. That thought stopped Gabe's fork in midair, and he had to swallow before he could chew. "How about I get a fireplace specialist out from Medford to see what's wrong with it?"

"Okay." He nodded and chewed.

"What color do you like on the walls?"

He shrugged. "Something that goes good with the light."

"How does white sound?"

"They are white."

"Clean white."

Jerry grinned. "That would be good." Funny, Jerry had amazing teeth. Really white and absolutely straight, like movie-star chompers, except for the little crossed tooth at the front.

"You must have had braces, right?"

"What?" Jerry looked really startled.

"Your teeth are so straight. I mean, except for…." He pointed at the little crossover, dropped his hand and wished he hadn't brought it up.

"Oh, yes, braces." He looked down at his plate and shoved a moo shu pancake in his mouth, chewed, then said, "They decided not to mess with my crooked tooth since people seemed to like it."

Gabe stared at Jerry as he took another bite of moo shu. Who were "they," and who were the "people" who seemed to like the tooth? He cleared his throat. Better to drop the subject.

He dug in his pants pocket and handed the papers to Jerry. "Here's the receipt for your washer and dryer. They'll be here tomorrow."

His eyes got wide. "You'll be here, right?"

"Uh, yes. I told them to come in the afternoon. I'm meeting the design builder to get his quotes at the same time. We may need to install the washer and dryer in the existing laundry room until I can get hookups put out by the garage."

Jerry smiled and nodded. "Here." He handed Gabe an American Express card. A black American Express card.

Gabe stared at it. "It's black."

"Yes."

"I've never seen a black card."

"It works, don't worry." He reached in his jeans pocket again and pulled out some money, which he extended to Gabe.

Gabe took it before he looked. "Wait. This is three thousand bucks. What's it for? You already paid for the washer and dryer on the card."

"That's for you."

"Me? Why?"

"You're doing all this work. I need to pay you." He took another bite.

"I've only been working for a couple days."

"Right. Tell me when that's used up, and I'll give you more."

"I'll give you an invoice, Jerry."

"Good. That's your retainer." He chuckled. "Like in *Good Will Hunting*. Remember?"

"Yeah, but—"

"Re-*tain*-er." He laughed again. "I love that movie. You like apples?"

Gabe had to smile back. "Well, I got her number. How do you like those apples?"

They both laughed.

Gabe set his empty plate on the floor and leaned forward. "Jerry, if you're going to live here, we need to make this house more comfortable fast. It's a big place, so we can find ways to create a private, comfortable space for you to hang out while other parts of the house are being worked on."

"Okay." He nodded.

"You need a microwave and an electric skillet or something to cook on until we redo the kitchen. You need dishes, lamps, a TV, and something to sit on."

"Okay."

Gabe just stared at him. *He wants me to get all that stuff for him.* "Don't you have anything, uh, for a house? Like kitchen utensils or anything?"

"Probably. But I'd rather have you choose all of it, okay?"

He might laugh—or maybe cry. "What about furniture? Don't you want to pick that out yourself? We could go together."

"No. Let's shop online. Anyway, next week I have to go away for a while. Maybe you could do some things while I'm gone?"

"How long will you be gone?"

"Four days. Maybe five."

"Okay, get your laptop, and let's get you some stuff. Do you have Amazon Prime?"

"I think so."

"Well, if not, we need to sign you up. Go on, get your computer."

Jerry bounced to standing and ran up the stairs.

Gabe stared after him, feeling half like he was sending his son to college and half like a newlywed.

He shoved his hand in his pocket and felt—paper. *Holy crap, I've got three thousand dollars in my pocket.* He sighed softly. *I sure hope Jerry didn't rob a bank to get it.*

CHAPTER SIX

AFTER TWO hours of selecting dishes, flatware, and stuff like dishtowels, Gabe drove back toward Medford, where he'd meet the guys. His brain felt stuffed with all the details of what needed to happen in the house, compounded by all the possibilities for improvements if Jerry wanted to go the extra mile—in other words, if he could afford the extra. Of course, Gabe's pocket felt stuffed with $3K cash, which was a pretty good argument for Jerry having some secret stash of money. Or he'd amassed all his cash and given it to Gabe, and from here on he'd be destitute. Gabe didn't have any idea which was true.

He pulled into the parking lot at the bar the guys from ImproveMart liked best. While he didn't feel much like going in, he'd more or less promised, and he didn't want to disappoint Harry. With Ellie working, Gabe didn't have to be home. No excuses.

He walked across the parking lot into the bar and then looked around the tables. At the back, he saw Harry sitting with Wilson, JZ, and three guys he didn't recognize. Must be the new men. As he got closer, his gaze settled mostly on one of the newcomers. He wore glasses and wasn't really dressed like the usual ImproveMart employee. A lot more—what? Nerdy? Collegiate?

As Gabe walked up to the table, Harry looked up and flashed a huge smile. "There you are, my man. We were starting to think you weren't coming."

"Sorry. It's my part-time gig—that you got me into, by the way. It takes a ton of time. So I'm ready for a beer." He shook hands with Wilson and JZ, and then noticed that the seat they'd left open was next to the nerd. No point making a point, so he sat.

Harry said, "Gabe, this is Murray, new in outdoor, and Jose. Jose's in lighting. Oh, beside you is Wilson's cousin Clark."

Gabe shook hands all around, getting a nice warm grip from Clark, and then ordered a beer from the waitress.

When he had his glass, Gabe turned to Clark. "Do you work at ImproveMart too?"

He smiled. "No, I'm a professor at SOU." He pushed up his glasses on a slim nose.

"No kidding? What do you teach?"

"English literature."

"That must be fun."

Clark smiled, and his blue eyes crinkled behind his glasses. A vision of mismatched blue and green eyes flashed in Gabe's mind, and he blinked it away. Clark said, "Yes. It is fun. I understand you build furniture."

"As kind of an avocation. Not many people around here buy custom." He sipped his beer. "So you live in Ashland?"

"Yes. In the Railroad district."

"Nice."

"How about you?"

"I have a home in Talent. For me and my daughter."

"Right. Wilson told me you had a child."

Obviously, the guys had been doing their share of talking. "Actually, I can hardly believe how grown-up she is. She's turning seventeen next week."

"It's hard to imagine you could have a teenage child." He smiled, which popped dimples in his cheeks. Once you got past the serious, studious looks, Clark was very cute.

Gabe talked to Murray and Jose for a while and gave them advice on how to thrive at ImproveMart. When he'd nearly finished his beer, Clark said, "Like another? My treat."

"Oh, uh, no thanks. My kid worked tonight, but she'll be home soon, so I need to get going."

"Is she okay on her own if her dad was to, say, go out for dinner?"

Gabe cocked a half smile. "I guess I'd have to get asked to dinner first."

"That can be arranged." Clark smiled back, and it really was charming.

Do I want to go to dinner with this guy? It's kind of crazy to devote a social life to having Chinese food on paper plates with a weird guy who couldn't sit here and carry on a conversation with this group of men— and probably doesn't prefer men in bed either.

"Yes, Ellie's fine by herself. I just don't like to leave her unless I've told her in advance."

"So maybe you'd like to tell her you'll be gone on Friday evening when you're having dinner with me?"

Gabe glanced at Harry, who was very conspicuously looking everywhere except at Gabe and Clark. *Total setup*, which gave Gabe a warm feeling since obviously Harry and the guys had taken Gabe's being gay seriously enough to try to fix him up. "Sure, I'd love to." He gazed at Clark with his nerdy but still costly clothes and refined manners. If Gabe ever needed to impress a judge with his upstanding associates, he could sure as hell produce Clark. Of course, he wasn't 100 percent sure what Clark saw in him—a guy who was good with wood and picking out washing machines—but he wasn't going to look a gift setup in the mouth. "Where shall I meet you?"

"How about I make reservations and come and get you?"

"Whoa, my parents will be impressed." He grinned.

For a second, Clark looked confused, then grinned back. "I think I need to impress your daughter. So give me your number." He held out his phone.

Gabe input his digits and handed the phone back.

Clark extended his hand. "Better get my number in case of emergency."

Gabe passed over his phone. When he looked up, Harry, Wilson, and JZ were staring with proud grins on their faces. The new guys looked a little confused, but Harry'd probably fill them in later. That'd be an interesting conversation.

Gabe swallowed his last mouthful of beer and pushed back his chair. "I better get home to my kid. Thanks for inviting me." He put money on the table, gave Harry a look, and shook hands with the new guys. To Clark, he said, "Guess I'll see you." He flashed Clark a smile and walked out.

In his truck, Gabe cranked the ignition, then paused. Harry and the guys had never taken an interest in his love life before. He was kind of flattered and kind of weirded out, but decided to go with the former. After all, they loved finding dates for the straight guys, why not him? And the fact that they thought Clark was the right kind of guy for Gabe was definitely complimentary.

He headed for home.

When he got out of his truck in the driveway and walked to the front door, the throb of drums and bass guitar rumbled from inside. As he opened the door, a blast of rock music hit him like a wall. He stopped. Wow. A lot of Ellie's music underwhelmed him, but this was amazing. Complex, soaring, but still low-down enough to grab your guts while it expanded your brain.

Ellie was bent over her homework on the dining room table. How exactly she could do anything besides listen to that he wasn't sure. She looked up. The music clicked off. "Hi, Dad. Sorry. I thought you'd hang with your friends longer."

He took off his boots, peeled out of his jacket, and stashed them all in the overcrowded hall closet. "I had plenty of time with the guys." He pulled out a chair at the table and sat.

"I brought you home some tacos from work in case you didn't get dinner."

"Actually, I had a late lunch with Jerry. Chinese. But I could manage a taco or two."

She got up, retrieved a paper plate from a bag on the counter, and set it in front of him with a cloth napkin—in fact it was a colorful dishtowel, but they liked big napkins. She resettled at her laptop. "Did you have fun with your friends?"

"Yeah." He picked up his taco and stared at it. "Remember I told you Harry seemed really anxious for me to go hang with him and the guys?"

She nodded.

"Well, I found out why."

"Hey, they don't need a reason. They like you."

"Yeah, well in this case, they were fixing me up." He took a big bite.

"Fixing you—wait, you mean like with a woman?"

He swallowed. "Nope. With a guy."

"You're kidding!"

"Not even."

She smiled. "Know what? That's actually pretty cool."

"I was a little, uh, conflicted about it, but I came to the same conclusion. And the guy's a professor at SOU, so we're not talking some loser here."

"That's really great. Did you ask him out?"

"He asked me. To dinner on Friday. And he wants to meet you, so he's even going to come pick me up."

She raised an eyebrow and put her hands on her hips. "Isn't it a little soon to be introducing him to the family?" Then she laughed.

"Actually, it is early, but that's what he suggested, and I figured you wouldn't be scarred for life if you didn't like him."

"Or if you don't."

"Exactly." He started on taco number two. "That was amazing music you were playing. I don't think I've heard it before."

She pressed her hands to her chest and sighed elaborately. "That's my birthday concert. Jet Gemini. I listen to him a lot, but mostly through the earphones. Great, huh?"

"Yes. I really liked it. So I get to hear this group too?"

"Yep. Can't wait." She clicked a few keys on the laptop and turned the screen around toward Gabe. In the video, a singer in skintight jeans and not much else but pale hair almost to his waist stalked around a stage backed by four guys who mimicked the jeans but added a bit more clothing. He strutted and danced like some personification of everything your mama warned you about, but the voice was soaring and angelic.

"Uh, wow."

She chuckled. "Yeah. They say his voice is nearly operatic, but it's housed in a bad-boy body." She clicked some more keys and turned the screen his way again.

This time, a slightly fuzzy photo showed the same long-haired man wearing a gaping leather jacket over his smooth, bare chest, sitting with a champagne glass in one hand, a curvy redhead in the other, and two gorgeous, twinky guys draped over his shoulders. He was kissing the girl with a lot of tongue.

Shit. Sexy. "Not exactly a role model for his fans, is he?" He smiled tightly.

"Yeah, well, all we have to do is listen. You can close your eyes if you want."

"Hey, it's your eyes I'm worried about."

"Dad!" She smacked his arm.

He chuckled. "So you put these child-morals-corrupting tickets on the credit card, right?" Ellie kept all their finances on track.

She snorted, then stared at him with her concentration crease between her eyebrows. "I've got a plan to pay it off fast, so don't worry. I paid off the other card, so I can use that money to—"

He reached in his pocket, pulled out the bills, held them between two fingers, and extended them to her.

"What's this?"

"My retainer."

"What?" She took the money, stared at it and then at him with an open mouth. "This is three thousand bucks."

"Yep."

"Wait." She grinned. "This is from Jerry the Weird, right? The one with two camp chairs and no washer?"

"That would be correct."

"Dad, what is this guy thinking?" Despite the fact that she was smoothing the bills lovingly, she actually frowned.

"Yeah, good question. I don't get him either. First, he gives me an American Express card. I mean, it probably has a limited amount of credit, but still, he barely knows me. Then he hands me three K and says let him know when it's gone." He shook his head. "So we need to put together an invoice accounting for my time at a reasonable hourly rate. He suggested a hundred bucks an hour, which is ridiculous."

"How about I research it for you and charge him whatever the going rate is for—what title shall I look for?"

"Construction supervisor?"

"No." She tapped her computer keys. "You're doing more than that. Sort of a design consultant, a personal assistant, and a supervisor, don't you think?"

"I guess." He wiped his hand and took his wrappers to the trash.

"Okay, so construction supervisors make about thirty or forty an hour. Personal assistants get less than that but they make a lot of bonuses. Design consultants make the big bucks. Up to three hundred an hour. So what if we settle on eighty-five an hour?"

"That seems like a lot."

"It's less than he suggested."

"Let's say eighty." He felt weird about that.

"So give me your hours, and I'll write up an invoice." She petted the money again. "And I'll put this in the bank."

He nodded. Maybe she ought to hurry.

"YOU'RE SURE we can remove this wall so we can expand the kitchen to here?" Gabe pointed at the far wall of the laundry room, then looked back at Jorge Alvarez and his designer, Morris Matthews.

Jorge, strong, solid, and silver-haired, banged on the wall that separated the laundry and kitchen. "Yes, this wall won't be hard to take out. Like you thought, it's not the dense plaster that a lot of the walls are. This is drywall, and I'm about 95 percent sure it's not structural."

"Okay, good. So can you do a layout for the kitchen? Give me a lot of island space, but not so much you can't reach the middle of it to clean it, and a gas range, double ovens, big pantry, the works. But put the mess over here, right? Put a smaller sink over in the island or somewhere, but the big sink and scullery area needs to be over here so it's not putting the dirty dishes out in front of guests. Make sense?"

Morris, a pretty, blond, supergay designer, nodded. "Can do. Lovely ideas."

"How soon will you have the drawings?"

"Give me a couple days."

"Okay." Gabe turned to Jorge and glanced over the phased plan he'd priced out. "Get all the electrical reviewed and modernized. Start the painting and redo the drywall where required. Plus get the fireplace working. I'd like the great room to be operational in a week."

"It's a lot, but we'll give it our best shot." He tapped a few things onto the keypad of his tablet.

"Get the plumber working too, okay? We've got to know if we need big, expensive renovations." And Gabe needed to know how much Jerry was prepared to pay for.

"You going to use some of your own furniture in that living room, Gabe? Man, it's made for it."

"Thanks, Jorge. But I don't want my client to feel obliged to use my stuff. We can buy furniture a lot less expensive."

"Not as beautiful, though. That credenza you designed for Mrs. Portico was the best piece of furniture I've ever seen. If she hadn't paid in advance, I would have kept it myself."

Gabe gave him a light punch on the arm. "Happy to make one for you anytime you've got a few thou lying around. I'll give you the friends and family price."

"Might just take you up on that."

Gabe shook his head. "Hey, I'm kidding. You don't need to spend money on my stuff."

"Can't think of a better investment."

They started walking toward the door. Gabe said, "The owner will be gone part of next week, but what I want to do is set up some safe spaces for him where he can have privacy and as little dust as possible. For now, you can renovate one of the other bedrooms and he can move into it while you do the master. I want to make big changes in there."

Jorge said, "So when are we going to meet the owner?"

Gabe raised his shoulders. "Not sure. He's pretty private. I'll keep him in the loop. Meanwhile, send a bill for the first third of the initial phase."

Jorge pulled a folded piece of paper from his jacket pocket. "Just happen to have that right here. Hate to ask, but since we haven't worked with this client before, I'd like to get paid pretty fast."

"Yeah. That's why I asked for the bill. I—" His cell phone dinged. *What?* "Sorry. Probably my kid." He glanced at the phone screen.

Give him the credit card.

Gabe glanced around but didn't see Jerry. He stuck the phone back in his pocket so Jorge wouldn't know they were being spied on. "Do you accept credit cards?"

"Sure. Be out of business if I didn't."

Gabe pulled out his wallet and extracted Jerry's card. "You can put the first payment on this, if that's okay."

Jorge took the card and frowned. "Is this legit?"

CHAPTER SEVEN

GABE STARED at the black credit card in Jorge's hand. "I hope it's okay. It worked once."

Jorge pulled a payment attachment from his pocket and plugged it into his laptop. After tapping a couple of keys, he swiped the black credit card.

Gabe held his breath. The bill was a lot of money.

Jorge chuckled. "Seems to work." He handed the card back.

Gabe exhaled very quietly.

He stared after Jorge and Morris as they left through the breakfast room door that had a far more direct pathway to the parking circle.

"I can't wait to see your furniture."

Gabe jumped a foot at the soft voice that came from behind him. He turned to encounter a smiling Jerry dressed in his usual sloppy sweatpants and massive sweatshirt. His pretty face, surrounded by the odd beanie, stuck out of his baggy clothing like a piece of art someone had wrapped in an old towel. Gabe tried to look stern. "Wouldn't it be easier to join in our meetings rather than lurking? That way you can make important decisions about your house."

"But I like the decisions you make." He turned and walked back to the refrigerator, pulled out a bottle of iced green tea, and poured it in two paper cups. He handed one to Gabe. "So what kind of furniture do you have, and how soon can we get it over here?"

Whoa. Talk about conflicted. He'd give a lot to see his furniture in that house, but making Jerry feel obligated to buy it was crap. Plus, if he was going to sell at a discount, he should offer the coffee table to Mrs. McRae, who'd expressed interest first. "You don't need to buy my furniture."

"No. I know. So when can I see it?" Jerry leaned against the island and sipped his tea.

"I can put a couple pieces in the truck. I have a coffee table that's dry and a credenza I'm using in my own house, but I guess—"

"You can make more for your house, and I bet your place isn't as empty as mine."

Gabe snorted. "The Great Pyramid isn't as empty as your house."

Jerry barked a laugh. "So go get some furniture."

"Now? It'd be better to wait until some of the work gets done. Otherwise, you have to cover it and move it around." Still, his heart hammered at the idea of Jerry seeing his furniture. Jerry might only have a couple of plastic chairs, but he'd picked the house, and that showed pretty amazing vision. Gabe glanced at his work boots. "You might not like it."

Jerry gave him a long sideways glance. "Only one way to find out, right?"

Gabe looked up. "You want to come with me? Then if you hate it, we can leave it behind."

Conflict played all over Jerry's face.

Gabe said, "I need help getting it into the truck if you do want it."

After flexing his bicep, which inside the massive sweatshirt was pretty funny, Jerry said, "Uh, okay." He inhaled deeply, then bounded out of the kitchen and returned a couple of minutes later with the damned sunglasses in place and a floppy windbreaker on top of the sweatshirt. *Seriously?*

Jerry led the way out the front door and locked it behind him, which made Gabe smile, since someone breaking into the house would assume a transient was squatting there.

At the truck, Gabe held the door and was tempted to help Jerry in, but with his usual grace, he sprang up into the high cab, causing the floppy sweatpants to tighten across his ass for a tantalizing minute.

Gabe turned on a pop radio station but played it softly. They rode quietly for a few minutes to the strains of Beyoncé, followed by John Legend.

Jerry kept glancing at Gabe. Gabe caught the movement in the corner of his eye. Jerry suddenly blurted out, "Gabe. Is that short for Gabriel?"

"Yes."

"I like that name."

"Yeah. Me too."

"It's biblical."

Gabe shrugged and looked at Jerry quickly. "I guess it is, but I doubt my mother knew it. She liked Gabriel Byrne. Named me for him."

He chuckled. "Good taste. The dark Irish type."

Gabe plastered on a smile to cover his flush. *Does that comment mean Jerry likes guys?* He swallowed. *And why do I care?*

They were both quiet for a few seconds, and then Jerry said, "It means man of God, or his strength is in God."

"It does?"

"Yes. I looked it up once."

Gabe pulled off the freeway in Talent, just a short drive from Ashland. When he stopped at the light, some people were standing on the corner waiting to cross. Jerry pulled his beanie down farther over his ears and turned his body more toward Gabe.

Before he could censor his mouth, Gabe said, "You seem pretty shy of people."

"Yeah. I guess." Jerry stared at his hands.

"But you talk to me okay."

"You're different." He flashed a quick glance at Gabe. "You're you."

Wow. "Uh, thanks."

"I like talking to you."

Gabe smiled softly. "I like talking to you."

"You do?" He looked surprised and as pleased as a kid in a toy store.

"Uh, we're here." Gabe nodded toward his house as he pulled into the driveway. His heart slammed. What if Jerry didn't like his furniture? Worse, what if he didn't like it and said he did?

Gabe stopped the truck. As Jerry reached for the door handle, Gabe put a hand on his arm. "Jerry?"

He looked back and smiled.

"I really want you to tell the truth about the furniture. Stuff like this is very subjective, so I won't be offended if it's not for you, okay?"

Jerry looked very serious. "Okay. I promise."

Gabe nodded and climbed out of the truck. By the time he got to the other side, Jerry was standing there waiting for him. "Nice house."

"Thanks." The fact that Jerry said that didn't portend well for his honesty about the furniture, but Gabe didn't say so. He walked to the door and unlocked it.

"Is your daughter here?"

Gabe couldn't tell from Jerry's sunglasses-covered eyes if he was happy or scared about Ellie's presence. "I don't think so. She told me she was studying with a girlfriend after school."

"Oh."

Gabe walked in and stood back to let Jerry cross in front of him.

"Oh my God." Jerry stopped in the middle of the living room and stared into the dining area.

"What?" Gabe followed his line of sight.

Jerry rushed into the dining room and ran his hands over the combination of polished and unpolished woods of the dining room table. "You made this, didn't you?" He looked at Gabe—or rather he pointed the sunglasses in Gabe's direction.

Gabe nodded.

"Can you make another one?"

"Uh, probably. No two are ever exactly alike."

"Make one for my dining room, okay?"

"Seriously?"

"Of course." He kept caressing the wood, but he raised his head. The noncaressing hand came up and ripped off the sunglasses. "Is that the credenza you spoke of?"

"Yep." Gabe was enjoying the show.

"And you're selling it?"

"I make furniture, Jerry. I sell it when I can. Not that many people in this part of the world can afford handmade furniture." There, he'd warned Jerry not to expect the prices to be cheap. He'd love to have his furniture in that house, but not enough to give away his hours of work. Of course, if he didn't give some of it away, he'd have a house full of furniture and no one but him and Ellie to enjoy it.

Jerry gave Gabe a quick glance. "I'll take it. How soon can you have another table?"

"What?"

"A table just like that, or as close as you can make it, okay?" He looked around. "What else?"

Gabe could hardly catch his breath. "Well, I kind of brought you to see the coffee table."

"Where's that?"

"In my workshop."

Jerry slid his hand into Gabe's. "Lead the way."

Gabe swallowed hard. While Jerry's hand felt ridiculously good, he'd never held the hand of a man in his life, even his own father. Hell, especially his own father. But Jerry didn't let go, so Gabe walked out of the kitchen door, across the garage, and into his workshop. Several pieces stood around the big space in various stages of creation——a small cabinet, a huge bookcase, and of course, the completed coffee table.

Jerry let go of Gabe's hand—kind of sad—and knelt beside the coffee table. "Wow. Just wow."

Gabe smiled. The table was a favorite. He'd embedded different woods into the border of the huge square table and woven it into an abstract pattern that was kind of Asian in its feeling.

"Say I can have it." Jerry looked up at Gabe and smiled.

"Well, if you want—"

"You have the card. Just put it on there, okay? And the credenza, and then make me a table, and—" His glance moved around the room. "Oh, that bookcase. I love that."

Gabe squatted beside Jerry. "I'd love for you to have them, but they're kind of costly, Jerry. They take weeks, even months of handwork. I can't sell them for too little. I mean, I can do a discount, but—"

Jerry's long fingers flew up and pressed against Gabe's lips.

Gabe gasped, his lips parted, and somehow, the tip of his tongue flicked against Jerry's skin.

Jerry's multicolored eyes widened and his soft hand curled around Gabe's cheek.

Gabe couldn't help it. He raised his shoulder and pressed Jerry's fingers harder against his own face. So few people ever touched him. After all, he was a big, strong guy. Ellie hugged him, of course, but a lot less than she used to as a kid. That was natural, but it often meant he only got touched by his own hand.

Jerry's fingers felt so nice.

Yeah, and he was crazy.

Without making a big deal out of it, he slowly moved his face away and sat back, then stood. Out of harm's way.

For a second, Jerry gazed at him with eyes that could only be described as dewy, and then he blinked. "You have the credit card."

"What?" He couldn't get his brain to focus. It was still back there where Jerry touched his lips and Gabe got a taste of heaven.

"For the furniture. Just charge it on the card." He got up all efficient and businesslike, and Gabe felt a loss of that other guy.

Gabe pulled in some air. "I'll send you a price quote—"

"Gabe, I want the furniture. Besides, I won't be here. Charge it. Let's get it loaded."

"Uh, okay, well I can sell you my dining table and make another one for myself later. And the bookcase is almost done. But all of it won't fit in the truck."

"Let's take what we can, and I'll hire some movers—or rather, maybe you can find some movers to manage the rest."

"I can get it there."

"Good." He stooped and grasped the bottom of the coffee table.

"Wait. I'll get some packing blankets for the truck, and we should start with the credenza."

Jerry nodded once. The mismatched eyes that had been so soft and misty now gazed at Gabe levelly and with evaluation. Another word for evaluation was judgment. *Shit.*

Gabe grabbed a couple moving blankets from the stack he kept in the corner of his shop and walked out toward the truck without looking back.

JERRY STARED at Gabe's retreating ass. Retreating was the active descriptor in that sentence. *He ran out of here like I set said ass on fire… instead of just coveting it. Talk about mixed signals.*

He extended his hand, leaned down, and ran his fingers across the satin surface of the amazingly beautiful coffee table. It was incredibly elegant, unique, unexpected, and artistic, but at the same time strong and solid. Like Gabe.

Gabe stuck his head in the workshop. "I've got the truck bed padded. Want to help me get the credenza out there?"

Jerry nodded.

The credenza proved to be even heavier than it looked. Good thing Gabe was like Superman, or at least Captain America. Jerry just managed to keep up his end, literally, while Gabe lifted the thing onto the truck like a champ. They followed with the coffee table.

Gabe stepped back when they'd managed to load both pieces. "I'll get the dining table and the bookcase over there while you're gone, okay? I mean, if you really want all of it."

Jerry pressed his hands together. "I want every piece you have for sale, and I can't wait."

Gabe smiled, and it flipped Jerry's stomach. Gabe said, "Get back soon and you'll see them."

Jerry looked into Gabe's crystal-blue eyes. "I will. I promise."

When Gabe turned and walked to the driver's door, Jerry ran a hand over his face. *Why am I even interested in this guy? Yes, he's attractive, but hell, so are a lot of men. When did I decide to go to the home improvement store and find a man? Am I really that desperate? Oh yeah, I better not answer that.*

Jerry walked to the passenger side and climbed in. As Gabe turned on the ignition, two teenage girls ambled toward the house on the sidewalk, talking animatedly. One of them, a pretty dark blonde, looked up, waved, and walked to the driver's window. "Hey, Dad."

Gabe leaned out the window as Jerry pushed on his sunglasses. Gabe said, "Hi, honey. Just taking some furniture over to Jerry's house. I won't be too long."

"Jerry's house? You mean…." She beamed and scrunched her head so she could see into the truck. Jerry pulled his cap down a little farther. She waved. "Hi. I'm Ellie Mason."

Jerry swallowed hard and waved back. "Jerry Castor."

"So you like my dad's furniture?"

"Yes, I love it, actually." He swallowed again. "Tell him to work faster." He smiled.

She giggled. "You have good taste, Mr. Castor. My dad's told me a lot about your house. From his description, I thought his furniture would look great in it."

He nodded. "I think so too."

He must have sounded nervous, because she took her focus off him and said, "Don't hurt yourselves moving that." She gave a little hop and said to Gabe, "So excited about the coffee table."

He didn't say anything back, but she walked toward the house as he closed the window and pulled out of the driveway. He glanced at Jerry. "She just loves that coffee table. She's excited that it will have a good home."

"Sh-she seems like a nice girl."

"The best. Amazing really. I don't know how many kids could be born to a seventeen-year-old father and a totally mismatched set of parents and wind up so bright and well-adjusted. Jesus, she keeps me together."

He seemed to realize he'd said a lot because he reached out and switched on his sound system. The soaring notes of "Higher Than Heaven" by Jet Gemini filled the cab at top volume.

Jerry glanced at Gabe, who smiled sheepishly and adjusted the sound. "Sorry. It's my daughter's current favorite."

"Oh."

"I've got to confess, a lot of her music goes right by me, but I like this too."

Jerry smiled, the song changed, and they rode in near silence back to Ashland and his house.

CHAPTER EIGHT

As THEY navigated carefully up the narrow drive in Gabe's truck, Jerry stared at the cracked walls around the pool, the sagging wooden decks, and the overgrown landscaping. He couldn't capture his sigh before it escaped.

Gabe glanced at him. "Problem?"

"Just realizing how much there is to do."

The corners of Gabe's mouth twitched upward.

"Okay, okay, I can hear you saying 'Duh' in your mind. You might as well say it out loud."

"We'll get it done. Don't worry."

Gabe's deep voice rumbled up Jerry's spine and made his eyes hot. "Thank you for helping me, Gabe. I don't know how I'd get it done if it wasn't for you."

"You'd have found someone." Gabe chuckled. "You're very persuasive."

"No. I was supposed to meet you."

"Uh, thanks." There was a moment of silence; then Gabe spoke very softly. "I'm glad you did."

Jerry pretty much smiled all the way through the unloading, which was damned hard and took an hour of trying to maneuver the huge pieces of furniture across the lawn and up the stairs to the nearest door. Once inside, they placed the credenza at one end of the dining room that looked over the pool. The gleaming wood of the cabinet glowed against the Saltillo tile floors and gave the room—which still needed paint, rugs, and a table—some promise.

When they'd wrangled the coffee table into place in the middle of the huge great room, Gabe laughed. "I guess we can call it a start."

Jerry threw his arms out and spun. "But it's sooooo beautiful." He kept swooping and twirling around the room until his head spun and the floor of the room and the wood ceiling far above kind of blended together. He threw his head back and laughed, his foot hit one of the rough places on the tile, and he staggered. "Whoa!" He slid and teetered toward the floor.

Before he could hit, Gabe snatched him into a full-body grab. "Hang on."

Jerry took him at his word. Wrapping his arms tightly around Gabe's neck, he hung on like crazy. Truthfully, he was too dizzy to stand up—

—and the Captain America arms didn't help that dizziness one bit.

Before he could really analyze his situation, he'd pressed himself full length against Gabe's tall, sturdy body, laughing tipsily.

Yes, the contact was pretty wriggly, and if he'd asked himself a hundred times whether Gabe might, just might, like guys since he seemed to look at Jerry like an hors d'oeuvre sometimes, he now got his answer. One formidable protuberance rose in the middle of the embrace and seemed to be matched in his own pants. Gabe's heartbeat pounded against Jerry's chest.

Oh fuck! Just one taste. Jerry slid the arm that was tightly wrapped around Gabe's neck up a couple inches and yanked Gabe's head down so he could lock their lips together.

The first touch produced an electric spark that slammed straight to Jerry's balls so hard, for a second he had to hold his breath to keep from embarrassing himself with wet sweats. As the first gasp came under control, a tsunami of heat washed through him, and he slid his fingers tightly into Gabe's shaggy, silken hair, as he pressed closer from lips to hips.

Gabe had been holding Jerry around the waist. His strong hands slid down and grasped Jerry's butt and squeezed. Jerry gasped at the amazing pressure, and everything in him wanted to climb Gabe like a tree and then plant that evergreen where it would do the most good.

Before Jerry could anchor a leg around Gabe's hips, he was gone, and Jerry was staggering backward to keep from falling.

Gabe gasped, "Oh God, I'm sorry. I'm so sorry. I hope you enjoy the furniture. Let me know if you change your mind about the other pieces. Otherwise I'll make sure they get here while you're gone." With that he turned, hurried from the house, and before Jerry even made it to the front door, had disappeared out of sight.

Jerry slammed the front door, leaned against it, then slowly collapsed to the floor. *Fuck-a-doodle-doo. Good job, asshole. Find somebody you actually like and enjoy being around and screw it up by being you.*

He dropped his head onto his bent knees.

GABE COULDN'T get his breathing under control. He pulled over to the side of the road about a block from his house, leaned his head back, and sucked air, long and slow, in through his nose. "What the hell did I do?"

He slammed his hand on the steering wheel, but at least on the bottom so nobody on the street could see. He pulled his cell from his pocket and held it so he'd look like he was being a responsible citizen and not driving while on his phone. *Responsible, my ass. I actually get a chance to do something good for Ellie, to sell some of my furniture and make some extra money for her college. All I had to do was be a responsible businessman, and what the fuck do I do? Jump my client's bones.*

Gabe shook his head. *Can I undo this? Jerry's going out of town, and I probably won't see him for a week. If he doesn't fire me tonight or tomorrow, maybe I can get a lot done while he's gone, and when he comes back, he'll be surprised. I'll act like the person he hired, and maybe—*

A picture of him and Jerry wrapped in each other's arms formed from the swirl of confusion in his brain.

Okay, wait—

Jerry hadn't been trying to get away. Hell, if he remembered right, Jerry actually kissed him. Sure, if he'd waited one second, Gabe would have been all over him, but he didn't. He started it. *Okay, so maybe he's not super upset. Or maybe he's pissed that I ended it—*

A knock on the driver's window startled him. MaryAnn, one of Ellie's friends, stood outside waving at him.

He rolled down the window. "Hi, MaryAnn." He gestured with the phone. "Just finished a phone call."

"Oh, cool. I just wanted to be sure everything was okay. Hey, I'm so jealous of Ellie's Jet Gemini tickets. Good going."

"Yeah, she's excited."

"She's going to record it for me. I know it's not allowed, but I promised not to, like, post it or anything. You're so lucky."

"I know."

"Well, so bye." She waved again and bounced away.

He closed the window. Okay, time to stop this shit and go home. Avoiding sexual crap was the smartest thing he'd ever done, even if his cock hated it. His agenda was clear—keep his nose clean, stay untangled, and get his daughter into a good college.

Oh yeah, everything below his belt hated that idea. Some things in his chest too.

He started the truck and drove home. As he pulled into the driveway, the front door of the house burst open and Ellie ran out full speed. He opened the truck door, laughing as she hurled herself at him for a hug.

"You sold the furniture. You sold it. Yahoooo!" She stepped back, and the smile faded just a little. "Are we sure he can pay for it?"

Gabe shrugged. "I've used his strange credit card a couple times, and it's worked. He says I should charge the furniture on it too."

"Wow. Maybe we should do it quick." She laughed and fell in beside him as they walked into the house. "How much are you going to charge him?"

"The same thing I was going to charge Mrs. McRae with a, uh, quantity bonus." He toed off his boots and shed his windbreaker by the door.

"Quantity?"

"Yeah." He chewed his lip. "You couldn't see it in the truck, but he also took the credenza."

"Holy crap." She glanced at him. "Cow."

They both laughed. Gabe said, "And he says he wants the dining table and the bookshelf too."

She pressed a hand over her mouth. "Dad, that's amazing."

He nodded, but he had to manage her enthusiasm a little. "But we shouldn't get too over-the-top. He's a pretty unusual person, and who knows what the future will bring." He sat on the couch, and she perched on the chair opposite him.

"That makes sense. We need to be excited about selling the two pieces and not count on anything else." She stared into space and nodded to herself. "I mean, seriously. Anyone who wears that beanie and those sunglasses at the same time can't be the world's most stable individual."

Gabe barked a laugh, but it hit his heart. "He's a nice guy, really. I just don't know much about him, so I don't want to count on his business." That was kind of the truth.

She stood. "Thanks, Dad. Anyone who makes us three thousand dollars and two pieces of furniture richer needs to be appreciated and not dissed. I apologize for my attitude. Beanies are beautiful!" She laughed and walked into the kitchen, then called, "Dinner in fifteen."

"I'll make salad."

"Tricky one. You're on."

He went to his bedroom, changed, and then headed for the refrigerator. As he washed spinach for the salad, Ellie said, "So what's he like?"

"Jerry?"

"Yeah."

"He's actually pretty friendly and even talkative one-on-one, but if somebody else shows up, he vanishes. The whole time I was meeting with Jorge, I guess Jerry was skulking and listening in, but he never showed his face."

"Why, do you think?"

"I don't know. Extreme social anxiety, I guess."

"He talked to me okay. I mean, he seemed shy, but not tongue-tied. What's with the disguise?"

Gabe frowned. "Disguise. You think it is?"

"What else?"

"Just part of his shyness, I guess. Hell, I walked in on him when he was taking a nap, and he was wearing that insane hat."

She shook her head. "Weird, I'll admit." She pulled a steaming casserole that smelled really good from the oven and carried it to the table. "I guess we have to go back to a card table again if Jerry buys this one." She grinned. "Know what? I won't mind that at all."

Gabe put his salad on the table too, and then carried two glasses of water to their places. Ellie sat next to him, and they dug into her casserole, which turned out to be mac and cheese and broccoli with lots of good tomatoes and herbs. "This is delicious."

"Thanks. I think we should get some steak or salmon on the weekend to celebrate our windfall."

"Sounds wonderful. Then next Friday, we'll leave early and have some good meals on the way to Eugene."

"Fun."

"By the way, I saw MaryAnn on my way home. She's really jonesing over the concert. You sure you don't want to take her? I can hang out somewhere in Eugene until you're done."

She looked up, chewing mac and cheese. She swallowed. "No, I really thought about it. Especially since you liked the music so much, I think it would be more fun to go with you. I'll tell her all about it later."

"Okay, if you're sure." He wasn't going to say how much her choice made him want to tear up. Being chosen as a companion by your seventeen-year-old daughter was pretty great.

She popped her dimples. "So tomorrow you're going on a da-aate."

Sweet Jesus, he'd completely forgotten. "Yeah, I guess I am."

"So a college professor, huh?" She grinned.

"He is that, yes." He stared at the last of his salad. He actually didn't love salad, but he wanted to encourage Ellie to eat her greens.

She was quiet for a minute. "Dad? Is everything okay?"

"What? Oh yes. It's great. But you know me. Lots of change at once unsettles me. I'm just a little uneasy."

"Well, if that's all it is, you're doing great."

"Thanks." He ate the last bite of mac and cheese.

She finished her food and stood to clear dishes. He got up too and grabbed his plate and glass.

"Dad?"

"Hmm?"

"Does Jerry look familiar? I mean, have you ever seen him before?"

He stopped. "Uh, no. I'm pretty sure I've never seen the man before. Why?"

"I don't know. I just thought there was something about him that rang a bell." She laughed. "Maybe weird guys are more familiar than I thought." She started loading the dishwasher.

Gabe rinsed the plates, handed them to Ellie, and desperately wished he knew what his favorite weird guy was thinking.

DAMN. THE phone rang so sharply in his ear, it felt like a migraine. Jerry swatted at it, and his back screamed in protest. *What the hell?* The phone rang again and he opened his eyes. *Damn.* He was lying on the floor in front of the door where he'd fallen asleep.

He felt for the phone. "Yes?"

"We need to pick you up. Where are you?"

Fred. Of course. "Hello to you too."

"Come on, Jerry, enough. There's a lot to do."

"I know." He sat up uncomfortably. "I'll meet you tomorrow."

"Why don't we have dinner tonight and plan?"

"I'd just as soon not."

"Come on, bro, you've got to unbury yourself sometime."

He stared at the floor. One more pizza or dinner with Fred? If he could have that pizza with Gabe…? He released a soft sigh. Fred was right. He couldn't walk away. "Okay, I guess."

"Good. Where?"

"Where are you?"

"San Francisco."

"Meet me in Ashland."

"Oregon?"

"No, North Carolina. Yes, Oregon. At Doves. It's in the old hotel."

"Okay. What time?"

"Text me when you get to Medford. I'll figure out my timing."

"Okay. Can't wait to see you."

"Yeah. Wear your hat." He hung up. Slowly, he rose from the floor. *So this is it. The end of… whatever this has been.*

He walked through the big house, room by room, entering the great room last. He stopped next to the coffee table, knelt down, and ran a hand across the wood. Then he settled on the floor, pressed his cheek against the table, and fell back to sleep.

CHAPTER NINE

"DAD, AREN'T you going to get ready for your date?"

Gabe looked up from the drawings of the desk he was working on at the card table in his workshop—the card table that would move to their dining room when Gabe took the other pieces to Jerry's. "Yeah. Be right there."

"He's coming here, so if you're half-dressed, he's going to know. Come on." She closed the door.

Gabe sat there. No part of him wanted to move. Creating another piece of furniture for Jerry seemed important. Going on a date didn't. *Come on, don't be dumb.* He might never see Jerry again, whereas Clark had gone out of his way to make the date happen.

He stood and walked into the house. He might not be taking the date seriously, but Ellie sure was. The house smelled like furniture polish and Simple Green.

Ellie planted her fists on her hips, and he grinned. "I'm going."

When he reemerged five minutes later, she looked up from her laptop and frowned. "This is it?"

He glanced at his black jeans and plaid shirt. "What? There's nowhere in Oregon I can't go dressed like this."

She bounced up and took his arm. "Come with me."

"Ellie."

She dragged him back to his closet and pulled it open. "Hmm."

"Right. Which pair of black jeans would you like me to choose?" He waved his arm at the meager collection.

"Okay, keep the jeans." She reached into the far back of his small closet and pulled out a white shirt. "Here."

"Come on. I wear that to funerals and weddings."

"Put it on." She crossed her arms again.

"Okay." He pulled off the plaid and put on the long-sleeved white button-down. "My funeral shirt. This could spell the death of the date."

She snorted. "Or you'll be setting a day for your nuptials."

"Don't get your hopes up." He tucked the shirt in.

She pulled an old jean jacket from the closet. "Put this over it."

"I haven't worn that in years."

"Because your life has been dedicated to plaid. Come on." She jiggled the jacket.

Making a face at her, he slid the jacket on. At least it still fit. If anything, it was a little loose.

She immediately went to work rolling up the sleeves and folding back the cuffs of the white shirt. She stepped back. "Very stylish if I do say so myself. Wear this to the concert, okay?"

"Anything for my birthday girl."

Their doorbell rang. Ellie's eyes lit up. "Showtime!"

He could have gone all day without thinking of the date in those terms.

She hurried out to the living room, and he followed more slowly. He'd been optimistic about the date the other night, but now when he thought of spending time with a guy, all he could feel were Jerry's lips. Right, and Jerry's ass.

By the time he got to the door, Ellie had completed introductions and was welcoming Clark inside. He instantly wanted to kiss his daughter. Clark wore a sports coat over his white shirt and jeans.

Ellie said, "Please sit down, Mr. Rickson."

Clark said, "Call me Clark."

"Thank you, Clark."

Yes, thank you, Ellie, since I didn't know Clark's last name. Gabe said, "Hi. Welcome to our house."

Clark smiled. "Thank you." He stepped forward, extended a hand, then pulled Gabe in for a one-armed guy hug. When Clark let go, he sat on the couch.

Okay, so he was serious about getting to know Ellie. Gabe sat in the slightly ratty chair across from Clark.

Ellie bustled over to the counter that separated the kitchen from the dining area and returned with some chopped veggies and dip. She set them on the coffee table—not nearly as nice as the one he'd taken to Jerry's—in front of Clark. "Can I get you something to drink?"

For a second Clark seemed to think about whether she'd be offended if he refused, then said, "No thanks. I think we'll be heading to dinner soon, but I'd love one of these carrots." He dipped it in whatever was in the bowl and crunched it into his mouth.

Gabe laughed. "You've earned points by getting Ellie to voluntarily eat extra vegetables."

Clark raised an eyebrow as he chewed. "I've only seen her *serve* vegetables so far."

Gabe laughed, and Ellie gave them both a look as she grabbed a carrot, drowned it in dip, and shoved it in her mouth.

Clark asked, "What grade are you in, Ellie?"

"I'm a junior."

"Have you decided on college?" He munched another carrot.

"Uh, no. I'm applying for scholarships all over the country."

"What subject do you plan to study?"

"Music, I hope. Maybe with an English minor."

"Well now, you just happen to know someone who teaches English, so if I can offer any advice, just call me, okay? Your dad has my number."

"Thank you, that's very nice." She stood. "So you two need to get to your dinner, right? Don't let me keep you."

Gabe wanted to laugh but managed to stay cool with his almost seventeen-year-old hostess. A few minutes later, she escorted them out the door, and gave Gabe a secret thumbs-up.

As they walked to the car, Clark grinned. "Do you think she's planning a party now that we're gone?"

Gabe shook his head. "If that girl wanted to party she'd have lots of chances. Nope, she's just that responsible. Sometimes I worry that she's had to be too mature too fast, but I think it's her nature."

Clark held Gabe's door, which made him want to blush, but Clark didn't seem to think anything about it. He said, "Trust me. Just because a girl has a single dad doesn't mean she's automatically mature. I see lots of kids that are forced into situations where they need to become grownups and they don't. They act out, get into lots of trouble, and generally screw up. I agree, Ellie's a responsible kid."

"I'm lucky."

Clark pulled away from the curb. "Probably also a good dad."

"Thanks. I hope so. Do you have kids?"

Clark glanced over. "Only the ones I teach."

"Never been married?"

"I knew I was gay when I was eleven."

"Holy crap. Seriously?"

"Yeah. I mean, I knew I was different. Then a couple years later, my mom sat me down and told me about the birds and bees and how sometimes birds like birds and bees like bees and how that's okay." He grinned. "She was a bit more educational than that. It didn't take long for me to understand why she told me. It was accepted in my family. I told my friends, and I was out."

"Man, some guys have all the luck." Gabe smiled and shook his head.

"I gather you were still experimenting with heterosexuality when you were sixteen."

"Yeah. My parents were too wrapped up in their addictions to notice anything about me. Plus, nobody ever believes I'm gay."

"I'd think in high school that'd be good. Hell, high school kids can be assholes."

"Yeah, but nobody ever assumed I was gay. Not my closest friends, even. So I felt different, but since no one ever guessed, I actually figured I was wrong. Maybe I was just gun-shy of girls because of my mother or something. I was dating this girl, and she wanted to have sex. I told her I didn't want to, and of course she said the magic words."

"What?"

"She said, 'What are you? Gay?' I had her on her back so fast they couldn't have recorded it on film. I guess the adrenaline and pure sixteen-year-old horniness got me through it. Of course I ejaculated without even wondering if she took the pill. And at the age of seventeen, I got Ellie."

"Jesus."

"Nope, he didn't help either." They both laughed, and Gabe glanced at the Ashland sign as they entered town. "I forgot to ask where we're going."

"I like Doves Restaurant a lot. How about you?"

"Haven't been there." He didn't say that was because their prices were above his pay grade, but maybe it would be okay to charge his meal, since he and Ellie were a little richer that week. Of course, that reminded him of Jerry.

"You okay?"

Damn, he'd been frowning. "Yeah, just thinking about work."

"I gathered you like your job. All your coworkers seem to think you're the best."

"I do like it. I just have some side gigs I need to wrestle."

"Your furniture business?"

"Uh, yes."

"I noticed the dining room table at your house. Did you make that?"

"Yeah."

"Beautiful and very original. I can't imagine how much work that takes."

"That's the problem. Hard to make it pay."

Clark pulled into a parking space beside Lithia Park. "Hope you don't mind a little walk."

"Not in Ashland I don't."

They both got out of the car and met on the sidewalk. As they headed toward the town plaza, Clark veered off to the right onto a bridge that crossed Lithia Creek to the park. The spring evening was still cool, but the days were lengthening. There was such a contrast between the light in winter and summer in the Northwest. In the park, a haze of green announced the reappearance of the leaves, and some trees even had full flowers. Gabe smiled.

Clark said, "I love this park. It's one of the great things about living here."

"I bet."

"Why don't you move to Ashland?"

"Can't afford it."

Silently, they walked past the lower duck pond and through the plaza, then up Main Street toward the hotel. The sidewalks were full since the Oregon Shakespeare Festival was back in action.

Gabe asked, "Do you go to the plays?"

"Yes, pretty much all of them. I assign them to my students, so I have to see them too. Do you?"

"I've been to a couple. I wanted Ellie to see Shakespeare."

"Did she like it?"

"Yes, a lot."

They walked into the small foyer of Doves Restaurant, and Clark gave his name to the hostess. Wow, he'd even made a reservation.

She walked them to a back corner table by the window.

Clark pointed. "Want the aces and eights chair or facing the door?"

"Hickok's fine with me." Gabe chuckled as he sat facing the wall, the chair position in which Wild Bill Hickok was shot from behind holding the famous aces and eights hand. Clark slid in across from him looking toward the elegant little restaurant.

They both ordered halibut, although Gabe cringed at the "market price." He said, "So tell me about you. I know you had a great mom. What else?"

"You're right about my mom."

"She still living?"

"Oh yeah. She's in Brooklyn with her second husband. Sadly, my dad died young."

"Sorry."

"He was great while I had him."

"Did you always want to be a teacher?"

"No. I wanted to be an astronaut. When I discovered astronauts had to learn math, I decided teaching sounded a lot better. My mom's a teacher, although she teaches high school."

Imagine having great parents.

The waitress brought their fish. Clark had a glass of chardonnay, and Gabe had beer. They chatted and chewed.

Gabe said, "This is really good."

"Glad you're enjoying it. Have room for dessert? I hear they—" He stopped and got an odd expression—half-amused and half-questioning.

Gabe started to turn around. "What?"

Clark grabbed his arm. "Don't turn yet. These two strange guys just walked in. They aren't seated yet."

"How strange?"

"They're both wearing hats and sunglasses. I'm not sure how they can see outside. One has on a cap. You know, like a ball cap. The other one's like a snow hat, which is odd right off since it's not very cold."

Gabe felt himself frowning. Sadly, the snow hat wasn't nearly as odd as it should be. He wanted to turn around so badly, but what if it was Jerry? *Hell, it can't be Jerry, can it? Unless whomever the man is that Jerry's with makes him not shy. Or maybe he was just faking the shyness. But why would he do that? And why would the guy eat pizza every night if he was perfectly able to go to a nice restaurant and eat?*

Brain exploding.

He couldn't stand it. He turned around, and his stomach dropped to his shoes. Three tables away, wearing the very familiar stupid knitted beanie and giant sunglasses, was Jerry. The man with him appeared to be young also, with a slim face and high cheekbones like Jerry's. Around the edges of the other guy's baseball cap, his hair was blond, and his sunglasses weren't quite as big as Jerry's, but still covered a lot of his face.

Gabe wanted to jump up, grab the guy out of his chair, and shake him until he admitted who he was and what he meant to Jerry. He forced himself to turn back around.

Clark stared at him with a crease between his eyebrows. "Are you okay?" He put a firm hand on Gabe's forearm. "You turned white. Do you know those men?"

He gulped some water. "No. I mean, one of them might be a client of mine."

"Client? Like furniture?"

"Yes."

Clark looked over Gabe's shoulder toward where Jerry sat and then back at Gabe. "I think we're done here, right? I mean, across the street is the best ice cream in Ashland. Arguably, the best in southern Oregon. How about we get dessert over there?"

"Sounds perfect." Gabe's stomach and chest didn't feel perfect. His exploded brain was flying in too many directions, most of them toward Jerry. Wanting to ask why Jerry had kissed Gabe. Wanting an explanation for whom the guy with him was and how he got to take Jerry out. Wanting to scream that Clark wasn't anyone special to him, which was a craptastic thing to be thinking about a nice guy. *Fuck!*

Gabe took slow, unobvious breaths as Clark negotiated the bill. Gabe pressed his credit card toward Clark, who shook his head, but Gabe insisted they split it. Especially in light of the not-at-all nice things he'd been thinking.

Finally, with the money wrestling match resolved and their credit cards returned, Clark put his jacket on, and Gabe did the same. They both stood, and Gabe took a moment to get ahold of himself before he turned around to walk out.

Every cell in his body knew the second that Jerry looked up and saw him. Gabe didn't look toward him, and Jerry wore the stupid sunglasses, but it was as if their eyes met and held in some kind of searing accusation.

I wonder what he thinks. I wonder if he wonders what I think.

CHAPTER TEN

GABE STOOD on the sidewalk, not entirely sure how he got there, but then he fell into step beside Clark and tried not to look shell-shocked. They hurried across Main Street at the crosswalk and slipped into the ice cream shop, which landed them in a considerable line.

As they stared into the glass case of ice cream flavors, Gabe forced a smile. "Dinner was great. Thank you for choosing such a terrific place."

"Glad you liked it. Wish you'd let me go through with my plan to take you out this evening."

He said the first thing that came to mind. "If we share, the money goes further."

Clark grinned. "Hmm. I could take that as a good sign that we might be sharing checks in the future."

Gabe laughed and hoped it didn't sound phony. Bless her heart, at that moment the young ice cream server said, "You're next. What would you like?"

Gabe had barely looked. To Clark, he said, "What's good?"

"I like the Rocky Road."

Chocolate and marshmallows. Maybe not. He turned to the girl. "Anything to recommend?"

"A lot of people like coconut crunch."

"Sounds like my kind of flavor. I'll try it."

"Single scoop?"

"Yes, please."

"Dish or cone?"

"One of those waffle cones."

When she handed it to him, his eyes widened. "Uh, I asked for a single."

She grinned. "You got it."

It was huge. He took a lick. "Oh man, that's good."

Clark said, "Told ya. Of course, anyone who doesn't choose chocolate is still in their adolescence tastewise."

"I'll keep that in mind." He took another lick. "Whoa. I've got to bring Ellie here."

Clark produced his credit card. "At least let me treat you to a cone."

"Thank you." As Clark paid, Gabe licked his cone and wandered what he hoped looked aimlessly to the window. He stared across the street toward the hotel and the restaurant. As he watched, the door to the restaurant opened and Jerry walked outside—alone. He looked in both directions through his sunglasses, then reached up and ripped them off and looked again.

Half of Gabe wanted to run across the street yelling, "Here I am." The winning half stood right where he was, his tongue suspended on its way to his ice cream cone.

Clark walked up beside him. "Want to stay here and enjoy your ice cream or walk and lick at the same time."

Gabe stared out the window as Jerry's shoulders visibly sagged and he turned and went back into the restaurant. *Right, to his date.* "I guess walking is a good idea."

Five minutes later, Gabe had eaten his cone, and they'd walked back through the park to Clark's car. Gabe tossed his paper napkin in the trash and climbed into Clark's Volvo.

When they were both buckled in, Clark started the car and then looked at Gabe. "Where to?"

Gabe swallowed. "Home, I guess. Ellie…." He drifted off because he couldn't quite bring himself to blame it on her.

Clark didn't say anything; he just flipped into gear and took off toward the 5 Freeway. A couple of minutes into the drive, he turned up the radio, and Gabe was vaguely aware that music was playing as he stared into the dark.

Before he knew it, Clark pulled up in front of Gabe's house and stopped.

Gabe blinked and glanced around. "Oh."

Clark looked at him with a smile.

Gabe swallowed. "Would you like to come in? I can't guarantee that Ellie's not awake."

"I certainly wouldn't mind seeing Ellie, but I have a feeling you'd just as soon I went on my way."

Gabe started to deny it—and stopped. "I'm sorry. It was a tough day, and I guess it wore me out."

"Tough day at the home improvement store?" Clark smiled when he said it, but Gabe met his eyes. It was the first time he'd gotten a hint of condescension from Clark. Maybe not surprising for a college professor evaluating a guy who worked in a retail store, but it still gave Gabe a weird feeling. Like he might not blame him, but he did.

"Actually, a tough day working on a home renovation, but it's all the same kind of stuff. Thanks for the evening. Sorry I wasn't better company." He opened the car door.

"Gabe?"

Gabe turned.

"I didn't really mean that the way it came out."

"No?" He paused. "Of course not, since you had to know what I did for a living when you asked me out. I kind of wondered what a college professor would see in a guy like me." He grinned. "But then I know what a sexy beast I am. Thanks again." He slid out of the car, closed the door, and walked into the house without looking back.

When he opened the front door, Ellie looked up from her laptop. "Hey, Dad, aren't you home early?" She gazed at him. "You okay? You look kind of shell-shocked. Did Clark turn out to be an a-hole? He seemed really nice."

"No, he was nice. I guess I just wasn't into it. I'm not a very good date."

"What? I'm so fun to hang with I've wrecked you for attractive gay men?" She chuckled, and he laughed.

"Must be it." He cocked his head toward the bedroom. "I'm gonna go get out of my fashionable clothes."

"Well, you're not quite ready for Christian Siriano, but you do look cute."

"I won't spoil my image by asking who that is." He walked to his bedroom, shut the door behind him, and leaned against it. *Why do I feel this way? I chose to take offense at a comment from Clark that most days I'd ignore. He's an attractive guy, and he went to a little trouble for the date. I blew it on purpose.*

He wiped a hand over his face. *Who the hell was the guy with Jerry, and why do I care?*

He pulled off his clothes, forced himself to hang them up rather than throwing them over the arm of his chair, and yanked on his sweatpants and shirt. With a flip, he sat on the edge of his bed and stared into space until a tap on his door roused him. "It's open, Ellie."

She stuck her head in, then pushed the door and let the rest of her follow. "Hey, Dad, what's wrong?" She crossed to the corner, plopped in the chair, and folded her fingers patiently like she'd wait all night for answers. "You aren't acting normal."

Reflexively, he started to say "nothing's wrong" but stopped himself. Did he really want to tell his not-quite-seventeen-year-old daughter the truth? Or something like it? He let out a breath. "You know my client, Jerry?"

"He who shall not be dissed for his weird hat because he might pay my college tuition?" Her dimples flashed.

"Yes, that Jerry."

He must have paused too long because her mouth and eyes opened at the same time. "You like him." It wasn't a question. "You've got a thing for beanies." She was keeping it light, but she looked really inquisitive.

"I barely know why, but I do. I like him."

"You like him like that?" Her eyes really widened at the thought.

"I'm not quite sure what 'that' is, but yeah, probably."

She crossed her arms. "You're sure you don't just feel sorry for him?"

He frowned. "Why should I?"

"Okay, if that's not obvious, you must definitely be hung up on him. Strange cap, can't talk to anyone but you, lives on pizza in a wreck of a house. Remember?"

"Yeah, well I saw him tonight in an expensive restaurant with another guy also wearing a weird hat and sunglasses, so maybe it's a frigging club." A club Gabe didn't belong to.

"You're kidding."

"No."

"There're two of them?"

"Apparently."

She raised her eyes, and this time they flooded with compassion. "That's why you're so upset."

Crap, he hated to admit it. "Yeah."

"So tomorrow, first thing, you go to his house and talk to him. Ask him so who's the guy. Tell him you like him." She chewed her lip. "Hey, he may have gotten the wrong idea about you. After all, you were with Clark. So you have as much explaining to do as he does."

"I can't."

"Come on. You're smart and a good talker. Look how much your customers love you. You can—"

"He's not there." He cocked half a smile. "And thanks for the compliments."

"Where is he?"

"No idea. I just know he's supposed to be gone for five or six days at least."

"Hmm." Her bottom lip disappeared between her teeth again. "You better call him. Otherwise, you'll never sleep. Do you think he likes you?"

"I'm not sure." He knew Jerry's cock seemed to like him, but that didn't mean his brain or heart agreed.

"Definitely, call him."

"And if he doesn't answer?"

"Text."

"What should I say?"

She cocked her head. "You saw him with this other guy, right? Did he see you?"

Gabe nodded.

"And neither of you said anything?" She looked at him like he was five.

"No. I didn't want to embarrass him or anything."

"In other words, you had no clue what to say."

"Correct."

She leaned forward on her jeans-clad legs looking thoughtful. "So tell him you saw him and you're sorry you didn't say hello, but you didn't want to interrupt his conversation. Say you're looking forward to seeing him when he comes back. That way, he has a perfect opening to tell you who he was with and where he's going."

"Or he might fire me and never speak to me again."

She sat up and spread her hands with a flourish. "Know what? Since your feelings aren't platonic, it's better to know now than to guess and jump to wrong conclusions."

"Don't forget the college tuition."

"I'm getting a scholarship."

"You are?"

"Of course. Brilliance runs in the family. Except you didn't get any gay social skills, but they don't give scholarships in that." She grinned.

"Damned shame." He grinned back. She was right. His fingers itched to dial. "Okay, I'll do it. Go away and let me die of shame on my own."

"You sure you don't want me to supervise? Coach?"

They were both laughing when his phone pinged with a new text. They both froze. He stammered, "Uh, it's probably Harry or work." Harry never texted him, and work seldom did. Gabe's heart slammed.

"Check it, quick." Ellie leaned forward in the chair. Gabe gave her a quick glance, and she made a face. "Oh come on, I at least get to know if it's Jerry."

He flicked his eyes toward his phone screen as if it was Medusa and he was about to be turned to stone. Another slam to the heart. "It is."

"Jerry?" She giggled with way too much excitement.

He pointed toward the door. "Out. Let me take my text lashing in privacy."

"But you're going to tell me what he says, right?" *Am I?* When he didn't answer immediately she repeated, "Right?"

"Right."

"Oh-kay." She huffed as she rose, took a longing look toward his phone, and walked with heavy steps out of his bedroom.

Gabe took a deep breath, then keyed in his code to wake up his phone and glanced away from the screen when the preview of the text message appeared. He clicked on home, then chose his text icon, saw the top message from Jerry, and clicked on it.

Hi. Where did you go? I chased after you but you were gone. I wanted to introduce you to my brother.

Gabe stared at the text, the word *brother* practically glowing like a neon sign. Still, it had taken Jerry a few minutes before he ran after Gabe, which reflected a little more uncertainty than the text suggested.

He practically called Ellie for help, but decided he was a big gay boy and could manage a text by himself. Hell, it was probably just a text to a client.

I didn't want to intrude. Sorry to miss meeting him. His fingers paused; then he typed, *Have you left on your trip?*

The bubbles danced and the answer came. *Yes. Do you have everything you need to manage while I'm gone?*

Gabe snorted softly. He wanted to type, *No. I don't have any full lips to kiss or a world-class ass to squeeze.* Instead he texted, *Depends on what you want managed.*

Getting as much done on the house as possible.

Gabe frowned. *There are a lot of decisions to make. You sure you don't want to be here for them?*

No. I want you to make them. Surprise me.

What if I paint the living room chartreuse?

Then you have to live with it.

Can a man smile and frown at the same time? What the hell did that comment mean? *Okay, no chartreuse.*

You have credit card. Use it. Make me more furniture too. Sure would like a place to sleep.

Another one of those comments that exploded Gabe's brain. *Don't have a key to house.* Jerry usually left the door open, but hopefully he hadn't done that this time.

Left a key under the mat.

First place a robber would look.

What will they steal? Pizza boxes? They can't lift my coffee table.

Okay, I'll try to get shit done.

Counting on you. See you in about a week. Call if you need me.

Just the thought of all the ways he could need Jerry made him sweat in his sweats. He typed, *Likewise.* Jerry could take that any way he wanted.

Gabe waited, but no more texty bubbles bounced, and he finally gave up and slid his phone back into his pocket.

A plaintive voice called from the other room, "You're sure taking a long time. Are you crying? Should I come and take the pills from your hand?"

He chuckled and walked down the hall to the living room where Ellie sat with her legs bent up in front of her on the chair, holding on to her knees. "So?"

"Sooooo—" He walked to the couch and flopped on it, lying on his back.

"Dad!"

He grinned. "The guy he was with is his brother."

She let go of her knees and thrust herself forward. "No kidding?"

"He said it was a shame I didn't stop and say hello because he wanted to introduce me to his brother."

She waggled her eyebrows. "Sounds like he went out of his way to make sure you know it was his brother."

"Yeah, now that you mention it, he kind of did."

"Of course, if you'd stopped, you would have had to explain who you were with, and that would not have been a relative."

"True." Weirdly, he'd been thinking so hard about who Jerry was with, he'd kind of forgotten he'd been on a date. *I wonder what Jerry thought.* Gabe gave him a few cool points. Of course, more likely it meant he didn't care.

CHAPTER ELEVEN

"So what else did he say?" Ellie gazed raptly at Gabe.

"Just business stuff. How he wants me to get as much done as I can while he's gone." He gave her a side-eyed look. "And how he wants me to make him more furniture."

"No shit?" She leaped up. The only thing she cared more about than Gabe's social life was selling his furniture.

"Ellie?"

"News that good deserves an expletive or two." She walked to the kitchen.

He raised his voice so she could hear him. "Yeah. He specifically wants me to find him a bed."

"What's he sleep on now?"

"A mattress on the floor."

She leaned over the kitchen peninsula. "Want an ice cream?"

"Had some tonight."

"Really?"

"Went to Zoey's."

"Oh yum. Should have brought me some."

"Seriously?"

"No." She sat back in the chair, chomping on an ice cream sandwich. "So Jerry's a strange one. How's he plan to pay for the bed?"

Gabe shrugged, lying down. "He says use the card."

"Well I guess he wouldn't cheat a man he was so anxious to have meet his *bu-ro—ther*."

He snorted. Truthfully, every time he used the card, he held his breath. So far so good.

"So I gather the date wasn't much?"

He sighed softly. "I like Clark. He went to some trouble, made a reservation at Doves."

"Wow. He paid like Sir Galahad?"

"He wanted to, but I paid half."

"You didn't want to owe him." She nodded sagely.

"Well, it was an expensive place."

"You're funny. I wish you could see the difference in your face when you talk about Clark versus when you talk about the beanie wearer."

"Clark's nice, I just—"

She held up a hand. "I get it. He's pretty clean for you."

"Uh, haven't I been taking enough showers or what?"

"You know what I mean. He's like white bread with no mustard. You like a little more sexual danger."

He sat up. "How would you know what I like? I never go out." Right. He never got any sex, dangerous or not.

"When you comment on actors or sports guys, they're always the sexy ones with a little edge."

"So I like dirty beanies?"

"I bet there's a little danger under that hat." She laughed, and the idea made him shift on the couch. She wiped her hands on the paper napkin she'd wrapped around her ice cream. "So remember that platform bed you made that they put on display at Sanderson's Furniture to see if anybody would spring for handmade pieces?"

He slowly nodded. "Yeah."

"I think that may just belong to Jerry."

"PUT THE mirror there, please." Gabe pointed at the wall in the long master closet.

Jorge stuck his head in. "Hey, Gabe, need to ask you something about the island."

"Be right there." Gabe checked on the progress in the master bath where they'd removed the back wall and framed the new bathroom addition, and then he trotted the length of the long hall and down the stairs to the kitchen. As he walked into the enormously expanded space, he wiped at his eyes.

Jorge said, "When was the last time you slept?"

"It's been a bunch of nights with a few hours sleep each, but I want to get as much done for the owner as I can while he's out of town." After the crews quit each evening, Gabe had been working into the night finishing bathrooms and installing bookshelves in the library, living room, and family room.

"That's devotion, man. But I understand. Who wouldn't want to do this house?"

"Yeah." Jorge got it. Gabe was in hog heaven getting to trick out the house the way he would have wanted it if the house were his. When Jerry came back, Gabe would feel like he had to ask more questions. At the moment, he was large and in charge and didn't want to waste a minute of it.

"How many men you got working on this place?"

"A lot." Gabe chuckled. Jorge's crew crawled all over the new kitchen, fireplace guys were cleaning the ducts and fixing the fireplace, a floor crew was going crazy trying to get wood laid all over the second floor at the same time painters and drywall guys were doing the walls. They were all running into each other, but as promised, shit was getting done.

"Well, let them do the work. You get some sleep."

Gabe cocked a half smile. "Nope. I'm taking my kid to Eugene for some big rock concert. We're celebrating her birthday."

Jorge gave him a look through his safety goggles. "You've got a kid old enough for rock concerts?"

"Yep. Seventeen tomorrow."

"Hey, man, you got somebody else doing your aging for you?"

"I had her when I was almost seventeen myself."

"Jesus. Well, that's quite a concert you're going to."

"It is?"

"Yeah. Jet Gemini. Man, big star."

"I've heard of him, I guess."

"He'd normally never show up in a place as small as Eugene, but I guess he went to University of Oregon, and this concert is a big fundraiser for the university."

"My daughter said something about that. Are you going?"

"No. The tickets sold out in a couple hours."

"Well, I guess I lucked out. So what's your question?"

They leaned over the frame of the island and looked at the drawings Jorge was working from. A piece of Gabe's brain wandered toward the impending rock concert. He had to not only stay awake tomorrow long enough to get to Eugene, watch the concert, and drive home, but he had to be alert and excited. No way he wanted to disappoint Ellie for even a minute.

When five o'clock came, all the subs were gone, and he was installing towel racks and a toilet paper holder in the one upstairs bath that was finished. He wanted a nice bathroom for Jerry to use while his master bath was being expanded out onto the deck.

When he finished screwing in the robe hook, he stepped back and looked. Nice. Really nice. This bath had come complete with a Japanese-style soaking tub made of glistening emerald-colored tile that, amazingly, had been in good shape. He'd installed a glass shower next to it, replaced the beat-up floor with heated marble, and applied paint to the walls. Aside from the fact that there were no window coverings, the room was ready for company.

"Need some towels." The two ragged things in Jerry's bathroom wouldn't do the job. Gabe could pick some up in Medford on the weekend. Of course, he didn't know when Jerry would be home. Since the text giving Gabe decision-making power, he'd heard nada.

He walked into the hall where the freshly laid maple flooring gleamed underfoot, dusty but beautiful. Gabe was lucky every bedroom had its own balcony so workers could enter that way on ladders to do repairs, and he was free to have floors laid without worrying about them getting wrecked.

He stepped across the hall to the big bedroom that would eventually be a guestroom, but in the short term would be Jerry's sleeping room while the master was being finished. From wood floors to polished beam ceilings to the reinforced balcony with a view of the pool, the room looked great. At least Jerry would have a retreat from the mess.

Okay, enough. I need to get home and sleep so I don't drift off on the road tomorrow night.

He trotted down the stairs and took one last look at the beautiful, soaring great room. *Man.* The room was painted, the ceilings polished, bookshelves installed, the huge ceiling fan that looked like palm fronds was operational, and so was the enormous fireplace. He knew that Jerry loved this room best. So did Gabe. In the middle of the room, the coffee table sat like some kind of icon. He hoped the couches he'd ordered arrived soon. Since they were pretty expensive, he hadn't wanted to add to the cost by making it a rush delivery.

He left through the front door and locked it behind him.

All the way home, his brain buzzed with details he needed to remember and to-do items that should be added to the list. When he turned onto their street, his foot faltered on the accelerator. Damn. Tiffany's car was parked in the driveway. Not even in front of the damned house.

He stomped the accelerator, pulled up in front of his house, hit the brakes hard enough to make them squeal, and was out of the truck and across the lawn in seconds. The screen door squeaked as he pushed it open.

Ellie sat on the couch between Tiffany and Irving. Despite the open package and pile of tissue paper surrounding her, Ellie looked miserable. *What's going on?*

Tiffany looked up and plastered on a smile that didn't quite warm up her eyes. "Hi, Gabe. I heard you'd been spending so much time at work, I thought you might not be here."

Gabe had to bite his tongue to keep from saying, "Sorry to disappoint you." Ellie shot him an apologetic look. Tiffany probably based her idea about Gabe's work on something Ellie had said. "Been working hard on this special project. Short-term thing."

"I thought you told the court that you keep that ridiculous ImproveMart job with its absurd salary because it's stable and gives you time with Ellie?"

He walked to a chair and sat. "What's going on, Tiffany?"

She frowned, although Irving's mild expression barely changed. "As you can see, we brought Ellie her birthday present, since she's not going to be here on her actual birthday."

He let all the bait lie. "How nice. What did you get, Ellie?"

Slowly, Ellie reached into the tissue and pulled out a white Bible. She held it up and stared at Gabe with such a determinedly neutral expression, he almost laughed.

"Oh, how nice. You must have picked that out, Irving."

Tiffany snapped, "What do you mean by that?"

"I mean he must have picked it out."

He smiled softly, like he was somehow receiving visions of celestial beings the others couldn't see. "Yes, I did pick it out. White for our pure angel."

Ellie jumped up, dropped the Bible on the coffee table, and walked out of the room.

Tiffany's frown got deeper. "She was fine until you came home."

Gabe said nothing.

Tiffany cleared her throat. "I'm glad we have a moment. I want to talk to you about Ellie's college."

"What about it?"

"Irving, uh, and I are prepared to pay for it, but she has to go to our choice of school."

He raised an eyebrow. "And what is your choice?"

She glanced at Irving, but his angelic mask didn't slip, so she said, "We'd accept Liberty, Biola, or George Fox."

"That's nice, you guys, but none of those are Ellie's choice to my knowledge. I'll certainly discuss it with her." He stood and gazed at them. *Message? Time's up. Leave.*

Ellie walked back in from the hall. "Thanks so much for coming to wish me a happy birthday." She said nothing about the gift.

Tiffany stood and Irving drifted up beside her. She said, "So what did you get Ellie for her birthday?"

"Concert tickets." He glanced at Ellie in time to see her grimace.

Tiffany pounced. "What kind of concert?"

"Actually, it's a special concert for charity, raising money for Oregon University. Lots of big names."

Ellie's lips twitched.

Tiffany looked somewhat mollified, but weirdly, Irving's sainthood descended into fire and brimstone. "That concert is the work of the devil. Our ministry has been protesting for weeks."

Tiffany glanced between Gabe and Irving. "What? Why?"

Irving's eyes widened, and his hands spread like he was feeling the brimstone. "Satanic, orgiastic rituals."

Gabe saw it coming but couldn't stop it. Ellie's eyes widened, her nostrils flared, and she yelled, "That's bullshit, and you know it."

Tiffany gasped.

Irving whirled on her and raised his right hand.

Gabe took one step forward, grabbed Irving's hand, and squeezed so hard it should have broken. "Don't even think about it."

"Ow!" he nearly shrieked. "Let go of me or I'll have you arrested for assault."

Tiffany shook her hands in front of her. "Let go of him, Gabe. Let go!"

Slowly, Gabe released Irving, who yanked his arm back.

Gabe said, "Don't ever think of raising a hand to Ellie, or Tiffany for that matter."

"Don't be ridiculous. I had no plans to hit our angel. I was simply raising my hand to gesticulate against her terrible choice of language."

"It could have been better." He took a breath and tried not to think of all the shit those two could stir up if they were provoked. Sadly, this meeting had been pretty damned provoking. "It's best you go now. Ellie and I need to make dinner. Thank you for coming to wish Ellie a happy birthday."

Ellie said nothing. Her lips were pressed together in an angry line.

In Tiffany's favor, she looked conflicted. She'd seen Irving lift his hand and probably had a helluva clear idea about his intentions. She didn't appear too excited about the idea of her fiancé hitting her daughter. She took a breath, walked to angry Ellie, and hugged her, though she didn't get a lot of response. "Happy birthday, dear. I'll have a couple other little things for you later." She looked at Gabe with a glare, but not a really convincing one. Nodding, she walked toward the door.

Irving gave Gabe a look that sure as fuck wasn't saintly or benign, then followed Tiffany out of the house.

For a second, Gabe and Ellie stared at each other, and then she burst into tears.

He covered the space between them in a second and gathered her into his arms.

She sobbed, "I'm sorry, Dad. So sorry."

He held her out from him and looked into her face. "What on earth are you sorry for?"

"M-making them mad." She sniffed.

"Sweetie, they came with an agenda. You're the one who deserves to be pissed."

"But-but what will they do?" Her sobs renewed.

He hugged her. "Come on, you've got nothing to worry about. You're seventeen. The judge is going to respect your choices, and there's nothing they can say or do about that."

"Really?"

Man, he wished that was true. Still, he walked her to the sofa, sat down with her, and held her tightly, rocking her like he'd done when she was a tiny baby and he was a teenager. "Come on, it's almost your birthday. We're going to have a great time. Take their birthday gift and flush it down the toilet if you want."

"Too hard on the plumbing." She sniffed and chuckled.

"Probably true, but if you want me to bury it in the backyard, hand it over."

She laughed. "I've been l-looking forward to the concert so much."

"You keep looking forward to it. I am."

"W-work of the d-devil."

"Yeah right, I'm thinking of taking my pitchfork."

She laughed.

"Let's make some food and look at all the restaurants near the campus. We can pick out the very best one for dinner." He nudged her. "Go get comfortable, and I'll start dinner."

She snuffled and dragged her feet toward her bedroom. Gabe would gladly have smacked Tiffany for wrecking Ellie's enthusiasm. Irving, on the other hand, he wanted to lay out like a cheap carpet—and would, given half a chance. The bastard had shown his true colors. No more holier than thou.

Gabe pulled some already chopped onions and garlic from the refrigerator and started sautéing them. For a second he managed to keep his own doubts at bay, but his worries about the evil Irving and what he might do—and persuade Tiffany to do—crept in. Yes, Ellie was nearly an adult, but if Tiffany and her asshole managed to convince the judge that Ellie was in some kind of danger or trouble, all bets were off. No way they'd let Ellie choose to stay somewhere the judge thought was really bad for her.

He sucked in a breath. But that wouldn't happen. Gabe might not be the world's greatest provider, but Ellie wanted to live with him. Plus working on Jerry's house would give them some extra money for Ellie's college. Hell, it was going to be a fantastic year, and then he'd be getting his own daughter ready to leave for the university, or wherever she wanted to go. That was a lot more than he'd gotten to do. Of course, the idea of watching her go gave him a queasy stomach. Since the fateful day when almost nineteen-year-old Tiffany had announced tearfully to sixteen-year-old Gabe that she was pregnant, his whole life had been about seeing that Ellie was happy and cared for.

Ellie walked back in wearing her pink sweatpants and a big T-shirt. Gabe crooked an elbow around her neck and gave her a quick kiss. "So right after dinner, I'll get out the black candles and we can get started."

She looked at him like he was nuts. "Get started on what?"

He widened his eyes innocently. "Don't we need to do satanic rituals before we can go see this rock star of yours?"

"Dad!" But she laughed, and as he'd hoped, it broke the tension.

"So tell me about this guy." He added olives and tomatoes to his mixture and slid half a package of pasta into a big pan of boiling water. "Is he a solo act?"

"No. It's a band, but the group has Jet's name. It's called Jet Gemini."

"That can't be his real name."

"It's not, but nobody talks about his real name at all." She grinned. "You're going to love him."

"I'm sure I will, but you can still change your mind and ask MaryAnn. I'm happy to wait for you guys and be your driver."

She shook her head as she pulled out a bag of already ripped-up lettuce and assembled two salads. "No, I really want you to see him."

"So I can be lured to the dark side?"

"Exactly." She poured some sparkling cider into two glasses.

"Well, I'm honored that you want me."

"Even if you're scarred for life?" She giggled.

"Looking forward to it." He reached for the glasses, handed one to her, and clinked them together. "To my almost seventeen-year-old daughter."

She raised her glass. "And to Jet Gemini!"

CHAPTER TWELVE

"THERE ARE sure a lot of trees on this road."

Gabe glanced at Ellie, who was staring fixedly out the car window at the beautiful but admittedly unchanging landscape. She'd given up on staring fixedly at her phone when the reception got shaky.

Her phone made a chirping sound. "Oh good. Reception." She grabbed it, and her head bent. "Wow."

"What?"

"MaryAnn's dad pulled some strings at Oregon U and got her a ticket to the concert, but she's going to be alone, so she'll come find us." Her thumbs flew over her phone keys. "I'm telling her our seat numbers."

Gabe smiled. "Good. You'll have someone with you who shares your passion."

"You said you liked the music."

"I did. It's just, uh, I'm not as familiar as MaryAnn, so you two will have more to talk about." And if he wanted to escape to the truck at intermission for a snooze, he could do it and she'd barely notice. "Is she nearby? Want to invite her to have dinner with us?"

"Oh, are you sure?" But she looked excited.

"Absolutely. Come on, we've got to have some fun from all those overtime hours I've been spending on my moonlight job."

"Thanks, Dad." The flying thumbs went to town; then she stared at the phone screen again. "Yes. She's close to campus. I guess her dad dropped her off at her aunt's or something. Anyway, she'd love to come."

"Get the address. We'll pick her up."

"No, she says her uncle will drop her off at the restaurant and then we can take her back after, if that works."

"For sure."

The thumbs clicked, and then Ellie looked up. "Yay. We're finally off the 5."

"Don't dis da 5. It's our road to everywhere." The 5 Freeway snaked up the entire west coast and was so central to Oregon transportation, people didn't have to say what town they lived in; only what exit. But they'd finally left the highway and were threading through the tree-lined streets of Eugene, a small city that looked exactly like what it was—a college town. Kids walked down the sidewalks, chatting, and bikes were parked everywhere. Most streets had at least one pizza parlor.

Ellie stared avidly out the window.

Gabe said, "Nice town, huh?"

"Yeah." She kept staring.

"The drive home's pretty easy. I mean, if you decide you might want to go to Oregon University. They have a good music school, right?"

She nodded, but there was a crease between her brows. "But here I'd need to pay room and board. If I go to SOU, I can live at home, and they have a great music program too."

"True, but SOU costs more, so it's a wash."

She glanced over her shoulder. "Trying to get rid of me?"

"Yep. Gotta make way for my wild gay sexual orgies."

"Right." She stared out the window again as they turned on the street where his map app said the restaurant was located. "Oregon gives a lot of financial aid. I read that. And since I'm in-state, I have a better chance of being accepted."

He blew a soft razzberry. "Ellie, you make nearly straight *A*s, you were sophomore president, and you still hold down a job. What college isn't going to take you?"

"You're biased." Still, she smiled.

"Here we are." He pulled into a small lot next to a sign for the Italian restaurant they'd picked, a few blocks from the arena where the concert was being held.

As they parked, Ellie started waving like a fiend through the window as MaryAnn climbed out of a nearby car. An older woman in jeans and a tailored jacket got out of the back seat and walked to the truck while MaryAnn bounded over, and Ellie jumped out to give her a hug.

Gabe slid out of the truck and smiled at the lady. "They're pretty excited."

She turned out to be MaryAnn's great-aunt and was satisfied when Gabe assured her that he'd keep an eye on MaryAnn and take her home afterward.

The lady shook her head. "You certainly don't look old enough to have a teenage daughter."

"She keeps me young."

"I think that's the opposite of what they say about most teenage girls."

"She's exceptional."

She smiled. "You're welcome to come and hang out with us while the girls are at the concert."

"No, actually Ellie insisted that I have to see the concert, so I have a ticket too."

She laughed. "Good luck with that."

"I'm pretty sure I'll need it."

What followed was a good dinner of decent Italian food, accompanied by a nonstop litany of history and praise about Jet Gemini. How tall he was—six foot one and a half. How much he weighed—156, which made him very slender. Previously, he'd been able to sit on his hair, but he'd cut a foot off of it a few months before and had sent the fan world into hysteria, but it ended up looking great.

No tats. He was afraid of needles.

He'd always wanted a cat but traveled so much, he didn't want to leave it alone.

Gabe managed to ask, "Where does he live?"

MaryAnn said, "California, naturally."

Ellie nodded. "San Francisco, actually."

"Right, San Francisco." MaryAnn said, "Did you see pictures of his place on *TMZ*? I died!"

Apparently dying was good. "So how old is he?"

"Oh, like twenty-five or something."

Ellie said, "Twenty-six."

Gabe struggled for more questions. "Is he married?"

"No." MaryAnn rested her cheek on her hand. "Never found the right girl."

Ellie said, "Some people say he's gay."

MaryAnn snorted. "They're just jealous of him."

Gabe cocked his head. "Jealous of his being gay?"

"No, silly, they just don't like how popular he is, so they spread rumors."

Ellie shrugged. "So what if he's gay? Not like we're going to get invited to be his girlfriend."

MaryAnn sighed dramatically. "I can dream."

Gabe laughed and looked at his watch. "We better get over there and find our seats. It's a big place."

Ellie said, "Twelve thousand."

"And it's sold out." Gabe shook his head in amazement.

"Oh yes, he sells out Madison Square Garden."

They found parking in the lot of the big arena that was on an off night for basketball, so it had been turned into a concert venue. After some thrashing around to find the right entrance, MaryAnn got directed one way and Gabe and Ellie the other.

Gabe said, "Shall we come with you to find your seat?"

MaryAnn shook her head. "I looked up the floor plan online. I know right where it is. I got a really good seat."

The two girls hugged, and MaryAnn hurried toward her entrance.

Gabe led the way to their seats, which also turned out to be pretty good. They could see the stage clearly with no obstructions. It wasn't close, but Ellie would be able to see her hero, at least, and hear the music.

Ellie sat, but she was practically bouncing up and down with excitement. Her phone dinged, and she looked at her screen. "OMG, MaryAnn's in the third row."

"I guess her dad has some clout."

"No. It's just harder to sell singles."

The lights went down, and after the audience was warned not to take pictures and to silence their cell phones, the warm-up act came out and started to perform. The four guys had a boy-band sound, and Gabe gazed around the arena in boredom.

Ellie leaned over. "Sorry. They're a little lame. I think the college must have chosen them; otherwise I don't think they'd ever have gotten to open for Jet."

The four guys ran off the stage, and with no preamble, a huge anthem-like song began. Four men, dressed in variations on jeans and T-shirts and playing their instruments, were lowered on wires into the arena.

Gabe whispered, "Which one's Jet?"

"None of them yet."

When the other musicians touched the ground, a big tower in the middle of the stage rotated open to reveal a man. From where they were, Gabe could make out that the guy was tall and slim, but mostly it was about the hair. Shimmering pale hair, like somebody had captured moonlight, flew around his head, blown by a wind machine.

And then he began to sing.

Holy shit. His voice, kind of high, kind of mellow, but with an edge and rasp that cut through and scraped along the nerves like a cat's tongue, filled the entire arena.

Ellie leaned over and grinned. "That's Jet Gemini."

"I guessed."

Jet Gemini sang his way through the first song while descending the steps of the huge tower, but he didn't walk. *Hell no.* He slithered, he gyrated, he slunk. He'd take a step down, then twist himself so he was leaning so far over backward it was a miracle he didn't pop a vertebra. Then he'd spin and run up three stairs, then slide his way down again.

The man could dance and move like he invented the concept, but what he really cornered the market on was sex. Every undulation, every twitch, reeked of carnal knowledge. Gabe wanted to hide Ellie's eyes— except if he stood up, his erection would have knocked over the women in the next row.

The girls in the audience screamed so loud, it was hard to hear anything but the bass line and the drums. Still, Gabe couldn't take his eyes from the rubber band of a body that managed to make you wish you were tied up.

He put his program on his lap to cover the evidence. His condition made him feel stupid. *Who gets a hard-on for a rock star? Come on, I know better than that kind of fantasyland.* But no amount of yelling at himself made a difference, since *el boner* wasn't going anywhere until Jet Gemini stopped strutting around the stage like a living wet dream.

After a bunch of songs, all of which Gabe liked a lot in all the wrong ways, they took a break for intermission. Gabe said, "How about I get some ice cream for our dessert?"

"That would be great, but first tell me how you like it."

"Oh, I love the music. It's, uh, original."

She frowned. "Is that another word for crappy?"

"No, honestly, I like it. A lot!"

He stood, still holding his program strategically, although his condition had improved. Ellie looked a little less disappointed, though not satisfied, but he really needed to walk and breathe before the second half. "Let me get the ice cream, and then we can talk more."

He hurried to the busy refreshment stand and got two ice cream bars, then added a third, thinking MaryAnn would probably show up during intermission. He should pack his dick in the three freezing desserts. It might get the thing under control.

When he carried the bars back to their seats, sure enough, MaryAnn was sitting in his seat, and the two girls were talking like they got paid for it. He distributed the ice cream.

MaryAnn said, "Thank you, Mr. Mason. I've got an idea. You know, my seat's really good. Why don't you go down there and I'll stay here with Ellie."

"I don't want to take your great seat."

"No, like, really, it would be fun, because then I can talk to Ellie and you get to see the show close-up. You'll like it. Seriously."

Some sensible piece of his brain wanted to run out of the arena and hide in the truck until this ordeal was over. It wasn't that the show was X-rated or something he didn't want his kid to see. No, this was personal. Somehow Jet Gemini pushed every one of Gabe's buttons, tweaked every fantasy, and vibrated through him like his own private melody. But no way could he walk out. In fact, he couldn't seriously turn down the chance to see this guy closer.

Hell, he was practically drooling.

He swallowed. "You sure?" He looked at Ellie. "Why don't you go take a closer look?"

For a second, MaryAnn looked uncertain. Sitting with her best friend's father clearly wasn't what she had in mind, but she rallied and clapped her hands together. "You could, like, for serious, El. I mean, I was so close I could, like, see his eyes."

Ellie gripped her sweater in her fist. "Oh, those eyes. Amazing." Then she shrugged. "But I think Dad should go. Then we can gang up and plot world domination."

MaryAnn looked a little relieved, and Gabe fought the whirlwind of elation in his gut. Getting to do his salivating in private and up close sounded like a dream.

He leaned against the seat in front of them and finished his ice cream while the girls compared enthusiastic notes. When the lights flashed, he collected their sticks and wrappers. "Okay, so you two sure you don't want to change your minds?"

"No, we're good." Ellie grinned.

MaryAnn told him the seat number and pointed down to the front, two sections over. "Down there."

"Guess I'm going."

Ellie gave him the side-eye. "Just don't become a rock-star groupie, Dad."

"Oh, thanks a bunch."

Ellie snorted, and MaryAnn obviously didn't get the joke. She knew Ellie's dad was gay, but it probably didn't occur to her that an old guy would find her heartthrob sexy too.

Gabe slid out of the row, which was filling up again, walked to the top of the aisle, dumped the trash, then hurried to the designated aisle two sections over and stepped his way down and down to the third row. Hellfire, talk about great seats. First row probably didn't see as well since it was so flat. The third row was perfect. He scooted in and sat.

A dark-haired girl with a lot of tattoos next to him said, "Oh, sorry. There's a girl sitting here."

"Yes, I know. We traded seats."

She barked a laugh. "Seriously? Were you sitting on the stage or something?"

He smiled. "I was sitting with my daughter. She's my daughter's best friend, and they wanted to sit together."

She narrowed her eyes but grinned. "Hey, man, who'd know you could have a daughter old enough to see the Jet."

"Yep, it amazes me too."

The lights started to dim, and Gabe drew a big breath.

CHAPTER THIRTEEN

IN THE blackness surrounding Gabe, Jet Gemini's voice, alone and clear as crystal, filled the arena and slid down Gabe's spine like cool syrup all the way to his groin. Nobody could say the guy got by on his hair. Hell, he could sing your ass off.

Gabe snorted at himself. *That's what I'm afraid of.*

Slowly, the lights came up, and the instruments picked up the melody. Jet stood in a spotlight, his head forward and his hair forming a curtain around his face.

A few girls started to scream, but they got shushed by other members of the audience, and the huge crowd became nearly still.

Jet began to sing in his pure voice about love that mended and never ended, a ballad that started in a mournful cadence but picked up and wrapped itself in joy. He swirled and spun, arms extended, hair whipping, his torso bare except for a silk vest with a huge red rose embroidered on it.

Gabe's heart thumped so loudly it should have added to the percussion of the music, and as the crescendo built, it seemed to live in his groin, throbbing and stretching.

Gemini stopped whirling and drew his hands beside his face to pull the hair aside. As the last notes faded, he raised his face, eyes closed, to the light, the flash of the spot reflecting on his perfect cheekbones. Breaking a smile, he opened his eyes and looked into the sea of passionate fans—

—and Gabe almost lost his ice cream. He pressed forward in his seat, and his lips formed the word: "Jerry."

His heart stopped for a second, then slammed against his ribs in a rush of adrenaline. *Nuts. Crazy. Of course it's not Jerry. Just somebody who....*

But even if every detail of Jet Gemini's beautiful face hadn't been identical, those eyes didn't lie. One blue, one green.

Gabe collapsed back in his seat, trying to take in enough oxygen. He wanted to jump up, run out, pound on something, but sliding past a whole row of avid fans sounded craptastic. *I don't get it. I've been played. But why? What possible use could I be to a world-famous rock star?*

Nothing quite made sense. Maybe Gemini was trying to get Gabe's help for the best price? But fuck, why would he want Gabe at all? He could have fifty guys, a hundred of the best craftsmen, working on his house. Why the fuck was Jet Gemini sleeping on a mattress on the floor and living on pizza? *It has to be a mistake. Jet has a twin. That's it. Jerry's his wacko twin.*

But the eyes. They had to be so rare. Would even identical twins both have those eyes?

The dark girl in the next seat cast a glance at him, then leaned down. "You okay? Are you sick or something?"

"Uh, yeah. I mean, no. Just a little light-headed. Not a lot of air." He tried to smile.

"Yeah, he has that effect." She winked. "Tell me if you need help. I'll be glad to give you mouth-to-mouth." She laughed and went back to whistling and screaming at Jet Gemini, but in Gabe's brain it was like someone had done a film overlay, and the top image blurred the one underneath. Gabe kept trying to make sense of tongue-tied Jerry with his shy smile stalking around the stage like a caged lion—growling, thrusting his hips, and tossing his hair. It made him dizzy even attempting to bring the two wildly opposite ideas together. His stomach flipped and shot a sour taste into his mouth.

Before he knew, he was moving. People were yelling and smacking at him as he pushed his way in front of them. After a couple of yells from people with hurt toes, he made it to the aisle and stopped, swallowing hard.

He couldn't help it. He wanted to keep running, but he looked back toward the stage. It might have been his imagination, but Jet Gemini was staring right at him.

Nonsense. The lights were too bright—weren't they?

But Jet stopped singing, just for a second, a breath. Probably more imagination. Probably he meant to pause there. Probably the fact that his lead guitarist gave him a startled look didn't mean anything. He seemed to blink and picked the melody back up so fast no one would know he'd stopped to look at Gabe.

Right, because he didn't.

Get the fuck out of here. Gabe hurried up the aisle and through the doors into the outside hallway. He wanted to keep on running straight to the truck, but he was afraid he wouldn't find the girls in the crowd, and they might not remember where the truck was parked in the big lot. Instead, he started walking around the circular hallway.

About halfway around the big circle, a security guard flagged him. "Can I help you, sir?"

Gabe grimaced. "Sorry. I brought my daughter and her best friend to see the concert. I, uh, just didn't have the same reaction they did, so I was taking a break."

The guard chuckled. "Man, I can get with that. You should hear some of the gar-bage I have to listen to on this job."

"But then the rest of the time you get to watch basketball, so I'm not crying for you."

They both laughed.

Gabe said, "Anyway, I'm getting in my 10K steps while I wait."

"Good plan. Excellent." He gave Gabe a pat on the arm, and Gabe kept walking. After a few steps, he let go of the smile. Now if he could just let go of his thoughts.

He rounded a turn and there was no one. Aside from the muted music drifting in from behind the wide doors, the hall was quiet. He stopped and leaned against the wall.

Assuming this was what it appeared to be—some kind of joke, if not a scam—the next question was what should he do? Jerry, who apparently was Jet Gemini no matter how insane that idea was, was also Gabe's client. One he'd spent a lot of time on, to say nothing of a lot of Jerry's money.

He gently banged his head against the wall. "So what do I say to him?" With a push, he launched himself from the wall and kept walking. *Do I pretend like I don't know? Chances are he didn't really see me.*

Craptastic idea. Jerry wasn't just a client. Gabe cared about him. Or maybe better to say he *had* cared about him. Maybe even for him. How did he ignore the kiss they'd shared? The way Jerry made him feel? To get to work on that house and save up more of Ellie's college tuition, was he willing to become a liar?

A huge explosion of applause poured from behind the doors. A minute later, one door opened and a couple hurried out, heading toward the exit. Probably wanting to be first out of the parking lot.

Get back. He turned and hurried toward the door where the girls would come out. As he passed the entrances, he could hear an encore going on.

At the correct entrance, he slipped inside and stood by the door, trying not to watch. No chance. He walked a few steps forward and stared at the stage. From that distance, the singer could be more Jet Gemini than Jerry Castor.

Wait, Castor. Wasn't he the twin of Pollux? Twin. Gemini. Shit.

He turned and walked back out the door to the hall. Suspending his brain for ten minutes, he waited while the music gave way to more clapping. The double doors swung open, and a flood of people poured out, laughing, chattering, and squealing. A minute later, Ellie walked through with MaryAnn behind her.

"Hey, girls."

"Oh, Daddy! Best birthday ever!" Ellie bounced toward him and threw her arms around his neck. He smiled since he hadn't been "Daddy" for a couple of years.

MaryAnn asked, "Did you like the seat, Mr. Mason?"

"Uh, yes, it was amazing." He waved toward the exit. "We better get moving or we'll be exiting the lot for the rest of the night."

They never stopped talking all the way to the truck. He loaded them in and input the address of MaryAnn's great-aunt into his app. It only took a few minutes, and they dropped her off at the door. She slid out and waved. "Thanks, Mr. Mason. Bye, Ellie. Can't wait to tell everybody."

Ellie hugged her, then crawled back into the truck.

Gabe turned on some music, and they drove quietly for a few minutes.

Suddenly, Ellie reached out and turned down the music. "Okay, Dad, tell me. You hated it, right?"

"No!" He frowned at her. "No. I really liked the music a lot. I thought he was an, uh, amazing performer."

"Come on, you don't have to say that."

"I'm not just saying it, Ellie, it's true. And—" He coughed. "—I'm pretty sure that Jet Gemini is my client."

She spun on the seat. "What?"

He nodded. "Yeah. Remember how you asked me if Jerry looked familiar? Well, I think you nailed it."

"Jerry?" It came out as a squeak. She leaned over the console. "Are you saying Jet Gemini is wacko Jerry in a beanie?"

"Yeah."

"I don't understand."

He let out his breath long and slow. "I don't either."

JERRY SLIPPED through the crowd backstage with a semi smile plastered on his face. Jet's face actually. He tried hard not to touch anyone without looking like that's what he was doing. *Just get away.*

He made it to his dressing-room door before a hand clamped on his shoulder.

"Great show, darling. You should bottle that charisma, you know?"

Jerry mentally slipped on his "Jet skin" so he wouldn't cringe, then turned languidly. "Hello, dear." He kissed the cheek of Bryson Anger, aging rock star turned wildly successful producer, who was responsible for some of Jet's albums.

Bryson said, "We're going out for drinks. Come?"

"Will you forgive me if I beg off? A show a night for five nights and still three to go. Need to save a little for the swim back."

Bryson laughed at the reference to their mutually loved movie, *Gattaca*. "You're forgiven. When will you leave all this botanical splendor behind and come see us in LA? I don't trust air you can't see and taste."

"I'll be a while. I need to spend some time writing before I can record." He kissed Bryson again. "Talk soon."

He opened his dressing-room door and stepped inside. Even Bryson knew that nobody followed Jet into his dressing room. Fred had done such a good job of striking fear into everyone's hearts that they all expected Jet to explode if a person invaded his space. *Close.*

The second the door closed, he twisted the lock, made a dive for the comfy chair he always requested in his dressing spaces, and curled into a fetal position. *It couldn't be, could it?* He couldn't have looked out past the blazing lights into the audience and seen Gabe scooting out of one of the front rows like he'd seen a ghost. Right, the ghost of Jerry Castor.

It couldn't be him. What would Gabe be doing at a Jet Gemini concert? But even as he thought it, Ellie Mason's cute face flashed in his mind. Hadn't Gabe said something about her birthday? *Oh damn shit hell fuck.*

Now he needed to do something, and all he felt was tired. Everything else aside, Gabe worked for him. Sure Jerry could have hired ten guys, fifty. Hell, he had an architect who'd designed his San Francisco home and a designer who decorated all his properties. So what? That wasn't what he wanted. Nobody else would get that Gabe gleam in their eye when they saw his house. No one else would work hard for Jerry, try to save him money, and worry about his pizza diet and sleeping accommodations. No one else had that amazing heart.

What does he think? That I'm a liar who played him? Jesus, what else could he think?

He clutched his middle tighter and moaned softly, mourning the one true relationship he'd thought for a minute he had in his life.

I CAN explain.

Gabe glanced at the text for the hundredth time, then shoved the phone back in his pocket. "Move that a little to the right." The two deliverymen positioned the huge butter-tan leather sectional around the coffee table and the abstract floral rug underneath it.

One burly guy, whose nametag read Hank, said, "Hey, this looks boss."

Gabe was pretty sure that meant good. "Thanks. I like it too."

He walked over with a tablet and handed it to Gabe. "Sign here for delivery."

Gabe signed and handed each of them a twenty from the cash he now knew Jerry could easily afford. The thought made his stomach clench. No way he'd let this ruin his fun. He was going to finish this house, or at least get as much done as he could before he got fired and replaced. Fuck, it wasn't every day he got a chance to earn a lot of extra money. He wasn't giving it up until he had to.

When the delivery guys left, Gabe ran up the stairs to check on the bathroom remodel. Since it had been five days since the concert and he'd only had the one cryptic text, not followed by a dismissal or even a return date, Gabe upped his schedule and worked twice as hard.

He and Ellie had talked it out in the car. *Keep going at top speed until Jerry gets back. Do a good job; bank the money.* Gabe had no doubts Jerry would pay him for the work done. After all, they had an agreement, and now he knew Jerry, aka Jet, had the money. God, it made him blush to think how hard he'd worked to keep costs down and how he'd cringed every time he used the stupid black credit card. *Right.* Ellie looked it up.

Only one of the most exclusive credit cards in the world. *He must think I'm a total hick.*

Which led back to the question, why had Jet Gemini taken the time and effort to con Gabriel Mason?

He stuck his head into the expanded bathroom. "Man, Jorge, this looks great."

The big room that had been pushed out onto the deck was fully framed and drywalled, and fixtures were halfway installed—a huge jetted tub, a walk-in shower with four showerheads, two sinks, each with their own storage and counter space, and a separate WC room for the toilet. And the view. Jerry could sit in his tub and stare at the trees and mountains beyond. Gabe swallowed. Thinking of Jerry in the tub—classically bad idea.

Jorge climbed out of the shower, where he was tweaking the glass shelving. "Did you look at the kitchen? We got the stovetop and ovens installed."

"When do the countertops come?"

"Tomorrow. I practically had to sell my mother to get them done that fast."

Gabe grinned. "Cheap at twice the price."

"Only got one mother, my man." He wiped his hands on his jeans. "So when's the homeowner expected?"

"I don't actually know. I guess he could show up anytime. That's why I've been rushing so hard. I want to get the most done possible before he gets back."

"Where is he?"

"Working."

"Long trip."

"Yeah." To discourage more questions, Gabe turned and walked back through the bedroom, which now boasted hardwood floors and perfectly painted walls, Jorge beside him.

Downstairs, Gabe walked to the kitchen, and he had to smile. *Wow. Just wow.* The kitchen was nearly twice as big, having taken over all the laundry room real estate. The biggest sink was hidden from view behind a lattice wall, but the rest was open. "Now that's a kitchen worthy of this house."

Jorge slapped his shoulder. "My thought exactly. Gotta say, great idea *we* came up with." He laughed.

Gabe joined him. "Let's look at the rest."

Beyond what had been the door to the mudroom, the "new" part of the house stretched out. The electrician and plumber had worked overtime getting the laundry with its red appliances set up, along with a big open room that Jerry could turn into whatever he wanted. It would probably make a good music studio, but what did Gabe know about that? There was also space for a gym, and finally they looked through the back door into the new garage that was complete with large translucent triple doors. Jerry would have a place to park when he got home.

It all made Gabe proud.

And nauseated.

When they got back to the kitchen, Gabe cleared his throat. "Uh, when the homeowner gets back, I'm going to turn the project over to him and recommend that he keep you and all the subs on. I'm pretty sure he will. I'll also suggest that you take over as the supervisor so he doesn't have to worry about the details."

Jorge frowned. "Why're you quitting, Gabe? You've got a real feel for this property. I can't imagine anybody, including me, can do a better job."

"Thanks, but I just have some other projects I need to finish." He pulled open the huge pantry and looked at all the shelves—again.

"Okay, well, I've never met this guy, so you'll have to introduce me. And I hope I can call you with questions."

"Yes on the questions. As to the intro, the homeowner's kind of shy—" A picture of Jet Gemini stalking the stage like a lithe caged animal flashed in his mind. "—so it's probably best if we just let him make contact with you however he wants to."

"So that's why we've never met him? He's shy?"

He wanted to scream, "I've got no idea why Jet fucking Gemini is hesitant to meet people since he plays in front of tens of thousands!" Instead he just nodded.

"That's kind of weird, but I guess we can put up with a boatload of strange to work on this house."

"So I'll leave you with a checklist and all my contact numbers. I'll give the same thing to the owner. You already know most of the projects, but the one thing missing is the front entrance. I've got a landscaper coming today to talk about developing a real entrance for the house so people know where to go when they drive up. I'll have to leave that with you." He swallowed. "So this room is looking great." He glanced at his boots. "I have some pots and pans and other household shit coming. Maybe you've got somebody who can arrange it in the kitchen."

Jorge gave him a sideways glance and frowned at what he saw. "Sure, Gabe. I'll have my interiors person help out."

"Perfect."

"You sure you wouldn't rather do it yourself?"

"Yeah, I—" The doorbell rang. "That must be my landscaper. You want to listen in?"

He nodded and tagged along to the yard. The landscaper, a guy who looked more like a painter than anyone who worked in dirt, caught on right away. He'd searched for the front door and understood what a problem it was.

By the time they'd walked the big front yard a few times, they'd conceived a Japanese-looking gateway with a stone path edged by boulders and shrubbery that wound between the trees. They considered covering it against the Oregon rain, but decided it would compromise the view, so they added a cover at the driveway and then umbrella stands where guests could grab a rain cover to get to the front door. On the porch, another set of stands received the wet umbrellas.

Jorge got into the swing and started trading ideas with the landscaper.

Gabe nodded. *Good.* But his agreement didn't make the lump in his throat go away. "You two keep at it. I've got to see to some stuff inside." He turned away. Weirdly, he was blinking against the hot tears that pushed at his eyeballs.

CHAPTER FOURTEEN

JERRY NAVIGATED up the narrow driveway in his Prius, blinking against the dimness of his one driveway light and his own exhaustion. When he'd finished his last concert in Reno, he'd pressed the accelerator to the floor and driven the five hours home from the busy freeways in Nevada, through the dense forest where there was no cell service, and over Mount Ashland on the 5. He'd barely kept himself from pulling over to sleep, but the lure of home—and the chance to maybe explain himself to Gabe—kept spurring him on.

Ahead of him on the driveway, three garage doors of translucent blue-green fiberglass shone in the soft illumination. *Oh my God, I have garage doors. Gabe gave me garage doors.* How nuts was it that the thought made his heart beat faster?

Of course, he still had to leave the car in the driveway since he didn't have an opener for the doors.

He parked and slid out, having to grab the side of the car to keep from falling he was so tired. With a yank, he dragged a small suitcase from the back seat and pulled out the handle. It wasn't heavy. Just a few Jerry clothes. He left all the Jet wardrobe with his assistants.

He started down the old pathway that led into the yard in front of his house—and stopped. There was some kind of paint on the grass, like somebody was plotting out a walkway and other stuff on top of what was there. *Must be Gabe.* He got another thrill.

Pulling his suitcase across the ragged grass and up the stairs to the front porch was tough going, but he made it and leaned against the wall as he unlocked the front door.

He stepped inside, dragged in his bag, and then closed the door behind him, settling into the dark inside his home.

Hmm. Interesting smells. Paint, wood, maybe cleaning supplies. He felt along the wall for the switch, flipped it and—*holy crap.*

His house. It was....

Wow.

The walls gleamed a fresh off-white, and the tile floors had been cleaned and polished. Across from the entry, he could make out the edge of the dining table he'd admired at Gabe's, now in his own dining room.

He stepped into the hallway, gasped, then rushed to the kitchen that had been a small cramped room and now was an open, inviting, expansive space full of polished quartz counters and shining stainless appliances. But most amazing was that the cabinets, at least some of them, were full. Inside two of the cabinets, which happened to be glass fronted, he could see some pretty dishes. He pulled out a dark wood drawer and found it full of brand-new pots and pans.

His fingers twitched to grab his phone and text Gabe a thank-you, but it was past two in the morning.

After pulling a few more handles and finding drawers, cabinets, and bins full, he wandered in awe back into the hall. He called it a hall for lack of a better word, but it was just an open central artery that connected the three-sided spaces that were the family room and dining room that faced on the pool, the kitchen, bath, and entry that lined the other side of the hall, and then the great room into which the hall ended.

Gazing at the almost unbelievably improved interior, Jerry wandered to the door that used to mark the end of the living area and the entry into the damp, cold mudroom and various unspecified spaces that finally led to the garage—the garage that now had doors.

Slowly, he opened the door. Warm air filled the space, and the walls had been painted. A bench, shelves, and hooks were built in on one side. It was a real mudroom.

He stepped down into the room, which had become positively cozy. He opened the door on the far side, stared into a hall, and then entered a large room.

Oh my God, what a perfect studio. It didn't open to the outside, so it was quiet and the light could be controlled.

He retraced his steps, closing the mudroom door behind him, and then headed to his favorite—the great room. Almost holding his breath, he approached the big room, which was dark except for the moonlight and twinkling stars shining through the two-story-high walls of glass.

He paused in the spot where the low ceilings of the hall gave way to the soaring ceilings of the great room. There was a light switch on the wall that hadn't worked since he bought the house. Just on a chance, he flipped it.

Whoa. A light went on in the middle of the huge room—on an end table next to a large sectional sofa that glowed a warm gold like seasoned butter melted in a pan. He walked toward it and realized that there was another lamp, which he also turned on. Now the whole sitting area came into view, the couch on top of a huge, beautiful rug, and in the middle of it all, the handmade coffee table.

Straight ahead was the big fireplace. All the beautiful venetian tiles were repaired, and there were big logs assembled in the hearth. He found the key that looked like it controlled the gas in the fireplace and a firelighter on the hearth beside it. He clicked the lighter, and with a touch to the log, the fire burst to life. He almost cried it was so beautiful.

Backing up, he walked to the sectional and collapsed on it. Wow, it wasn't just the color of butter, it was that soft to the touch. Lying there with the two lamps on their lowest setting, the fire dancing happily and the moon still shining like a giant gift through the windows that were somehow magically clean, Jerry felt totally at home, maybe for the first time in his life.

He reached out and touched the table, running his hand back and forth over the silken wood. In that sweet comfort, his eyes closed.

"Mr. Castor? Sir?"

Jerry heard the words and blinked. Brilliant light flooded behind his eyelids, and his eyes flew open. He sat up and scooted back. "What? Where? I mean, who are you?"

The stocky man in work clothes smiled at him. "I'm so sorry to wake you, sir. I'm Jorge Alvarez, your design-build supervisor. I've been working with Gabe, and he gave me all the instructions for how to move forward. I wouldn't have bothered you except the guys are installing the bookshelves in here in a few minutes, so I thought you might want to go upstairs so nobody'd bother you."

Jerry touched his shoulder. Fuck, his hair was hanging down and, of course, no sunglasses. But the man seemed clueless and harmless. "Uh, sorry. I got home really late and fell asleep." Jerry glanced around the big room, glistening with morning light. "I guess that's obvious." He swallowed. "Where's Gabe?"

For the first time, the man looked uncomfortable. "Uh, he had another—I mean, he handed off the to-do list to me to supervise, uh, assuming you agree, of course. There's still a lot to do, as you can see, but Gabe really got the ball rolling, and I feel good about taking it from here…."

The man—did he say Jorge?—kept talking. He seemed nervous. But what was he saying? Jerry glanced around again. No sign of Gabe. "So where is Gabe?"

"Uh, I guess he's at work. He said he left you a report. Didn't you see it?"

"No. No report."

"Did you look in the bedroom he finished for you?"

"What?"

Jorge was looking confused and… patient. "The bedroom? Upstairs? The master isn't done because of the bathroom build-out, so Gabe got one of the guest rooms ready for you. Uh, he worked really hard to—"

Jerry jumped off the couch and started running toward the stairs.

Jorge muttered behind him, "I guess that's a no on having looked in the bedroom."

Taking the stairs two at a time, Jerry made it to the second floor. He stared into the guest room across from the staircase. Floors and walls done, but empty.

On his left, he peered into the bathroom with the soaking tub. *Holy crap.* It was gorgeous. There were even towels. Big, fluffy dark-green towels.

Turning quickly, he took the four steps to the door of the next guest room—and stopped.

If the bathroom had been great, this was—no words. Beautiful jewel-colored rugs dotted the maple floors, drapes and sheer curtains stretched across the whole back wall, and the room was dominated by a king-size bed made up with crisp sheets that probably had a million thread count and a quilt in muted silk folded across the foot.

I could have slept here last night in this perfect haven that Gabe made for me.

Heat stung the back of his eyes, and he inhaled and blinked. All he wanted was to curl up in that cozy nest—preferably not alone. He strode closer, and that's when he saw the papers lying on the cover.

He stopped. *It's a report. A schedule. That's what Jorge said, right?* But it didn't feel right. Hadn't Jorge said something about a to-do list and taking it over? The words *good start* trickled into Jerry's mind.

He didn't want to look at the papers, but he sighed and picked up the top page. Carefully typed and printed, it was headed "Interim Report: Renovation of South Mountain Property for Jerry Castor, aka Jet Gemini."

Shit. He didn't want to read any further.

But he did.

The report listed every action that had been undertaken, its state of completion, and the precise expenditures made in pursuit of that aspect of the renovation. It went on for pages, listing every charge and purchase down to the penny.

In a separate document, he detailed Jorge Alvarez's credentials and cited his trust in his abilities. He recommended that Jerry keep Jorge as supervisor.

Last, he'd attached his final bill. It was a lot, but compared to the work that had been done, the bill was a pittance. Only the furniture he'd provided—the dining table, three bookcases, the credenza, a bedframe, and the perfect coffee table—were charged at what Jerry thought of as a fair price. *At least he respects his own art.*

Jerry sat on the bed. It was wildly comfortable, but not as much of a haven as it had felt a few minutes before. *Choices.* He could lie down and go back to sleep. Let events unfold as they'd been so meticulously planned. Chances were good that Gabe wouldn't tell anyone who Jerry was, and Jerry would never have to see Gabe Mason ever again. Yeah, sleeping was an option.

GABE LEANED against the shelves on aisle eighteen, pulled his phone from his pocket, and glanced around. It was a slow day. He should check out lumber and see if he could help over there, but first....

He clicked on the links that had become pretty familiar in the last week—the gossip and so-called entertainment news sites. With a deep inhale, he tapped in *Jet Gemini.* True, it was pretty unlikely that there was anything new since the last time he'd searched a few hours before. In fact, he got a story he'd seen promoted on one of the other pages he'd looked at. It was a story about Jet and his band at a club in New York. It showed a photo of Jet sitting on a couch with a beautiful woman on each side. He had a glass in his hand, his head was thrown back, and he was laughing.

Man, he was gorgeous—and lying through his gorgeous teeth. Not only was he someone other than who he'd told Gabe he was, but also, as far as Gabe could tell, he wasn't shy in any way, and despite one very memorable kiss, Jerry Castor wasn't gay.

Gabe sighed and ran his thumb across his phone screen. *Shit, I'm not usually an effing masochist.*

"Gabe?"

Gabe looked up at Harry as he clicked his phone off. "Yeah, sorry. Just checking some stuff. Slow as maple syrup in Canada today."

"He's back."

"What? Who?"

"The weird guy. Weren't you doing some work for him?"

Stomach to the floor, heart in the throat. "Where?"

"Uh, I told him to wait over on sixteen."

"Look, I don't really want to see him. We didn't end up too well. So would you tell him I'm working on a project offsite? Just get rid of him? Sorry to ask you to lie, but I'll go back to lumber, and that's kind of offsite, so it's not too bad."

"Jeez, Gabe, can't you just talk to him? I think I scare the shit out of him."

"You don't. Trust me. He'll be fine." He took a few steps backward. "See, I'm heading offsite." Gabe turned and practically ran toward lumber. When he got to the end of the aisle, he looked back and saw Harry walking in the opposite direction, but he glanced back once with a really grumpy expression. *Man, I'm gonna owe him.*

Gabe waited on a couple of people in lumber and then started cutting two-bys, an activity that was soothing. He could be useful and focused and not have to think. Thinking was the enemy. Unfortunately, he was under enemy attack.

Why did Jerry come here? Maybe he should rephrase that—why did Jet come here? What could he possibly hope to accomplish? *What does he want from me?*

Just run the saw.

An hour later, he'd cut so much lumber, he was running out of space to store it, so he gave up and pulled off his safety goggles and gloves. He waved to the guy coming on the late shift as he walked back to his own department.

It was close to quitting time. Maybe he'd stop and get some takeout for him and Ellie and—he paused in the middle of the aisle.

Sad. He felt sad. How strange.

He shook his head and continued to the department counter. He stopped and checked the computer, then fished his windbreaker out of the drawer of the desk.

"Gabe?"

Gabe caught his breath because he didn't even have to look to know whose voice that was.

CHAPTER FIFTEEN

BRAIN EXPLOSION.

Jerry Castor had been waiting for him for almost two hours.

Gabe turned and frowned. "What?"

"Hi."

There he was. Stupid cap. Stupid sunglasses. Shoulders stooped in that shy, diffident way. Stupid way.

"What the fuck, Jerry? What's with the stupid act?"

He glanced around nervously. "Could we go somewhere and talk?"

"No. What's there to talk about?" It was Gabe's turn to glance around. For the first time that day, he was glad it was so slow. "I don't get it. Why the hell would you want to take the time and energy to con me, of all people? Jesus, why didn't you just buy the store? Then you'd have owned me." He paced a couple steps, then turned back. "And why did you come to ImproveMart to buy some drawer pulls? Couldn't you have sent ten employees? They could each have carried one knob home." His voice kept rising, and he tried to control it. "Living on pizza? Bullshit. Do you know we were all worried that you'd spent your last dime on that wreck of a house, and we thought your credit card wouldn't work, and I was trying to hire people who'd charge you the best rates so you didn't go bankrupt? Damn, Jerry, why? Why'd you do it?"

Jerry stared at the floor and mumbled something.

"Fuck, I can't hear you when you pretend to be some social misfit."

Slowly, Jerry looked up and pulled off the glasses. His two-color eyes met Gabe's. "I am a misfit. I can't be who I am because no one wants him, and the one everyone wants lives a life I hate." Gabe's face must have shown his cynicism, because Jerry said, "I know, poor little rich boy. So misunderstood." He sucked in a long inhale. "I let you think those things because no one else ever cared enough to think them before." He pulled an envelope from his jacket pocket and held it out to Gabe. "Thank you."

Gabe stared at it. "What?"

"Payment of your invoice."

"Okay." He took it. "You should let Jorge stay on."

"Sure. I already told him. I appreciate you taking so much time from Ellie. Give her my best."

He turned and started walking toward the front of the store where the exit doors were, perfect ass in baggy sweats flexing.

"Jet, look over here!" The shout was accompanied by flashing lights, and suddenly four people, three men and a woman, came running toward Jerry. The woman held a microphone out in front of her, and a guy with a video camera chugged behind her. The other two both flashed expensive cameras.

Jerry's expression looked panicked, and his arm came up to hide his face. He bumped against the shelves beside him and stumbled. The woman shoved the mic in his face as he tried to catch himself. "Jet, what are you doing in ImproveMart? Have you got a girlfriend near here? Are you trying to show the world what a regular guy you are?"

One of the men yelled, "Jet, what's with the cap. Come on, show us your hair."

As the vultures closed in on Jerry, Gabe's feet moved on their own. He rushed forward and put himself in front of Jerry, who cowered against the shelves.

"Get away from him. Stop harassing our customer. Please leave."

Cameras flashed in his face. Gabe grabbed Jerry and, using his shoulder to block the reporters, rushed Jerry from the store. Outside, he said, "Run. Come on."

They broke into a fast canter, and Gabe led the way to his truck. The reporters were after them, but he unlocked the doors from several yards away, and they each dove into a side. Gabe clicked the locks and had the engine revved and them moving before the photographers could even get a picture, much less reach a vehicle.

As they raced out of the parking lot, Gabe said, "We'll go to my place. It's closer, and they're likely to see us on the freeway if we drive all the way to Ashland."

Jerry just nodded, but his hands were clenched in his lap, and the guy looked freaked.

"How in the hell did they know you were there?"

He sighed. "Someone in the store must have recognized me and called them."

"Seriously? Who'd do that?"

"Lots of people, I guess."

Gabe said, "Does this happen to you all the time?"

Jerry shook his head. "It happens to Jet all the time."

"Uh, you are Jet."

"I know." He didn't say anything else. He just closed his eyes and rested his head against the window.

Ten minutes later, Gabe pulled into his own driveway, looked up and down the street and saw nothing out of the usual, then got out, walked to the passenger door, and tapped against the glass.

Jerry's head popped up, and Gabe opened the door. "Come on in."

Jerry slid out of the truck, but he looked like somebody had beat on him with a stick. The cap sat cockeyed on his head, and his sunglasses were askew. Gabe walked beside him to the front door, then opened it and gestured for Jerry to go in.

When Gabe followed, he found Ellie sitting at the dining room card table, her laptop open in front of her, staring at Jerry with her mouth open.

Gabe grinned at her stunned expression. "Ellie, you remember Jerry Castor."

She nodded, but her wide eyes narrowed. "Hello."

Jerry glanced up at Gabe like maybe he wanted rescuing, but Gabe said nothing. He really wanted to see what Jerry would do next.

Jerry's chest expanded as he visibly took a breath, then walked over and slid into the chair beside Ellie. "Did you come to the concert too?"

She looked confused, but she nodded.

"It was your birthday, right?"

"Yes."

"I hope you enjoyed it." He smiled shyly.

For a second she just gazed at him. Easy to understand. Even behind sunglasses, that was quite a face. Then her eyebrows lowered. "I did until my dad told me that you were the person who'd been pretending to be his friend and he had no idea why you'd done it."

From where he stood, Gabe could see that Jerry held her gaze. "I wasn't pretending. I am—I hope I am—your dad's friend."

"But you lied to him."

"Not exactly. My name is Jerry Castor—legally. My own brother calls me Jerry. When I met Gabe, I...." He ran a hand over his head, pulled off the cap, and let the world-famous moonlight-blond hair fall around his shoulders and down his back.

Ellie actually gasped.

He looked up. "Oh, I'm sorry, I—"

Gabe said, "Ellie, why don't we let Jerry go sit on the couch and watch TV while we make dinner? Then he can tell us whatever he wants to."

She looked torn. *Poor Ellie.* Of course, she wanted to gush over her hero, but she wanted to be loyal to her father too.

Jerry held up a hand. "I don't want to keep you from your dinner, but I want to say that when I met Gabe, I wasn't looking for a friend. I just wanted some drawer pulls." He looked up at Gabe and then back at Ellie. "Then I met your dad, and he was so kind and nice to me, and he didn't know who I was." His voice rose. "I was trying to have a life. A life of my own. No one knows about my house, and when I met Gabe, he seemed like someone who could help me without my having to reveal my private place to all the people who take care of Jet." His Adam's apple bounced. "I didn't mean to lie or hurt anyone. Especially not you." He looked up at Gabe. "But I couldn't imagine that you'd care if I was Jet Gemini or Mickey Mouse." He stared at his hands, the glowing hair covering his face. "I'm so sorry."

Gabe gazed at Ellie. He didn't want to take the decision on forgiveness away from her.

Ellie said, "So are you really shy and tongue-tied?"

"Yes, but it's made a lot worse because I know that most people could recognize me, and then I get chased and photographed, and I don't have any freedom or personal life." He dug his fingers into the mane of hair and pulled it off his forehead, then let it go. He looked so sad a person would have to be a real hardass to stay mad.

"You should have been honest with my dad and not let him think you were a regular guy who blew all his money on a run-down property."

Jerry looked up at Gabe. "You thought that?"

Gabe nodded.

"I'm sorry. I gave you the card. Did you think it wasn't good or something?"

"Yeah. I'd never seen the black card before. That's not your fault, I realize."

Jerry half smiled. "I really loved that you were looking out for my budget so carefully. No one ever does that. I didn't know you were being so cost conscious because you thought I was broke."

"Yeah, sorry." Gabe pointed toward the couch. "Why don't you get comfortable?"

Jerry stood from the dining room chair. Suddenly, he touched the card table. "Wait. You gave me your table. I didn't mean for you to do that."

Ellie said, "That's okay, Jerry. We always meant to sell it. We were just using it until we had a buyer." She put her hand on his arm. "Don't worry, we were super careful."

He smiled softly. "I really love it."

"Good." She stood up, all lady-of-the-house efficiency. "Go rest while we make some dinner. Dad says you eat way too much pizza."

"Well, I guess he'd be right about that." He gave Gabe another of those shy smiles. "But I do like pizza a lot."

Ellie grinned. "That just means you're smart." She walked toward the kitchen.

Jerry said, "I'd like to help make dinner too."

"Oh." Ellie looked surprised. "Okay. Dad, you guys make salad."

She started banging pots and pans, and for the first time, Gabe looked at Jerry head-on. They were both standing, and Jerry's unique eyes were almost on a level with Gabe's.

"You're tall."

"Almost six-two." Jerry spoke quietly. "I'm so sorry. I didn't intend to lie to you."

Gabe raised an eyebrow.

"I mean, I knew I was hiding a part of my life, of myself, from you, but I didn't exactly think of it as a lie. More like a sin of omission. It was so much fun having someone who just treated me like everyone else. Like a regular person. I thought of telling you about, you know, Jet, but I couldn't bring myself to spoil everything." He stared at his feet.

Gabe frowned. "But like I said before, you *are* Jet."

"Not really. I mean, Jet's an act. I'm me."

"Seriously? Don't you spend more time doing your so-called rock-star act than being the shy, pizza-eating nerd we know and love?"

"You do?" Dimples flashed in his lean cheeks, and then he dropped his eyes. "That was why I bought the house. To try and have some private life." His light brows pulled together. "But they're everywhere. No one lets me just live." He glanced up. "Sorry. Poor me again."

"I've got to admit, those reporters were crazy."

Jerry nodded. "Let's make salad." He walked to the kitchen via the piano and ran his hand over the keys.

As they ripped prewashed lettuce, Ellie asked, "So how the heck did you become Jet Gemini?"

"My brother."

Ellie said, "Freedom?"

"Yeah. Fred."

"Seriously, that's his name?"

"Yep."

"So how did he make you Jet Gemini?"

Jerry leaned against the counter. "When I was little, I could sing."

"News flash. You still can."

He smiled and started cleaning carrots. "I was a freshman in high school, and there was a big talent contest in our town for some TV show or other."

"What town?"

"Outside Portland."

Ellie nodded and kept cooking chicken in a big pan.

Jerry said, "My brother dragged me to the high school to sing. I threw up, but at least I didn't do it on the stage." He chuckled. "Somehow I managed to perform by pretending I was somebody else. Someone cool and exciting. I called him Jet in my head." He shrugged. "I won. An agent who'd come to the show to support his nephew saw me perform. He came backstage where Fred was trying to keep me from passing out. They talked. The guy was Herb Flores. He's still my agent."

"What happened with the TV show?"

"Nothing. I never signed a contract because Herb already had a potential record deal going."

Ellie said, "The stories always say you made Herb Flores a rich man."

"I guess he made me one too." He stared at his shoes again. "The only thing was, I never wanted to be rich. Don't misunderstand, I'm not complaining. Rich can be a pain in the ass, but it's—nice. It just wasn't ever a goal. The famous part was the bitch." He shuddered and put down the knife. "A little bit famous is fun. Having a few people know your name and say they like your voice makes you smile. But I can't imagine any person who's ever been really famous actually likes it. They may appreciate what goes with the fame—the influence, money, power, whatever—but the famous part, the 'no privacy, you don't own your life' part? No. Not many people like that when they have it." He picked up the knife again and kept chopping.

Ellie glanced at Gabe with compassion flooding her eyes. "So you gave up your privacy and the life you wanted to have a whole lot of stuff you don't care about?"

He shrugged and swiped chopped carrot into the big salad bowl. "When I started, I was too young to have any idea what I wanted, so I guess I learned by trying out what I don't want."

"If you could do anything you wanted, what would it be?"

He glanced at Ellie with the shy smile. "I'd teach music."

"Really?" Her smile radiated. "That's what I want to do too."

"So the piano's yours?"

She nodded. "I also play guitar."

"Maybe we can play together?"

Her eyes got huge at that thought, and she quickly turned back to the chicken, which was smelling heavenly. "What made you want to teach?"

"My father was a teacher. I guess I always liked that idea."

Gabe asked, "He's no longer living?"

"Oh no. Both my parents are alive. But he retired when I bought them a new house. Now both of them mostly play golf and go boating in their retirement community in Florida." He gave a wry grin. "Turns out he didn't love teaching as much as I thought."

It took a few minutes to get all the food on the card table, and then they sat to eat.

Jerry said, "I feel like I deprived you of your beautiful table, but I'm not giving it back. So next time, we'll all eat at my house." He glanced up uneasily, seeming to realize what he'd said.

Ellie put her hand on his arm, easy in such close quarters. "I can't wait to see your house. Dad talks about it all the time."

Jerry smiled and glanced at Gabe.

Gabe said, "Ellie's especially anxious to swim in the pool."

"How about tomorrow?"

Gabe laughed. "It's pretty cold to swim."

"I told the pool man to turn on the heater."

Gabe said, "Holy crap, uh, cow. Do you know how much that costs?"

Jerry glanced up through his lashes, and Gabe snorted. It just wasn't possible to keep remembering that this shy, quiet guy was one of the world's biggest rock stars—even with his hair hanging down.

They ate quietly for a second. Jerry said, "This is so good."

Ellie laughed. "Uh, you've had too much pizza. This is just mushroom soup on chicken."

"Will you show me how to make it? I've never learned to cook."

"Sure. It's dead-on easy." She chewed. "The thing is, Jerry, if you want to be a teacher, you have to learn how to economize."

"I do?"

"Um-hum." She dabbed her lips with her napkin. "If you give up the whole rock-star gig, you can't keep spending money like water. Much as I hate to say it, you should probably wait until summer to use the pool. That way, you won't be burning up dollar bills."

"What if I install solar?"

Her eyebrows went up. "That's a good idea. Just don't cut into your savings too much because you'll need the money later. But solar will cut down on monthly expenses."

She cut her chicken, and Jerry's lips twitched. He was definitely trying not to laugh at her bookkeeperish advice. He looked up, and his dual-colored eyes met Gabe's, sending a jolt of heat into Gabe's gut.

When they'd finished eating, Gabe said, "Why don't you two go relax, and I'll clean up."

"Thanks, Dad, but I can help." She glanced at Jerry. Maybe the prospect of making small talk with her idol seemed a little overwhelming.

Gabe waved a hand. "No, go on. You made most of the food."

Jerry pointed at the piano. "Come on. We'll give each other lessons."

For the next half an hour, while Gabe took more time than he really needed to scrub the frying pan and put the plates and flatware in the dishwasher, the sounds of music and laughter came from the living room.

Gabe sidled around the corner and watched them. They'd been playing a piece that was probably a Jet Gemini song, then segued into "Chopsticks" and practically bumped each other off the bench reaching across to play higher and higher notes. When they were laughing so hard they couldn't find the keys anymore, they stopped, and Ellie moved over and collapsed on the couch.

Jerry rested his fingers lightly on the piano keys, swayed, and started to play.

Gabe mouthed, "Holy shit."

Jerry's fingers flew across the old piano keys like they were a single entity, a piano-playing machine.

Ellie sat, eyes wide, mouth open, for the minutes that Jerry played. Then he just stopped.

Ellie leaped up. "That was Liszt. Oh my God, you played Liszt!"

Jerry turned and nodded. "*Transcendental Études*. Just showing off."

She pressed a hand to her heart. "Show off anytime. My God, you can play like that? You should, like, join the symphony or something."

He laughed. "Too much competition."

She nodded. "Right. And nobody else wants to be a Grammy-winning rock star."

Gabe watched them both and let air slip between his lips. Whether he was a rock star or played with the symphony, Jerry Castor was so far out of Gabe's league, he might as well have lived on a different planet.

Oh well, not like this is a relationship.

After sipping some tea and eating another ice cream sandwich, Gabe said, "I forgot to ask how you got to ImproveMart today."

"I drove." Jerry took a healthy bite of his dessert.

"Shall I take you back to pick up your car?"

"Oh." He finally seemed to grasp that he had to leave. "Uh, I guess so."

Ellie shook her head vehemently. "No way. What if the paparazzi are waiting for him by his car?"

Gabe raised an eyebrow. "They didn't see Jerry's car. They did see my truck. They're more likely to find him if he's riding with me."

Ellie got that master planner look on her face. "Okay, you take Jerry home. Tomorrow, I drive to work with you, get Jerry's car, and take it to him. Then he can drive me to school."

"Even for you, that plan's a little overworked, don't you think?"

She turned to him and gave him big eyes. "No. It works perfectly." She did everything except wink. He felt half-embarrassed and half-excited at her heavy-handed manipulation. With a turn, she looked at Jerry. "Right, Jerry?"

He grinned, fished in his pocket, and produced a set of keys. "Blue Prius."

"Oh good. They're easy to drive. I'll find it and bring it to you at about seven, okay? I have to be at school at eight twenty tomorrow."

"Deal."

"You guys better get going." She yawned elaborately. "I have to get to bed since I'm getting up extra early, so night, Dad. Sleep well." She kissed his cheek, and he could actually feel it warm with a blush. Then she turned to Jerry. "I'm glad the reporters chased you because this way we got to find out you're not an asshole, and I'm so glad you're not, because that would have been way disappointing." She leaned forward and kissed his cheek. "See you tomorrow." She waggled her fingers and disappeared down the hall.

Gabe shook his head. "Sorry about that."

"I'm not."

Gabe didn't dare ask what he meant.

CHAPTER SIXTEEN

IN NOT quite relaxed silence, Gabe and Jerry got into the truck and headed for Ashland. To cover the quiet, Gabe turned on the radio, then flipped it off, because coals to Newcastle after all. Questions pushed at Gabe's lips.

"Can I ask you something?"

Jerry made a funny sound, half-laugh and half-gasp, in his throat. "I wish you would."

"Well, I saw some pictures of you online."

"Of Jet?"

"Yes." Gabe cleared his throat. "You were at a club sitting with your arms around two women."

"Yes." That word conveyed a world of strain.

"So are you gay, bisexual, or not out? I mean, I got the idea you were gay, but when I saw the picture, I realized I might have assumed too much."

"I'm gay." He blew breath between his lips. "Jet isn't entirely out. There are a lot of rumors, but he, uh, I never have a boyfriend, so nobody can really assume. I'm seen with a lot of women, but I never imply that one of them is my girlfriend. The press has even started guessing that I'm asexual."

"Why don't you ever have a boyfriend?"

He shrugged. "Not fair to anybody. Some guy who'd hook up with Jet wouldn't want me, the real me, and chances are I wouldn't want him. I've had some hookups, but the men never know who I am, and it's just for sex, so nobody loses." He glanced over. "What about you?"

"For me, life's all about Ellie."

"She seems to want you to, uh, have a boyfriend." His voice rose in half a question.

"Ya think?" They both laughed, and that relieved the tension a little. "She wants me to be happy. The trouble is, her mother's new fiancé is a homophobe who'd love to find a reason to take Ellie away from her perverted father."

"Fuck that. He can't do that, can he?"

"Probably not. Ellie chose to live with me. But I don't want to give the courts any reason to question my fitness as a father. I always figured if the neighbors saw guys going in and out of my house, that'd be bad."

"So no boyfriends? Not even the guy I saw you with at the restaurant?"

"No. That was my first date with him, and likely last. Some friends fixed us up. He's a college professor. Doesn't need to be dating a blue-collar dude like me."

The awkward silence struck again; then Jerry blurted out, "Do you want to go out with him again?"

"What? Oh, no. I told him no thanks, more or less. He's not my type."

They reached the top of Mountain Avenue. Gabe made the sharp turn into the driveway and climbed to the top of the hill. When the translucent doors came into view, Gabe hit the button on his visor, and the doors silently slid open.

Jerry chortled. "You left my keys, but you can still get in."

Gabe said sheepishly, "Yeah. I kind of forgot I programmed your doors into my truck." He pulled into the garage. "Did you leave any lights on inside?"

"No. I never thought I'd be coming home so late."

"We can program some motion detectors so they turn on automatically." Gabe looked toward the door to the inside. "But for now I better check to make sure no asshole photographers are lurking around."

"Oh, yes, you better check."

They both sounded like they were reciting a script, and neither of them believed for a half second that some rabid reporter was lying in wait.

Gabe slid out of the truck and heard Jerry behind him. His pulse throbbed so hard he could barely hear. With a press of the button, the garage door closed, leaving them in the timed light on the garage door opener.

Like the mighty hunter, Gabe opened the door to the house, stepped inside, and flipped the light switch beside the door. Jerry came in behind him, so close Gabe could feel his heat and smell his cinnamon scent. They were in a slate-tiled hallway that led from the garage to the mudroom, with doors to the two big extra rooms on one side.

Gabe looked through the first door. "I thought one of these rooms would make a good gym and the other one could be a music studio, but they'd be great as a lot of things."

"Actually, did you notice the big, barnlike building beside the driveway?"

"Yes. I wondered what it was."

"It's mine. I thought about turning it into a music studio. Since it's separate and private, it shouldn't bother anyone." A crease popped between his brows. "But to use it, I'd have to tell people where I am, and right now, nobody knows. Not even Fred." His inhale was audible. "Anyway, it's a big building and it's there, so it can be part of the plans for the property."

A huge elephant called Is Gabe Still Going to Work on the Property walked into the room. Gabe said, "Good to know."

Gabe kept moving down the hall, passed the reinforced door that led to the pool equipment, and then walked into the mudroom. The slate floor carried through there, but it was heated so people wouldn't freeze when they took off their boots or shoes.

They both slid off their shoes, and Gabe led the way into the main part of the house. He flipped on the light in the open hallway and had to smile. The house was really....

"Beautiful," Jerry breathed the word for him. "Seriously, Gabe, I knew this house had potential, but I never dreamed it could look like this."

Gabe felt his smile spread. "Look. The countertops." He walked into the now open kitchen and ran his hands over the silken smoothness of the golden-white quartz.

Jerry pressed a hand against his mouth. "Oh my gosh." He rushed over and followed the smooth surface with his finger over what they called the waterfall edge—stone cascading in an unbroken surface all the way to the floor. "I love this."

Suddenly, Jerry whirled and threw his arms around Gabe's neck. "Thank you. Thank you for this wonderful gift. I've never had anything of my own before."

The simple statement hit Gabe in the gut, and he tightened his arms around Jerry's slender frame. "My pleasure. You helped me too. Getting to do this project will let me save some money for Ellie's college."

Jerry looked up slowly through his lashes in that way he did. He released his arms from Gabe's neck, which was disappointing. "But you're not done, right? You'll keep working. There's the other building and the patio, and you can't let anyone besides you oversee the path to the door. No one else would understand how important that pathway is."

Funny how Jerry understood it. Gabe thought he was the only one.

Jerry's face got serious. "Please, Gabe. Let me pretend I have a life for a little while longer."

Hell, what had Jerry ever done for Gabe that wasn't good? Not his fault he was some rich, famous guy. Gabe nodded.

Jerry's smile started slow and gathered speed, glittering out of the blue and green eyes. He mouthed, "Thank you." All it did was focus Gabe's gaze on those lips that ought to not be so soft and sensual looking.

For a second, they just stared at each other.

Gabe's ulterior motive in checking for paparazzi hung in the air like Kobayashi Maru, the unwinnable scenario from *Star Trek: TNG*. The man in front of him with the moonlit hair hanging around his near-perfect face could claim to be meek Jerry Castor all he wanted. He looked like Jet Gemini. All Gabe had to do was reach out, but where the hell would that get him? Continuing to work for Jerry was one thing. Following up on the obvious invitation in his eyes….

Jerry snaked out a hand and grabbed Gabe by the neck. "You're thinking too hard." He closed those too-soft lips over Gabe's, and they weren't too soft at all. Just right.

In fact, everything about Jerry was perfect. The right height so they could press together and their erections rub with perfect friction. The right-shaped ass to fill Gabe's palms like they were made to go together. The right soft, seeking tongue exploring Gabe's mouth while perfect little moans and mewling noises provided the musical accompaniment.

Gabe's body ate it up like the starving man he was. It was tempting to write this off as getting some desperately needed sex, but he couldn't fool himself that much. Gabe had been with other men. This was special. Perfect, like he'd thought.

Jerry climbed him, one leg wrapped around Gabe's hip and both arms tightening around his neck. Gabe slid an arm under Jerry's ass and hoisted him so both his legs could circle around Gabe's hips. *Oh shit!* Jerry started riding him like his favorite merry-go-round animal, sliding up and down so their bulges pressed and throbbed together.

Gabe staggered back so Jerry was pressed against the kitchen counter, but it was too high to sit him on. Instead Gabe used the counter for leverage so he could rut against Jerry's crotch even harder. Each thrust sent bolts of pleasure lightning from his balls into his cock, which was so hard he could have sold it to Craftsman for their tool chests. From his dick, the electricity seemed to shoot up his spine and explode some piece of his brain.

One goal. Orgasm.

"Oh God, Gabe." Jerry's head hung back so his mane of hair brushed the shining counter. His hips bobbed and bumped as Gabe ground against him. So close. So close.

"Oh shit!" Somehow, the crossover from excruciating pleasure to release happened without conscious thought—an eruption in his balls and a wash of ecstasy that filled every cell and shot a flood of hot stickiness into his jeans.

Jerry yelled so loud his voice echoed through the not-yet-full rooms of the house. "Oh, oh God. Oh!"

Gabe held him up for seconds as they both shook and shuddered through orgasm together, and then Jerry's legs seemed to collapse down Gabe's sides, and his feet made it to the ground. He rested his head against Gabe's shoulder. Breathing became top priority.

As his gasps subsided, Gabe noticed how Jerry felt under his hands. Whipcord slender but strong, just as he'd looked stalking around that stage bare-chested. Still, Gabe probably outweighed Jerry by forty pounds, and he liked that feeling of being the shelterer, the one keeping the stress and danger away from Jerry.

Jerry pulled back and looked up at him with his face soft but serious. "Are you going to chalk this up to extreme horniness and say that you have too much to lose to be around a guy like me?"

Gabe opened his mouth, then closed it and shook his head. "What is a guy like you? I'm not sure I can draw general rules about a sweet dude I met in a home improvement store who doesn't like talking to people and occasionally struts around a stage half-dressed singing like an angel to twelve thousand screaming fans."

"Confusion's a good start. Take off your pants."

"What?" Gabe barked a laugh.

"Unless you want to wear your cum home, I'd suggest trying out my new washer and dryer on both our pairs of jeans."

He glanced down at the dark spot on the crotch of his pants that was partly drying into a light, stiff blotch. "Good plan."

"Come on." Jerry took his hand and led him out of the kitchen. Now that they were moving, the stickiness in his drawers was definitely an issue.

Gabe made a little hop, trying to get the goopy situation away from his softening cock. "I haven't done anything like coming in my pants since I was in middle school."

"Yeah, I think we get to try out the shower too." He trotted up the stairs, still pulling Gabe with him.

"It should work."

Jerry grinned. "What about the soaking tub?"

Gabe tried to keep from leering back. "Prime operational condition."

Jerry made a left into the bathroom. "It's even clean." He closed the drain and turned on the tap. Gabe held his breath, but the water poured into the huge tub in a wide flow. Jerry slapped his hands together. "Perfect." He grabbed Gabe again and pulled him into the finished guest bedroom that Gabe had created for him.

Gabe looked at the pristine sheets and comforter, exactly as he'd left them. "Didn't you come home last night? Where did you sleep?"

Jerry gave him a sheepish look. "I fell asleep on the couch. Your guy found me there this morning."

"My guy? Oh, Jorge?"

"Yes. He told me you'd left a note for me. I ran upstairs, found it, said no fucking way, and ran out the door." He waved a hand. "Take off your clothes and I'll wash them."

"Uh, you have about a hundred miles of not-yet-covered windows, and while the neighbors aren't close, they are out there."

"True that." He pulled open the bottom drawer of his dresser, which Gabe had moved from the master bedroom, and fished out two pairs of sweats. "You can probably wear these. They're my biggest ones. Come on, give me your clothes."

Gabe peeled off his shirt, then his jeans. "Yuk." His boxer briefs sported a big wet stain. He quickly glanced at Jerry, who was gathering Gabe's clothing. They might have ridden each other's erections, but they hadn't seen them. With a quick breath, Gabe ripped the shorts down to his ankles and stepped out of them.

When he picked them up, he found Jerry staring. Gabe swallowed. "Uh, getting a complex here."

Jerry raised his saucer eyes to Gabe. "Holy crap, you're hung."

"Yeah, well, I'm six-three."

He cocked his head sideways to stare at Gabe's groin. "It looks like it."

Gabe snorted. "Am I doing a strip show, or will you be joining me?"

"I'm going to strip in the laundry room. Go turn off the water and get in."

Gabe yelled, "No fair," but Jerry trotted down the stairs carrying Gabe's jeans and underwear. Gabe turned off the water in the big tub across the hall, tested it, and found it hot but delicious. He climbed the steps to the top, then slowly lowered himself into the deep tile-covered tub.

Oh man. It was that hot that seared the edges of your skin but soaked into your muscles and tendons like soothing balm. While he'd been finishing the tub, he'd dreamed about sitting in it like this.

He heard soft, fast footsteps on the wood floors, and Jerry came tearing around the corner. "Brr. It's a little chilly in the laundry room. I guess because it's next to the garage."

Gabe didn't respond. Frozen—and not the kids' movie. *Holy hell and little fishes.* On the stage, Jerry had reminded Gabe of a prowling leopard, wild and dangerous. Here, shivering adorably with his beautiful hair falling over his soft tan nipples and his long, long dick showing off between his legs, Jerry made a picture Gabe couldn't find words to describe. He couldn't have told Jerry how beautiful he was even if he could have gotten sounds out of his dry mouth.

Seemingly oblivious, Jerry mounted the steps and sat on the edge of the tile. "Ooh, that's cold on the butt. How is it?"

"Uh, hot. Slide in slowly so you get used to it."

Jerry put weight on his arms, biceps popping, and slowly lowered himself into the water across from Gabe. He opened his mouth wide and gasped as his slender torso slid under the water, his hair floating around him.

Holy crap, I'm in a tub with Jet Gemini.

Jerry closed his eyes and moaned—as if Gabe needed any more sensual sound effects. Jerry whispered, "This is so great."

Gabe couldn't close his eyes. He might miss something.

Suddenly Jerry's lids popped open. "It's important that you get all that sticky off you." He slid forward, probably onto his knees because he had to raise his chin to keep his mouth above water. "Here. Let me help."

Before Gabe even registered what Jerry said, a strong hand wrapped around his cock and started to stroke. Just the sight of Jerry in the nude had gotten Gabe back to half-mast. The hand did the rest of the job. "Shit."

"You like?"

"You kidding?"

Gabe slid down so he was on his knees facing Jerry and grabbed his own handful. Staring into each other's eyes, they jerked and massaged, their breath coming hot and fast.

Jerry leaned forward. "Will you fuck me?"

Gabe about lost it just at the thought. "Not in the water. Need lubrication."

"I've got it." Jerry pointed to the thick tile top of the tub. "Sit there." He climbed out, just as erect as Gabe, ran out of the room, and came back carrying a tube of lube. He held it like a trophy. "My jerking-off lube."

Unceremoniously, he pushed some into his own butt.

"Have you got a condom?"

Jerry paused. "No. But I've been tested at least once since I had sex with anyone but my hand."

Gabe nodded. "Me too."

Holy shit, he was about to go from no sex to bareback with the hottest man alive.

Jerry climbed onto the edge of the tub, leaned over, and captured Gabe's big dick in his mouth.

"Holy crap, warn a guy."

Jerry made a snorting sound around his mouthful and sucked hard, then pulled his lips off and started lubing Gabe's cock. He looked up. "For a guy who hardly ever gets fucked, you're kind of an advanced class, but I love the idea of it."

"You don't have to bottom."

"No, I really want to." He grabbed two hand towels from the rack beside the tub, straddled Gabe's hips, and put the towels under his own knees before taking Gabe's well-lubed cock and placing it in the perfect spot. Then with a look of wildly sexy concentration, he pressed down. Nothing happened.

He rose up again, repositioned, and pressed harder. Gabe slid his fingers under Jerry's smooth-as-silk ass and insinuated a finger between the edge of his cock and the target. Wiggling, he slid it in.

Jerry gasped, then made a humming sound.

"Gotta walk before you can run." He pulled out the index finger and substituted his thicker middle finger. Jerry started bouncing on his finger, and Gabe chuckled. "I think he likes it."

They were both gasping so hard they could barely talk as Gabe pulled the edge of Jerry's slick channel outward so the pressure of his cock got some traction and—holy wow!—the tip slid in.

"Oh God, Gabe. Yes. Yes." Jerry pushed like a crazy man, gaining real estate with every thrust.

"Don't hurt yourself, sweetheart."

"Want more." He was rising and falling on his knees as he pushed Gabe's big cock deeper and deeper inside him.

Gabe looked up. *Oh my God.* The mirror over the sink reflected Jerry, riding Gabe's erection like a madman, wet hair flying, his head thrown back, eyes squeezed shut and mouth open.

Nothing Gabe had ever seen compared.

Jerry cried, "I love this. Can we do it all the time? I want you to fuck me on every surface in the house. Please."

Gabe chuckled. "Guess if you're begging, I'll have to say yes. I'm a good guy like that."

They both started to laugh, and then Jerry screamed, "Oh God, I'm coming," and spurts of cum decorated Gabe's chest. Everything, the friction, the smell, the silky texture of Jerry's skin. *Too much. Oh man, oh crap. Oh*— The image of his cum flooding Jerry's body filled his brain just before it exploded.

Moments later, they both slid into the still very warm water, locked in each other's arms. Gabe murmured, "We better be careful not to drown."

He suspected he meant that in more ways than one.

CHAPTER SEVENTEEN

"I DON'T even believe this."

Jerry smiled at Ellie as she stared out the family room door at the swimming pool. As promised, she'd brought his car from ImproveMart and was taking a quick tour of the house before he drove her to school.

Shaking her head, she wandered onto the patio, up the steps, and into the pool enclosure. "This is huge." She knelt by the edge of the pool and trailed her finger in the water. The raised-eyebrow look she gave Jerry made him laugh.

He held up his hands. "I know, I need to be more sensible, but I'll call and order the solar panels first thing Monday."

She shrugged dramatically. "Just sayin'. I know you're this big rich guy, but rich people are rich because they're careful with their money."

"I know. I'm not great with money, so I have other people who manage it. I promise to pay more attention." He cleared his throat. "But I can't turn off the heater until the pool guy comes the next time, so, uh, maybe you want to come over and swim while it's still warm?"

She looked at him, her dimples accenting her pursed lips. "Very tricky. Think you can lure me with my love of swimming, right?"

He crossed his arms and grinned. "It crossed my mind."

She jumped up like a cheerleader. "Well, it worked! When can I come?"

"If you're not busy tomorrow, you can come anytime and swim all day."

"Can I bring my dad?" She asked it with a smirk, so Ellie definitely wasn't in the dark about her dad being gay.

"Sure, if you want." He also said that with a smirk, and she laughed. "So we better get going if you're to be on time for school. We can do a more in-depth tour tomorrow. I'll show you the tower."

"The tower?" Her eyes got wide, and she looked up at the roof. "Oh, is that it?"

"You have to wait until tomorrow." He crooked a finger. "Come on."

At the front door, Ellie said, "I brought you a cooler cap." On the built-in cabinet beside the entrance she'd put a bag. From it, she took a newsboy cap in a small checked pattern. She handed it to him.

"Hmm. Think I can get all this under it?" He held out a long hank of hair.

"It's pretty flexible." She pulled a ponytail holder from her pocket. "Bend down."

He did, and she gathered his hair and pulled it into a tight tail, then wrapped it around his head and slid the cap over it.

Hands on hips, she cocked her head. "Totally cool. Look." She pointed toward the bathroom, and he stepped into it and gazed into the vanity mirror.

"Damn." He barked a laugh. "You're right."

"This cap looks like you wear it on purpose, not because you're trying to hide something. But it still covers your hair, and who's Jet Gemini without his hair, right? So who's going to recognize you?"

Jerry took another look. He looked good, not stupid. Amazing. "You get to dress me from now on."

"With pleasure. Now put on your glasses, and let's get going."

When they got in his Prius, Ellie said, "I listened to your playlist. Hope you don't mind. It's mostly classical."

"Yes."

"So when you teach music, it'll be mostly classical, not rock?"

He tried not to make a face. "I don't really know. I mean, the chances I'll ever get to teach are pretty slim, at least before I'm, like, fifty or sixty."

"Why?"

"Well, uh…." He turned onto the 5 Freeway, heading toward Talent and Phoenix. "I'm still pretty popular."

"Okay, understatement of the century."

"So I guess there're still people who want to hear my recordings and go to my concerts."

She looked at him. "Of course there are. There probably always will be. But your fans aren't the boss of you. If you want to do something else, do it."

"Truthfully, Ellie, I'm kind of an industry. All popular performers are. There are tons of people who make their living from my work. I can't just quit."

She chuckled. "It's nice that you're worried about the people who work for you, Jerry, but would they do the same for you? I mean, if General Motors can close plants and lay off thousands of workers, I think you can become a teacher if you want to."

Whoa. No one ever told him he should quit.

"Not that I'm encouraging you to give up being Jet. You're my favorite singer ever. But I live with a man who pretty regularly gives up what he wants to do in his life for somebody else, namely me. It's great, but it's not a sustainable strategy."

"You think your dad should be doing something different?"

She sighed loudly and pointed at the next street. "Turn right up here." She shifted so her left cheek rested on the seat back, and she faced him. "I don't know, Jerry. He's given up so much for me. I mean, he's gay for crap's sake, and he married a woman for me—and we'd never even met. He gave up college and a social life and moving to a city where his furniture business might thrive. Instead, he stays with ImproveMart because it's steady and gives us benefits and he can point that out to the court."

"I think that's what good dads do, isn't it?"

"I guess. I mean, he had such bad parents, he overcompensates." She straightened in her seat. "My school's up there."

Ahead Jerry saw cars pulling into a large school parking lot. He got in the queue and put on his blinker.

Ellie looked at him, then at her lap. "The worst thing is, he doesn't really try to find someone he could love who'd love him back. He just tables it because he doesn't want to take any chances with the court. It's sad, and I feel responsible."

Before Jerry could even think of what to say, they were at the head of the line, and Ellie gathered her backpack and purse. "Thanks so much, Jerry."

"Thank you for rescuing my car."

"I didn't see any paparazzi, but they're sneaky. I'll see you tomorrow, and I'll bring the big guy."

"Deal." He smiled at her.

She scooted forward, kissed his cheek, then got out of the car, slammed the door, and waved at another girl as she trotted toward the school.

Jerry touched his cheek. *She's an amazing kid.* At seventeen she seemed smart, capable, even sophisticated, but not jaded. Still a kid—

something it sounded like her dad had never been. *Gabe gave up his childhood to assure she had hers. Pretty damned special guy.*

Jerry grinned as he pulled out on the street and pointed the car back toward Ashland. For the first time in forever, he couldn't wait for tomorrow.

Don't get attached. Don't get attached.

Gabe lay back on the chaise lounge he'd picked out for Jerry's deck. There was an iced tea beside him on a small table, his daughter was ecstatically swimming from end to end of the huge pool where she'd occasionally peek up to be sure they—no, make that Jerry—was appreciating her, the sun shone down in full spring attempts at warmth, and Gabe was resting for the first time in weeks. Man, this place and this guy would be so easy to get used to.

Since their evening of wild sex two days before, Gabe had worked like a crazy man at ImproveMart to try to make up for any cutting of corners that might have resulted from his juggling two jobs. Jorge was still tacitly in charge of supervision at Jerry's house, but he'd been pretty glad to discover Gabe was still participating. Plus, the landscaping of the front entrance had just begun, and while Jorge was enthusiastic, he didn't know much about gardens or hardscape, so Gabe was in charge of that project.

Ellie bounded out of the pool, grabbed a towel, and walked over to where Jerry lay on a chaise beside Gabe. He had the cap Ellie had gotten him over his hair and his sunglasses on, probably because of the workers who were still in the house and yard, but at least he'd worn slim-fitting jeans, not his baggy sweats. Ellie said, "Dad and I brought ingredients. Is it okay if I make us all some lunch in your new kitchen?"

Jerry sat up. He really seemed to like Ellie, even at her bossiest and most intimidating. "Sure. We can help."

"Okay, but give me a few minutes to scope out the appliances and find everything."

He grinned. "Good. You can teach me when you've got it mastered."

She wrapped her towel around her curvy, cute figure in her not-very-daring bikini and padded into the house through the mudroom entrance, where they'd installed a shower and an infrared sauna.

Gabe said, "She sure loves your pool. She's having a hard time yelling at you for spending the money to heat it."

"I promised her I'd have solar installed right away." Jerry smiled. "Do you know somebody?"

"Yeah. Got to keep the budget police off your case." He chuckled.

"Actually, it's fun to have somebody worry about spending my money. Most people forget I work for a living." He glanced at Gabe. "I appreciate both of you looking out for me."

Gabe lifted his brows. "I've spent a lot of your money with that weird black card."

"Yes, but you account for every penny, and you're not exactly using the most expensive sources. I really am grateful. Nobody could have gotten this much comfort and style for such a reasonable price."

The compliment shut Gabe up. He'd only thought of himself as a stopgap—a way to get things done when Jerry didn't want to do them himself. The idea that he brought something special to the process made him blink.

Ellie's voice came from the family room door. "Okay, ready for helpers."

Gabe followed Jerry into the house, enjoying the view of the slim hips in tight denim gently swaying. Any way he could come back to Jerry's after he took Ellie home? He sighed softly. Not fair to leave his daughter by herself while Gabe sneaked out to get laid, even if she'd tell him to go.

He stepped into the kitchen and caught his breath. Ellie had a big pot of homemade soup she'd made at their house and was heating here on Jerry's shiny new professional-quality range. She'd spread out all the salad makings they'd brought on the quartz counters. The whole scene looked kind of like an ad for the cooking channel, but best of all was Jerry, who stood with a hand over his mouth, staring at his own kitchen. Gabe walked up beside him and settled a hand in the small of Jerry's back.

He whispered, "You okay?"

Jerry nodded but didn't get any words out.

Gabe smiled. "Looks like a real home, huh?"

Jerry shook his head again, then turned and burrowed his head in Gabe's shoulder.

For a second, Gabe looked uneasily at Ellie, but she glanced up, grinned, and winked. Gabe tightened his arm around Jerry's back and gently patted him until he raised his head.

Jerry slowly shared a smile. "Sorry, it's just so nice to see—all this. Thank you for making it happen." He wiped a hand over his eyes, turned to the already washed lettuce and spinach, and started ripping them into a big wooden bowl that Gabe had bought for the kitchen. Jerry sniffed as he grabbed an avocado.

With a grin, Gabe started washing tomatoes, and ten minutes later the three of them sat down at Gabe's handmade table that was now installed in Jerry's dining room.

Jerry looked down at the pretty patterned soup bowl and plate in front of him. "We're inaugurating this room." He raised his iced tea glass. "Thank you, Ellie, for this great moment."

She blushed and raised her glass. "My pleasure. I put the extra soup in your freezer, so all you have to do is remember to defrost it, and you don't have to eat pizza for one meal."

Jerry started singing the song from *Oliver* about glorious food, and Ellie joined in. Jerry jumped up and segued to "Let It Go." He waltzed around the room singing something about looking like he was the queen while draping his head with a place mat. Gabe and Ellie rocked in their chairs, but despite the laughter, Gabe could have listened to that voice all day. Man, could Jerry sing.

After they ate, they cleaned up the kitchen, then Ellie asked, "Can I take one more swim? Is it okay, Jerry?"

"Sure."

"Okay. I'm going to turn on the dishwasher and then change back into my suit."

Gabe and Jerry walked back out into the early afternoon sunshine. Jerry glanced at the door, then rested his head against Gabe's shoulder. "I didn't know I could have a day like this."

All around them, the branches of the trees Gabe still hadn't had time to get pruned were starting to leaf. Gabe sighed. *Perfect.*

"Jerry! Hey, Jer, where the hell are you?"

The shout came from inside the house.

Jerry stiffened and leaped back like someone had stepped on the cat's tail.

Or his dreams.

CHAPTER EIGHTEEN

"Jerry!"

Gabe turned. Jerry stared toward the source of the voice like he'd heard an oracle of doom.

Through the family room doors came the guy Gabe had seen sitting with Jerry at the restaurant that night, but this time he wasn't wearing a hat. His hair was cut in one of those styles where the top's long and the sides are short, and the color was almost white with a streak of blue shooting through it. He was shorter than Jerry and stockier, but the resemblance was there.

Jerry started to say something, then gasped as three other men came out of the door after the blond guy. They looked familiar. Gabe was pretty sure these were the musicians who'd played with Jet Gemini.

Jerry clenched his teeth. "Shit!" He took a few steps forward. "What in the bloody fuck are you doing here?"

The blond stopped a few feet away and raised his hands. "Hey, bro, come on. We've been cooling our heels in San Francisco waiting for you to show up." He glanced at Gabe. "Finally I figured we needed to come to you."

Jerry's voice was icy. "How did you know where to come?"

The guy looked up uneasily. "I figured you were coming back to Ashland. I, uh, had somebody follow you when you got off the freeway."

"Goddammit, Fred!" Since there was more than one exit, it meant Fred the Asshole had more than one spy following him.

"Come on, kiddo, I had to make sure you were all right and nobody was, uh—" He glanced at Gabe again. "—taking advantage of you. You can be such an easy mark." He plastered a smile on his face and stuck out his hand to Gabe. "Hi. I'm Fred Castor."

Gabe shook Fred's hand automatically, then looked at Jerry.

Jerry gave him one glance that seemed to contain all the pain and longing of his life, but it only took a second for his expression to cool and harden. "This is Gabe Mason. He's heading the construction on my house."

The words were only true—but they froze his blood. Gabe dropped his hand.

Fred said, "Hi." His gaze moved back and forth between Gabe and Jerry like a Ping-Pong ball. How much had he seen?

Ellie's voice preceded her bounding entrance through the mudroom door, singing. She stopped, staring at the men who openly ogled her. "Oh, sorry."

Gabe said, "Ellie, we best be going. Please get your things."

"But—"

"Get your things, please."

She turned and walked back into the house.

Gabe mumbled, "I'll check with the landscaper before I go."

"Good, thanks." Jerry kept glaring at his brother without a glance for Gabe.

Gabe stalked into the house, wanting not to feel hurt and stupid, except it would *be* stupid not to *feel* stupid. Ellie met him at the door holding her still-damp bikini. She said, "I left the extra food here."

Gabe just nodded.

"That's his band. And his brother. Did Jerry invite them here?"

"No."

"Is Jerry okay? He looked really weird."

He acted really weird. "I'm sure he's fine. Let's go."

Gabe trotted down the front porch steps, checked with the guys working on the landscaping of the entry path, and walked toward the driveway. As they came around the corner, Gabe thought he saw a person scoot past the edge of the wall that surrounded the pool. He glanced at Ellie. "Did you see something?"

She seemed distracted. "What? Oh, I wasn't watching. What happened?"

"I thought I saw somebody wandering around out here."

She shrugged. "Probably one of your landscapers. Or maybe another member of the band got lost."

"Yeah." They climbed in the truck, and Gabe wound down the narrow drive.

As they pulled onto Mountain Avenue, Ellie said, "I'm worried about Jerry. He really seemed different. Upset, I think."

Gabe softly sighed. "I think he was embarrassed."

"What do you mean?"

"That the big rock star was caught socializing with his hired help."

"Come on, Dad. Jerry doesn't think of you that way."

"Sure he does. Why wouldn't he? That's what I am. He only invited us because he's grateful that I got his house partly done." He flashed her a big smile and hoped it reached his eyes. "And I got paid well to do it, so no complaints." The great night in the soaking pool had merely been his bonus.

"But you like Jerry." Surprisingly, he saw a glitter in her eyes like tears.

"Sure I do. He's a great guy." He took a breath. "But he lives in a different world from us, honey. Once his house is done, he doesn't have any reason to see us. Not like Jet Gemini's going to be dropping into ImproveMart."

"He did once."

"Yeah." He stopped talking, afraid his voice might shake, and flipped on the radio. It was still on the local classical channel where Jerry had set it last time he was in the truck. Gabe swallowed and changed to a country western station.

PERCHED ON the edge of the chair in the second guest room, Jerry glared at Fred. "What was it about me wanting some time and privacy you didn't get?"

Fred frowned. "Come on, Jer, is this time and privacy?" He waved an arm. "I leave you to yourself for a few weeks, and you buy a ramshackle house and hire some home-improvement dude to fix it up? Jesus, you've got a perfectly great penthouse in San Francisco and a palatial mansion in LA. Whatever possessed you to buy this?" He looked around in disgust. "You're the one who's always telling me I need to be more careful with money."

Jerry opened his mouth to answer, but Fred, as usual, pushed on. "And your fix-up guy?" He sneered. "You don't care about his skills. You just like his ass. Seriously, Jer. I thought you'd grown out of that phase. Just when the rumors start to die down, you go back to your old tricks. At least the guys saw that cute girl. Hopefully they think you're balling her."

Jerry sprang to his feet. "Fuck, Fred! She's seventeen years old! She's his daughter."

"I didn't say you were sleeping with her. Plus, they don't know how old she is." He leaned forward on the bed where he'd planted himself, leaving the band downstairs in the family room sipping beer and watching some sports or other on the TV that Gabe had worked so hard to get attached to the solid plaster walls. Damn, just thinking of Gabe made Jerry's chest hurt. *What's he thinking?* Gabe had looked so shocked and offended. *And Ellie?*

Fred said, "Since we lost Marty until his mom gets well, we need to rehearse with Swizzle on bass, and we've got the big performance in Vegas."

"So instead of calling me and asking me to meet you, you thought you'd just have me followed like some kind of cheating spouse to see whether I was behaving in accordance with your exalted standards."

Fred narrowed his eyes, an expression that had cowed Jerry lots of times as a kid. "I don't make the rules, Jerry. I don't give a shit if you're gay, but your fans do. Older women don't care, but young girls get squigged out by sex, to say nothing of their parents keeping them home. Theoni's told you that a million times."

True. His publicist didn't actually know he was gay, but whenever there was a rumor, she preached how bad it would be for his career. Gay might be cool in most circles, but not for movie and rock stars. Sex symbols could dress in spangled tights as long as they had a woman on their arm.

Man, I'm tired of this shit.

Fred got his sincere face on. "I'm sorry I had you tailed. I've got to admit, you kind of made it a challenge." He grinned just a little, probably hoping for a smile back. He didn't get one. "Anyway, I may not get this whole house thing, but I'll defend your right to have it. And since you do have it and it's as big as Colorado, how about we set up and rehearse here?"

"No."

"What?" He looked shocked.

"You and the guys get out of here. I'll meet you back in the studio in San Francisco tomorrow."

"Come on, that's dumb. We're here."

"And I didn't invite you. This house is mine. Get back on a plane, and I'll meet you tomorrow."

"Jesus, Jer, you're acting like a crazy man."

"That's what comes from spending twelve years living everybody else's fucking life." It took all his guts to stare his brother down. Too many years where Fred was the only one on his side. Of course, he was more on his own side. Jerry said, "There are lots of flights from Medford. Get on one and go home." He kept staring, arms folded over his chest.

"Well shit." Fred rose and stomped out of the bedroom, scowling.

Jerry walked to the top of the stairs and listened as the guys grumbled, laughed, clomped around, and finally slammed the front door behind them.

Jerry padded down the stairs quietly, peering along the hall, afraid some other member of his team would leap out at him. Everything was quiet.

He rushed back to his interim bedroom, grabbed his phone from the nightstand where he'd left it, and dialed before he could lose his nerve. It rang. And rang. Third ring.

It went to voicemail, and for a second he heard Gabe's recorded voice. Jerry clicked off and immediately dialed again. It rang. After another ring, it stopped, but no voice came on.

Jerry said, "Hello?"

No answer.

"Gabe?"

"Jerry?" It wasn't Gabe; it was Ellie, and she was whispering.

The words tumbled out. "Hi, Ellie. I'm so sorry about what happened today. I didn't know they were coming, and I didn't want them to stay. That's why I didn't introduce you. I didn't want them to know anything about you or your dad because you don't need to be involved in that world. Will you tell him that, Ellie? I'm so, so sorry about—everything. Please."

"Jerry, I can't talk. I grabbed Dad's phone from the couch, but he doesn't want me to talk to you. I'll try to tell him you're sorry, but—" The phone clicked off.

Damn.

He dialed again. Ring. Ring. Ring. Voicemail.

He hung up and dialed again. Ring. Ring.

Gabe bellowed into the phone. "Dammit, Jerry, what the hell—"

"I'm sorry."

"Come on, you were embarrassed, and I totally understand." He breathed out. "I like you more than I should, but what can we possibly have going, Jerry? Are we going to meet in secret from time to time hoping that no one finds out? Let's face it, the likes of you doesn't mingle with the likes of me. I forgot that for a little while, but now I remember. There's no Cinderella in real life. The guy from ImproveMart doesn't get to end up with the handsome prince. So thanks for the reminder. I'm really glad I got to—" His voice broke and the phone went dead.

Jerry stared at the phone. "Fuck this!" He ran down the stairs, into the mudroom, and through the hall to the garage.

He was pretty sure he didn't take a full breath on the twenty-minute drive to Talent.

ELLIE'S WARM hands on his back were the only thing keeping him from flying into a million pieces.

"Come on, Dad, call him. I believe him. He's really upset. So are you. How does it make sense to not talk to each other?"

He just shook his head. He was acting like a big baby, but he couldn't stop. Too much longing pressing against a huge wall of reality. How could it be that the one guy he'd really liked in most of his adult life had to be—who he was?

The sound of the doorbell made him jump a foot.

Ellie yelled, "I'll get it!" She was out of his bedroom so fast there should have been speed lines.

He heard voices from the living room, Ellie's soprano and the lower sound of a man's voice. Gabe strained to hear who it was, but no go. *Don't get your hopes up. Why would he come here?*

Things got quiet, but there was no sound of the front door closing, so he turned to go see and gasped. Jerry stood in his bedroom door, pale hair hanging around his face and shoulders.

Gabe's heart slammed so hard it should have bruised his ribs. The anger, hurt, and shame all dissolved in a burst of elation. *He came!*

Gabe took a step forward, and Jerry did the rest. He cleared the space in one jump and landed with his arms around Gabe's neck. After a serious nose bump, he managed to fuse their lips together, his fingers digging into Gabe's hair.

Gabe wrapped his arms around Jerry and pressed their bodies together. All he wanted was to kiss until he didn't have to think anymore.

It didn't work.

Gabe might be going up in smoke, but his well-trained dad brain reminded him that Ellie could be right outside the door. He pulled back, looked into Jerry's face, and that was all it took to realize nothing had really changed. "Wait."

Jerry opened his beautiful, odd eyes. "Do I have to?"

Gabe smiled and flicked the hair from Jerry's eyes with a finger, then trailed it down the lean, pale cheek. "Yeah."

Jerry sighed. "You're right. We need to talk."

Gabe gazed at the crease between Jerry's brows. *How can I care so much about something so impossible?* Gabe said, "Sadly, I don't think there's much to talk about."

"Yes there is. Come on." Jerry took Gabe's hand and led him into the living room. Ellie sat at the dining room card table putting on a big show of working. *Likely story.*

Jerry sat on the couch and pulled Gabe down beside him. Ellie seemed to get the message that she was included, because she walked in and sat on the easy chair with her legs tucked under her.

Jerry stared at their clasped hands. "I didn't tell my brother who you were because I don't want that part of my life to be a part of this part of my life. Jet can be Jet, but this is *my* life, and I want you both to be a part of it."

Gabe squeezed his fingers but still shook his head. "It's not very realistic, Jerry. Your brother found you, and other people will too. You're afraid to go to the home improvement store without a disguise. You are who you are, and you don't get to snap your fingers and become a regular person."

Ellie leaned forward. "I'm afraid I agree with Dad. I'll admit, it's easy to forget you're Jet Gemini when we're just hanging out, but for how long? The paparazzi are going to find your house eventually, and then you'll need your bodyguards and barbed wire." She looked up with compassion in her eyes. "Plus, your fans don't know you're gay, Jerry, right? I mean, I'm a big fan who follows all the stories about you, and even though I've heard rumors, I've never seen any of them confirmed. So what are you going to do? Suddenly show up with my dad? The reporters will go apeshit, and so will the fans."

Suddenly Jerry buried his face in his hands.

Gabe knew how he felt. The truth hurt like hell.

CHAPTER NINETEEN

HIS CHEST hurt so badly. Jerry pressed a hand against his sternum to help catch his breath, then raised his head and looked at Gabe and across the room at Ellie. Funny how these two people had become so important to him so fast. Maybe it was because they were the first friends he'd made who hadn't known who he was. They liked Jerry, shy and pizza eating, and even though they now knew he was also Jet Gemini, they didn't seem to expect him to morph into the rock star at any moment. That was comfortable and restful and fun. *Fun.* Not something he had a lot of, regardless of what his life looked like online.

Truthfully, he'd have liked Gabe and Ellie no matter how he'd met them—assuming he ever had. There was the problem. In his regular life, he never would have come across this wonderful man and his terrific daughter. If Jerry hadn't broken away, sneaked off to a small, arty town in Oregon, bought a run-down house, and paid an ill-advised visit to a home improvement store, he would never have found Gabe. The thought gave him chills. *No Gabe.*

He felt himself shaking his head before he said, "No. There has to be some way to make this work. There are famous people who get to have happy lives. Lots of them."

Ellie leaned her chin on her bent knees. "True. I don't think most of them are rock stars with a powerful desire for privacy." She smiled, but her eyes looked sad.

Jerry sucked in some more air. "I have to leave tomorrow morning early for San Francisco, and then I'm doing a huge one-night benefit show in Vegas. While I'm gone, I'm going to talk to Fred, who's my manager, and some of my other people. I'm going to work out a way where I get to have a life that doesn't belong to the press or the fans." Damn, even to his ears, the claim sounded like fantasyland. "When I get back, I'll put it into effect."

Ellie smiled encouragingly, but Gabe just ran a hand over his calf and stared into space. He said, "How long will you be gone?"

"I hope to be home by Friday."

He nodded but never looked up. "I'll make sure some work gets done while you're gone. At least you'll have a house to come home to."

Jerry wanted to yell, "Will I have you?" But that wasn't fair. It wasn't Gabe's life that made it impossible for them to be together. "Thank you."

They were all quiet, and not in a comfortable way.

Finally Jerry said, "I guess I better go and let you get some sleep." He desperately wanted to ask Gabe to come home with him. That wouldn't happen. Gabe wouldn't leave Ellie, and Jerry wouldn't ask him to.

Slowly he stood, some piece of his heart begging for them to talk him out of it. He'd happily sleep on their couch.

Ellie cleared her throat. "You can stay here, Jerry. Uh, I mean, if you want."

Gabe frowned. "Jerry has to pack for a trip."

Ellie nodded. "Sure." She clasped her hands. "I didn't think of that."

Jerry couldn't hold in the words. "I could stay. I don't actually do much packing. All my touring clothes are in San Francisco."

Gabe said, "What time's your plane?"

"Uh, I don't exactly know. I need to make a reservation for tomorrow morning."

Ellie leaped up. "I can do it." She raced to her laptop, set up on that ridiculous card table that was all his fault. She clicked a bunch of keys, and Jerry glanced at Gabe. He didn't look delighted but also not really angry.

Why am I doing this? It wasn't like he and Gabe were going to have hot sex while Ellie was in the house. Plus, he actually should go home in the morning and get a few things, although he didn't really have to. Still, it seemed important to be with people he cared about. Even though he loved his house and his privacy, at that moment the prospect of driving to Ashland felt lonely.

"Okay, here are some choices," Ellie called.

With one more glance at Gabe, Jerry walked over and sat beside Ellie. Together they picked out a flight that left at seven and booked him a first-class ticket.

She bounded up. "You can have my bedroom, Jerry. I'll sleep on the couch."

He shook his head. "No way. I'll sleep on the couch, and then I can sneak out at five and not bother either of you."

She side-eyed him. "You're pretty tall for that couch."

"You should see some of the places I've slept on the road. No worries."

Gabe stood from the already reserved couch. "I'll get some sheets and a blanket." He still hadn't smiled.

When Gabe walked out of the room, Ellie said, "Don't worry. He really wants you to stay." She gave him a grin, and he had to return it.

Fifteen minutes later, they'd made up the lumpy couch for him, and Ellie had found him a toothbrush. Now the three of them stood staring at the couch.

Ellie yawned. Make that fake yawned. "I'm heading for bed. Why don't you guys watch some TV for a while?" With elaborate stretching, she walked out of the room.

When her bedroom door closed, Gabe snorted. "I don't think she'd better plan a career in acting."

"Aside from her acting skills, she's pretty fantastic. You're so lucky."

"Yeah. I know." He smiled, and that carved-in-granite face softened. "Since she went to so much trouble to set this up, want to watch something?"

"Sure."

They both sat on the couch made up as a bed, and Gabe turned on the large flat-screen TV that dominated one wall.

Jerry whispered, "That's a pretty guy TV."

"Maybe I use it to watch *Dancing with the Stars*? Or reruns of *The Sound of Music*."

"Do you?"

Gabe gave a mock sigh. "No, I'm a football guy."

"I suspected that when I saw the size of the television you installed in my family room."

"Yeah, I was having TV envy."

Jerry whispered, "Size does matter."

It was good to hear Gabe laugh. He flipped through the channels and landed on a rerun of *Groundhog Day*.

Jerry bounced. "I love that movie."

"Me too." Gabe turned up the sound on the scene in the coffee shop.

Jerry said, "What if God isn't omniscient? What if he's just been around so long he's seen everything?"

They both laughed and launched into the next half hour of trading quotes from "Don't drive angry" to "Any kind of change is good."

As Bill Murray and Andie McDowell walked out the door of the B and B in the snow, Jerry said, "I guess we all have to learn the definition of insanity in our own way."

Gabe looked at him. "Doing the same thing over and over and expecting a different result?"

"Yes. You want something different, you've got to do something different. Give something different."

Gabe frowned. "But what if by changing one thing you change a lot of other things you didn't intend?"

Jerry smiled. "I heard a story once about how they used to catch monkeys in India or someplace like that. They'd put a banana in a small jar that was roped to the ground. The monkey would slide his hand in the jar and grab the banana, but the opening was so small, he couldn't get his hand out while he kept holding on. To be free, all he had to do was let go of the fruit, but he wouldn't do it and he'd be caught." Man, he hadn't thought of that story for a while. "Wealth and fame and all the shit that goes with them are a really shiny monkey jar."

"And a big banana." They chuckled, and Gabe looked up from under his dark brows. "Yeah. I guess I was like most people. I always figured money and fame gave you a lot of choices. I never knew how much they can own you." He sighed. "But we're all owned by something, aren't we?"

"I guess. Are you?"

Gabe raised his arms and stretched. "Yeah. Giving my daughter what she needs to live a happy adult life, starting with a decent college education. It's the only thing I want. The only thing I can afford to want."

"What about a happy adult life for you?" Jerry smiled and turned to face Gabe on the couch.

"Worrying about shit like that's for single guys, not single fathers."

"Ellie told me you'd given up so much for her. I think she feels responsible."

Gabe wiped a hand over the back of his neck and let out a breath. "I know she does, but I don't know what to do about that. She has to be my top priority."

"I think she wants to see that you're happy."

"Why can't she see that I am happy taking care of her?" He sounded frustrated, like this wasn't the first time he'd thought about it.

"She knows you love her, Gabe. She's one of the happiest, smartest girls I've ever met. You've done an amazing job."

"Thanks."

They were quiet, but it had a peaceful feeling.

Gabe said softly, "I'm going to miss you."

Jerry collapsed sideways so his head rested against Gabe's shoulder. "Not as much as I'll miss you. This is my last contracted engagement for a few months. I'm supposed to have a break to work on new music and then go into the studio with the band to record."

"Where do you do that?"

"San Francisco."

"You could install a studio in your house or in the other building."

Jerry leaned back against the couch. "I know. I'm thinking about it. But once my whole crew starts hanging out at that house, I'm afraid it'll feel like everywhere else. Like it's not really mine anymore. The only reason I'd do it is to be able to spend more time in Ashland." He didn't say "with you."

Gabe leaned over and gave Jerry a warm kiss. "You've got to get up really early. You better get some sleep."

"Yeah, I guess so."

Gabe turned off the TV, rose slowly, stretched so his flat, ridged stomach showed under the hem of his sweatshirt, then walked out of the living room, turning off the lights as he went.

Jerry made a fast trip to the bathroom, then felt his way across the dark space, settled onto the couch, and pulled some rumpled covers over himself. He was glad he'd stayed. The more time he spent with Gabe Mason, the more he liked him. "Liked" was such a high school word, but in Gabe's case it applied. On top of all the lust, passion, and complicated feelings Jerry had for Gabe, he genuinely liked him.

A scuffing sound made Jerry raise his head. A big dark shadow moved across the room.

Jerry suppressed a giggle and scooted against the back of the couch, making room. Gabe barely fit, what with the erection the size of Delaware pushing out the front of his pajama bottoms.

He whispered, "Ellie's sound asleep. I checked. Be real quiet." Then he wrapped one of those big, callused hands around both their cocks and made Jerry happy to get no sleep at all.

"WOW, WHAT an amazing building." Ellie looked up.

Gabe stood at the door to the big two-story open-space studio building that occupied a corner of Jerry's property near the road. The first time Gabe had seen it, he'd thought it was a neighbor until he saw the ground plans. Ellie wandered around inside.

The building had obviously been used as an artist's studio in the past, with swipes of paint on the concrete floors and a big exhaust fan in the corner where a firing kiln had once stood. A second-story balcony enclosed an office, and below was a full bathroom, complete with a shower. The rest of the huge building was open space soaring two stories high with a band of high windows as well as lower windows at the floor level.

Ellie called, "Dad, this would be an amazing music studio. Listen to the great acoustics." She bounded up beside him.

Gabe said, "Jerry's not sure he wants his band in here."

"I don't mean for the band. I mean for, like, music lessons." She flashed her dimples. "You know. When he becomes a music teacher."

Gabe laughed. "Right. As if he's going to leave audiences of twenty thousand to start teaching kids to play 'Twinkle, Twinkle, Little Star.'"

"Could happen." She spun around. "So what are we going to do in here?"

He grinned at her use of *we*. She really liked Jerry, and Gabe had a pretty good idea it wasn't about being a fan of Jet. She just liked Jerry. Yeah, well, that made two of them. Didn't change anything. There must be five hundred guys who liked Jerry and ten times as many who liked Jet. *Get in line, idiot.*

He cleared his throat. "I've got specialists coming to check the overhead lighting and the heat and air systems. We'll clean the place, paint, polish the concrete floors, and I guess let Jerry decide the rest."

"No. Let's do it and surprise him." She pressed her hands together in enthusiasm.

"Like what?"

She ran across the floor and waved her arms. "We could build a soundproof studio over here and put in all the recording systems and turntables and sound controls."

"I thought we were just playing 'Twinkle, Twinkle' in here."

"But Jerry's still going to be writing his own music. Plus he might want to record his students or maybe bring in an orchestra so Jerry can play with them. I mean, did you hear him play Liszt?"

Gabe laughed. "I don't think Jerry's as ambitious for himself as you are for him."

She frowned. "Somebody has to see to it that the man has a happy life. If he keeps on like he is, his life's going to slip away, and he'll never have lived it."

Gabe's mouth opened and closed. He couldn't get a word out since he felt like he'd been punched in the gut.

A few minutes later, Gabe held the door for Ellie, then followed her outside.

She said, "We need a better walkway out here. It's hard to find the entrance."

"That's a common theme on this property. Yeah, we need to put an entrance on the driveway and use this as a back door."

As they walked around the corner of the building, a car cruised slowly down the street below them, which was odd since that road led nowhere except to Jerry's property. Cars might get too far and have to turn around, but they didn't linger since there was no reason to be in that spot. If you were coming to see Jerry, you'd turn up the long driveway.

Gabe took a couple of steps down the drive toward the road, staring hard at the car. As he did, the car's tires squealed, and the thing took off in a cloud of dust.

"What was that?" Ellie glared after the retreating car.

"Don't know. Somebody lost, I guess."

Ellie shrugged, and they walked back to the house to check on Jorge's progress.

CHAPTER TWENTY

JERRY PINCHED the bridge of his nose. It had been a long Sunday, starting at 4:00 a.m. when he'd gotten into his car and driven quickly to Ashland to gather his toiletries and a few other things. Then he'd rushed back to Medford to get on his plane, fly to San Francisco, and spend the day rehearsing with his band.

They hadn't quit until almost 7:00 p.m. He was tired and hungry, and he wanted desperately to be back on a couch cuddled with Gabe or sitting at dinner laughing with Ellie.

Fred punched his arm. "Let's go get a drink."

"I want food."

"That too. Theoni's joining us. She wants to talk about the tour."

"Okay." He glanced at Fred. "Are the guys coming?"

"No, this is administrative stuff. Just us."

"Okay." Damn, this could be a chance to talk to both of them.

Thirty minutes later, they were sipping wine at a table at a quiet upscale restaurant on a high-rise rooftop. Theoni had laid out a plan for two magazine covers and a potential appearance at the American Music Awards. "Plus, I've got a surprise. Right after the concert, you're scheduled for the *Late Night Show with Bobby Breeson*. He's hosting the benefit, so he agreed to shoot the show from Las Vegas." She grinned.

Fred rocked back in his chair. "Good job, Theoni! That's fantastic exposure and will help keep the buzz going while Jet's off tour."

She said, "Thanks. Speaking of off tour, it'd be ideal if you have a new recording in time for the AMAs."

Jerry rubbed his forehead again. "I'll have to have time to write some new songs first."

She put her hand on his arm. "Are you okay, Jerry?"

He looked up at her. "Tired. Very tired."

"I thought you were getting some rest. Isn't that where you've been?" She smiled with that deep concern of someone whose whole income was based on him working.

"I rested some."

Fred smiled sweetly. "Jerry's been having a bit of a retreat, but no writing got done."

Fuck. Jerry pushed his chair back with a scrape, which took him out of reach of both of their oh-so-concerned hands. "Look, I've told you both, I want more time to write, play, and record. I'm tired of touring."

Fred sounded placating. "We've already cut back on the length of tours so that you have time off in between."

"You know that touring is what makes you a rock star versus just another recording artist. We've talked about that, Jerry." Theoni gave a strained smile.

"Maybe I don't want to be a rock star."

The look of panic that flashed across her face before she got control of her expression said it all. People wanted the best for him, and they knew exactly what that was—it was whatever was best for them.

Fred might have been talking to a sulky child. "You say that now, Jerry, but just wait until your popularity starts slipping and your fans stop screaming. Then you'll be yelling at me and Theoni because we let you do this to your career."

Jerry stared at his brother. "How much do I pay you, Fred?"

Fred's eyes widened, and he glanced uncomfortably at Theoni. He cleared his throat. "I receive a small salary plus bonuses."

Yeah, bonuses he paid himself. Jerry smiled. "What about you, Theoni?"

She laughed uncomfortably. "You must know how much you pay me."

"I can't remember offhand. Remind me."

"Uh, I make three hundred thousand." She rearranged her flatware. "Have you saved a lot of it?"

"What?"

He smiled. "It's always smart to save for the future."

Her lips turned up. "I'm only twenty-eight. I have time."

"Umm. Time. We never have enough of that, do we?"

GABE HAULED another pallet of tile to the shelves and started stocking.

"You sure look happy."

"What?" Gabe looked up at Mary, who'd come up behind him and he hadn't even noticed. "Sorry, you startled me."

"You were so absorbed in your happy thoughts." She winked at him. "Must be somebody special." With that, she bustled off down the aisle.

Special. Yeah. It was a sad commentary on Gabe's present state of kidding himself, but having Jerry say he wanted to find a way for Gabe to be in his life had given Gabe a permanent sappy expression. If Jerry wanted it to happen and Gabe wanted it to happen, maybe the sheer idiocy of the idea could be overcome.

He hauled another armload of tile samples and stretched to place them on a high shelf.

A weird click behind him made him turn. A woman dressed in jeans and a suit jacket, carrying a large tote bag and a phone, smiled at him. He'd seen an expression like that on the wildlife channel just before the lion ate the wildebeest. "Can I help you?"

"Yes. What nice tile. What do you call it?"

He glanced at the name on the edge of the sample. "Summer Sunrise. Do you want some?"

"You're Gabe Mason, aren't you?"

He tried to keep the crease from between his brows. "Yes. How many pieces would you like?"

"You're a regular employee here at ImproveMart?"

"Yes. May I ask why you want to know?"

She smiled. "Yes, I just wanted to know what it feels like for an improvement-store employee to know his daughter is the girlfriend of one of the world's biggest rock stars. I mean, how did you work that out?"

"What in the hell are you talking about?" He slammed the samples he had in his hand back onto the cart he'd carried them on.

She widened her eyes. "Your daughter's sleeping with Jet Gemini, of course. How old is she? I mean, isn't she in high school?"

"I don't know where you got the idea that my daughter is Jet Gemini's girlfriend."

"The same place everyone else did, Gabe. The pictures in the Daily Quest online. The same place I saw the picture of you and Jet cuddling away. So I guess the rumors about him playing on both sides of the fence must be true, right?"

"Get the fuck out of this store!" he roared, and the woman backed up.

"Don't you have a comment for my blog?" She snapped a couple of pictures as she ran backward.

Two more people, one with a video camera and the other snapping pictures with his phone, raced down the aisle, and Harry and two of the guys ran behind them.

Gabe yelled, "Get these people away from me." He took off running and made it to the stockroom, where he locked the door and flattened himself behind it. People yelled in the aisles outside the door, and Gabe couldn't breathe. *No. Can't be happening. Can't be.* Over and over like a mantra, the words repeated in his head.

Hammering on the stockroom door made him press harder against the wall.

"Gabe, it's Harry."

Gabe unlocked the door, and Harry rushed in. "What the hell is going on, my man? What are they talking about? The whole store's in chaos. I guess some of the employees saw the pictures of you and Ellie with Jet Gemini. I mean, seriously."

Gabe shook his head.

"Is Jet Gemini…?"

Gabe nodded. "Your weird customer, yeah."

"Holy fuck."

Gabe's cell started ringing. He pulled it from his pocket. *Ellie. Sweet God.* "Hi, honey." He held up a finger to Harry.

"Dad, do you know what's going on?"

"Yeah, a bunch of reporters showed up here at the store. Are they at your school?"

"When I tried to go to lunch, there were some reporters outside. I ran back in the school, and they won't let them in, but I'm scared to go out to get on the bus."

"I'll come and get you."

"What happened, Dad?"

"Remember I thought I saw somebody outside the wall at Jerry's?"

"Damn, a paparazzi, right?"

"I think so, yes."

She snorted. "And they decided from me swimming in that pool that I'm Jet Gemini's girlfriend? Jesus, somebody's desperate for a story."

"Yes, I think you're exactly right. Look, I'm going to leave here as soon as I can. I'll text you. Meet me at the back of the school, and we'll try to get home."

Harry waved his hands and mouthed the words, "Alejandro wants to see you."

Fuck. Alejandro managed the store, and he was usually an ally, but…. "I'll get there as soon as I can, honey."

"Okay, Dad. Hang in there."

"You too." He hung up and said to Harry, "Is Alejandro in his office?"

"I think so. He was helping to drive the reporters out of the store, but we can't really keep them out since we can't tell if they're customers or reporters."

"I'll go find him." He peered tentatively out of the stock room, saw no one who looked like they were about to take his picture, and slipped out, then circled through the lesser used back aisles to get to Alejandro's office.

He tapped on the closed door.

"Come in."

He opened the door. Alejandro was on the phone. He waved at Gabe to come in and was saying, "Thanks, Mac. I may need to call in a few extra security guards. Yeah, thanks." He hung up and looked at Gabe. "What the hell is going on?"

Gabe ran a hand through his hair. "You know all the stuff I've been buying for this home renovation I'm overseeing?" Might as well prod Alejandro's self-interest.

"Yeah. You mean my Christmas in April?"

Gabe nodded. "I didn't know it when I started the job, but the client's Jet Gemini."

"What the hell? How could you not know it? The guy's, like, famous."

"I'd never heard of him until I went to the concert with Ellie. He disguised himself. Even she didn't recognize him, and she's a huge fan."

"So what's this paparazzi shit?"

"Ellie loves to swim. He has a big pool. He invited us over so she could swim in his pool. Some paparazzi must have found the house and taken the photos over the wall."

"Yeah, well, what about the picture of you?"

Gabe gave a long, loud sigh. "He's an emotional guy. He was happy about everything that had been done in his house, and he gave me a hug. The photo leech caught the end of that. Then Ellie walks out to go swimming. It's total crap."

"I can see that." Alejandro ran a thumb over his chin. "But I also can't have the store being disrupted. Maybe you should take a few days off."

Gabe shook his head slowly. "Come on, Alejandro. I'm saving my days so I can take Ellie to see colleges. I can't—"

"Sorry, Gabe, I don't have any policy that lets me give you extra days. You'll have to use your vacation until this bullshit dies down."

"Damn. Okay. Thanks." He stood.

"You think he'll be spending more money at the store?"

Gabe frowned. "I don't know if he'll ever be back to Oregon." He stomped out of the office. Breathing hard, he pulled his keys from his pocket, decided to forget about his windbreaker, slipped out the back door, and ran to his truck.

For a second, he sat there and stared at the steering wheel. This was what Jerry had to put up with every day. Much worse for him. People chasing him, making up stories about everything he did. No privacy at all. What a crock.

He started the truck and drove out the back exit of the parking lot. Nobody seemed to be following, but what would it be like if paparazzi chased you down every street and each time you got in a car? What a nightmare.

When he pulled up behind Ellie's school, she ran out and hopped in the passenger seat. Gabe said, "Duck down so they don't see you."

She did, and they managed to pull out of the school driveway without anyone seeming to see. No such luck at their house. A bunch of unfamiliar cars dotted the parking spaces all the way down the block, and there were a couple of people lurking on their front lawn.

"Shit." He glanced at Ellie. "Excuse me."

"I second the motion."

"Okay, here we go. I'm going to pull into the driveway and hit the opener at the same time. Jump out, run in the garage, and as soon as I get in, close the doors."

"Deal."

He drove sedately up the street. He couldn't drive into their garage since he'd converted most of it to his workshop storage, but the door still worked.

"Get ready."

Ellie poised at the door.

In one move, he pulled into the driveway and hit the opener.

Ellie jumped out of the passenger door. The paparazzi seemed to come alive at the sight of her running into the garage, and they leaped out of their cars.

Gabe braked, piled from the driver's seat, made a charge at the reporters who got too close, scattering them, and then ran headlong into the garage with the door closing after him.

Ellie slapped him a high five, and they gasped for breath. Outside the garage door, they could hear people yelling and milling around.

Gabe opened the door into the house and walked straight to the living room windows to close the blinds. "Maybe I should call the police to get them off our lawn."

"Give them a few minutes and see if they leave. We can't be that big a story. Who'd ever believe I'm Jet Gemini's girlfriend? I mean, except for some of my stupid classmates. Seriously, my personal currency has never been this high. They think I'm denying it to be cool." She snorted. "Was it tough at work?"

"Alejandro was pretty supportive, but he has to worry about the store. So I have to take vacation days until this thing dies down."

"That's craptastic, but maybe you'll get more done at Jerry's house."

He flopped onto the couch, flipping on the light on the end table against the self-imposed gloom. "I think the reporters all know where Jerry's house is now, which is sad for him. But going there's pretty sure to put me directly in the paparazzi's sights." He shrugged and rubbed the back of his neck as the reality of the whole mess washed over him. "Now that everyone knows where the house is, Jerry may not want it anymore. After all, the place was about his having something of his own. Private. Remember how he kept saying that?" He glanced at Ellie and she nodded. "It sure doesn't qualify anymore." He swallowed hard against the tightness in his throat. The end of Jerry's dream. *Mine too, I guess.*

CHAPTER TWENTY-ONE

"Have you called Jerry?" Ellie put a warm hand on Gabe's arm for a second.

"No. I'm not sure what that would accomplish. If he says something to the press about the photos, it'll just assure that the story lasts twice as long."

"But he could explain that it's all a stupid mistake."

Gabe rose, walked to the kitchen, poured iced tea, and snapped the venetian blinds shut there as well. He turned and faced Ellie, holding out the glass. She went over and took it.

Gabe spoke softly. "Have you seen the photos?"

"A couple kids waved them in my face, so I looked them up."

"Are they bad?"

She pulled her phone from her jeans and clicked, then held it out to Gabe. Almost scared, he glanced at the screen. *Ouch.*

There were more photos that he'd expected. "Holy—they must have followed Jerry here when he came over after me."

"Yep."

The first photo was the one Gabe had expected. Him and Jerry standing on the pool deck, Jerry's head against Gabe's shoulder and Gabe's arm around his back. But also as he'd guessed, the shot might have been midhug and could be explained as a moment of gratitude—if you didn't really look at their expressions.

The next shot showed Fred and the musicians gaping at Ellie, who stood looking surprised and totally adorable in her modest bikini.

But then came a series of grainy photos taken through the front window of Gabe and Ellie's house—Ellie and Jerry on the piano bench, the two of them dancing around the living room singing, her standing at the door welcoming Jerry with a big smile.

To Gabe, who knew what had happened, every photo looked innocent, but then he read the headlines and captions.

Does Jet have a new girlfriend?

Robbing the cradle?

Is Jet taking a page from the old Elvis and Jerry Lee catalog?

A reference, Gabe guessed, to the fact that Elvis and Jerry Lee Lewis married very young girls.

And then the huge cringe. *Does Jet like father and daughter?* Yuk.

He looked up at Ellie. She was trying to be strong, but she couldn't erase the frown entirely. Gabe said, "I guess I better call him."

"If for no other reason than to warn him not to go home." She sipped tea. "I really feel badly for him. He wanted that house so much."

Gabe glanced at his watch and dialed his phone. It rang three times, then went to voicemail. Gabe said, "Hey, Jerry, it's Gabe. Call me, okay?" He clicked the phone off. "I didn't want to say anything in voicemail. Don't know his schedule at all. He's probably rehearsing or traveling or something." He set the phone on the counter.

Gabe moved to the front blinds and looked out. There were still a couple of strange cars, but no one was tromping on their grass. "I'm grimy. I'm going to take a quick shower and then let's make some dinner."

"Deal."

He walked into his bedroom, trying to shake the feeling that someone had stuffed his head with cotton. Right, cotton soaked in hot sauce. The disgusting prurience of the stories wove in and out of the sappy optimism he'd felt that morning. Which one was more unreal? Had he honestly thought that he and Jerry had a chance? Maybe not, but he also hadn't dreamed that just knowing Jerry could drag him and Ellie through the internet sewers.

As he turned on the water, he might have heard the sound of a phone ringing. For a second, his heart leaped, but the sound didn't repeat, so he stepped under the water and did a quick wash. He didn't shave, just soaped, rinsed, and dried. In his bedroom, he pulled on some sweats, brushed his hair off his face, then opened the bedroom door.

The sound of Ellie's sobs slammed him in the chest. He almost broke his neck thrashing into the living room to find her crumpled on the floor beside the kitchen counter, the phone lying beside her.

He fell to the ground. "What's wrong? Are you hurt? What happened?"

Ellie raised her red, puffy-eyed face to Gabe. "Mom. Mom's taking you to court for sole custody. Child endangerment."

JERRY FINISHED the last chorus and wiped his face with the edge of his T-shirt. "That's good. We've got it." He walked downstage and sat on the edge as the band milled around behind him. Out in the massive showroom, he could see Fred and Theoni with their heads bent together. They looked serious and intense. As usual.

Al, his drummer, sat beside him. "You think the sound's okay with Swizzle?"

"Yeah, don't you?"

Al, a tall, thin guy with red hair, nodded. "I like him a lot. He brings great performance value."

Jerry nodded. "Just in time for us to end the tour."

"I never got to tell you, I really like your house."

Jerry wanted to frown, but he didn't. "Thanks."

"You going back there after we close in Vegas?"

"Probably."

He barked a laugh. "You sure you're going to like living someplace where the most exciting thing that happens is a performance of William Shakespeare?"

Jerry sighed softly. "We'll see." He liked Al and all of the band members, but he hadn't chosen them. They weren't like the Beatles or Queen. Fred picked musicians as they needed them for their tours, and the players changed as schedules and music changed. Jerry—no, Jet—wrote everything and was the draw. The guys were backup.

Jerry hopped off the stage, grabbed a sweatshirt to keep his muscles warm, and walked up the aisle toward Fred and Theoni. "Hey, guys, I'm starved. Let's eat."

Theoni glanced at Fred kind of nervously.

Fred said, "Why don't I go get takeout?"

Jerry glanced back and forth between them. "Why? I like the restaurant in the hotel."

"No point in doing all the autograph seekers and lookie-loos when you have to perform tonight."

Jerry frowned. Fred always wanted to see and be seen. "I'm going." He started up the aisle. Fred and Theoni scrambled to get beside him. Fred waved a hand at the two giant humans he'd hired to be Jerry's bodyguards in Vegas, and they hurried over to join the parade.

Jerry looked at Fred as they walked. "What's going on?" He hit the double doors at the top of the aisle and pushed out into the huge lobby of the giant showroom and—

At least a hundred reporters pushed toward him with cameras, microphones, and notebooks poised.

"Jet, Jet. What about the underage girlfriend?"

"Is that why you've never gotten married? Do you like them young and sweet?"

"What about the guy? Why were you hugging a man?"

"Jet, are you gay or straight?"

Jerry fell against the doors, and the bodyguards flanked him, pushing him back into the relative quiet of the massive auditorium.

Jerry just stood there, processing.

Fred said, "Those fuckers, they just won't leave you alone. Let's get someone to go for food, and you can rest in your—"

Jerry clenched his teeth but got the words out between them. "What the fuck is going on?"

"It's just more of the same old crap, Jet. Don't worry." Fred grabbed Jerry's arm.

Jerry ripped his arm away. "If you expect me to perform tonight, somebody better start talking."

Theoni shot Fred a vicious look and touched Jerry's arm. "Come on, honey, I'll tell you."

She led him to a quiet part of the auditorium. Fred tried to tag along, but she shook her head. Jerry's stomach was tied in knots before he even sat down.

When he and Theoni were finally face-to-face, she said, "I guess Fred and the band came to Ashland and found you, right?"

"Yes."

"Apparently a couple paparazzi followed them. They took pictures of you with your friends, the man and the girl."

A sour taste rose up the back of Jerry's throat. "Show me."

She did.

"I'm assuming she's not your girlfriend."

"She's the daughter of the guy who's renovating my fucking house." He clenched his fists. "She's seventeen years old, Theoni. What the fucking hell are these vultures thinking?"

"You're news, Jet. They're going to make it any way they can. I'll have the lawyers on the publication in an hour. We'll get them to print a retraction."

"As if that will do any good." He leaned back in the chair, trying to get enough air in his lungs to scream. He snapped his fingers. "Where's my phone?" He never carried it onstage since he'd broken about five phones crashing them to the floor as he danced.

"Fred has it, I think."

"Fred! Give me my damned phone."

Fred rushed over, pulling the phone from his jeans pocket as he came. He stopped a few feet away. "Who are you calling?"

Jerry jumped out of his seat. "When that becomes your business, I'll have it published in the fucking *Enquirer*. Give me the phone now!"

Fred fumbled the device but managed to get it into Jerry's hands. He flipped it on. Missed call from Gabe.

Jerry hit return call. It rang, rang, rang, and went to voicemail. "Shit. Shit!" He pressed a hand against his chest and glared at Fred. "If you'd left me alone, if you'd never come to Ashland, they'd never have found me and this would never have happened. My friends—"

Fred seemed to snap. "Come on, Jerry, I'm sick of this mealymouthed crap. You wanted to be a big star, and I made you one. What do you think? You can start hanging out with some retail clerk and that's not going to be news? For fuck sake, it's better if they think you like the girl. Get your head out of your ass, sell that stupid house, and get back to San Francisco where you can be protected. Beyond that, I don't want to hear about it. Something of your own? For Christ's sake, this is all yours. You made it. Own it." He turned and stalked out of the showroom.

Jerry stared after him. He knew truth when he heard it.

GABE HELD the phone in one hand and embraced Ellie with the other. "For God's sake, Tiffany. You know damned well those stories aren't true. Some idiot photographer shot some pictures of Ellie and Jerry having fun and gave them a smarmy interpretation."

"It doesn't matter if it's true or not. That's not what—you know what I mean. As long as you're associating with immoral people, I can't let you have any say in Ellie's life or future."

"Jerry's not even close to immoral. He's a kind, gentle man who treats Ellie like his own daughter."

"Oh, right. I've seen him prancing around the stage."

"Listen to yourself. There was a time you would have loved Jet Gemini. Do I have to remind you that I could have gotten sole custody of Ellie when you were going through your ugly second marriage, but I had faith you'd pull out of it, and I wanted you to have a relationship with your daughter? We've always been a team, Tiffany."

She paused, and he could hear her breathing. Then there was a muffled voice in the background. Tiffany seemed to take her finger off the microphone. "I'm sorry, Gabe. This kind of pornography is inexcusable. I'm calling for an emergency hearing tomorrow." She hung up.

Gabe stared at the phone, then dialed his lawyer, a friend of a friend from work who hadn't charged much mostly because he didn't do that much. "Hey, Mitch. It's Gabe."

The lawyer laughed. "I figured I'd be hearing from you."

Gabe scowled. "What does that mean?"

"I saw the stories. Holy crap, how'd you ever meet Jet Gemini? Did he see Ellie and call you for a date with her?"

Gabe hung up the phone.

Ellie asked, "What did he say?"

"Not a good time to talk." He glanced at his phone. "I missed a call from Jerry."

She sat up. "Call him back."

Gabe tried to keep his hands from shaking as he hit the return. Just like last time, it rang three times and went to a nondescript voicemail. He hung up, pressure so intense in his chest he couldn't believe his heart was still beating.

"No answer?" Ellie's eyes were big.

"No."

She pointed at the time on the phone. "No wonder. Jet's practically on stage. Turn on the TV. They're showing it live."

He wished he could say he didn't want to see any Jet Gemini concert, but that would be a bigger lie than the one he told himself about how content he was with his life.

He flipped on NBC. The view of the huge Las Vegas showroom packed with fans gave way to a shot of the host, the late-night guy Bobby Breeson, who welcomed everyone and told them how important the concert was and all the charities it helped. The cameras cut to a phone bank where a lot of big-name actors and ball players were answering calls and giving thumbs-ups as the donation chart climbed in the background.

A famous comedian came on, and Gabe and Ellie stared at the screen without laughing until finally Breeson said, "And now, the guy you've been waiting for. Ladies and gentlemen, Jet Gemini."

The stage went up in sparks and flares, the throbbing beat of the same anthem he'd started with in Eugene began playing, and Jet made his grand entrance.

He was astonishing. His charisma ate the screen, and it was like his talent blasted the doors off the showroom to fill the world beyond. Gabe felt himself shaking his head.

Ellie must have had the exact same thought. "Who'd ever believe that god even knows us?"

"Yeah."

After a few commercials and breaks to show the climbing donation chart, the MC said, "Jet says he has something special for us, so show him how excited we all are by pumping up the donations even more."

Jet walked onto the stage, took the microphone, and started reading off the names of people who were donating. The phones went wacko as people tried to hear their names read on TV by Jet Gemini.

When the donation chart leaped to another milestone, Jet said, "Thank you for your amazing generosity. As promised, I want to share something—a little different." He raised his face to the light, and it shone off his mane of hair and those cheekbones like cut glass. "I want to dedicate this to a dear friend who I hope won't mind my telling you she is like a little sister to me. Or in my heart, more like a daughter."

Ellie caught her breath.

Jet said, "Anyone who tells you anything different is lying through their teeth. This is for Ellie."

He strode across the stage in his skintight jeans, vest, and bare flesh, sat at the piano, and began to play.

Ellie sobbed as the strains of Franz Liszt filled the showroom. The cameras cut to people in the audience pressing hands to their mouths in astonishment. A couple of minutes into the piece, which Ellie assured Gabe was one of the hardest in the world to play, Jerry stopped, stood, and bowed. The place erupted.

His face serene, he strolled down to the microphone in a single spotlight. "I know I usually sing my own music, but sometimes another songwriter has better words. So I'd like to share a song that was written by Meredith Wilson, was covered by the Beatles, and now says the words I want to say. The song's called 'Till There Was You,' and it's for Gabe."

This time, Ellie held on to Gabe as he wiped tears from his cheeks and watched Jerry stand at the microphone and sing about how he hadn't known there was love all around—*until there was you.*

As the credits for the show rolled, Ellie whispered, "Jet Gemini sang you a love song."

Gabe shook his head. "But it doesn't change anything."

"He came out on TV!"

Gabe wiped at his face. "Not really. Come on. His PR people will invent some supermodel named Gabriella and claim he was singing to her. And even if the press knew about me, what would they print about the rock star and the home-improvement clerk? Seriously."

"Do you really care what people think if you can have the guy you love?"

He gazed at her. Reality check from his seventeen-year-old. His phone buzzed in his pocket, and he grabbed for it.

Ellie squealed, "Jerry!"

Gabe glanced at the phone and frowned. "It's your mom." He looked at Ellie. And clicked the phone. "Tiffany, you okay?"

"Will—will you come and get me?" She was crying.

"Where are you? I'm there."

"In front of Irving's."

He covered the phone. "You know how to get to where your mom lives?"

Ellie nodded.

"We're coming. Are you safe?"

"I don't know. I left."

Gabe grabbed his car keys from the overstuffed cabinet by the front door as Ellie pulled her jacket from the closet. Gabe said, "Here, talk to Ellie while I drive."

CHAPTER TWENTY-TWO

JERRY STOOD offstage and watched as the charity drive barometer climbed over its wildest predictions, the audience applauded their hands off, and Bobby Breeson said, "Jet will be my guest on the *Late Night Show* tonight, and I promise to ask him all the questions on your minds, so tune in." He glanced offstage and grinned at Jerry.

Swigging a water, Jerry took off for his dressing room. The hotel had let Bobby set up his show in their smaller theater, and a live audience was being gathered to add the applause.

Fred fell in beside Jerry, with Theoni rushing in her high heels to catch up. Fred said, "What the hell was that all about?"

"If you couldn't tell, I must have been doing it wrong."

"Come on, bro. In some kind of fit of God knows what, you're liable to do shit you'll regret. Let's sit for a few minutes and strategize what you're going to say on Breeson's show."

Jerry got to the dressing-room door. "That's exactly what I plan to do. Thanks." He walked inside and closed the door in Fred's face.

Quickly, he crossed to the makeup table and checked his phone. A missed call from Gabe. Jerry punched the Callback button.

It rang once and instantly was answered. There was rustling and bumping.

Jerry said, "Hello? Gabe?"

A breathless female voice whispered, "Jerry?"

"Ellie, hi. Where's your dad?"

"He's driving. We saw your show. It was amazing, but it's been a hard day around here."

"Jesus, I'll bet. I'm so sorry. I didn't know anything about the photos or what was going on until it was almost time for my show. I tried to call but didn't get an answer."

"That's because my dad was on the phone with my mom. She and her idiot fiancé were talking about taking Dad to court to try to get full custody of me." She sounded pissed.

"Wait. Are you saying this has something to do with the photos?"

"Yes. They were claiming child endangerment. But now my mom's left her fiancé, or at least she's waiting on the curb, so maybe she's changed her mind. We're on our way to get her."

"Wait. To get her. Where's the fiancé?"

"We're not sure. That's why we're hurrying. Trust me, he's not a nice guy. I've got to get back to my mom, Jerry. She's on the other line."

"Call me and tell me what's happening." His stomach clenched. "And don't worry. Sometimes there are real good reasons to have a lot of money, and hiring the best lawyers is one of them."

She snorted. "Can I be defended by Gloria Allred?"

"We'll have to see if Gloria's available."

"Gotta go. I hope we're home in time to see you on Bobby Breeson's."

"I hope so too. Love you."

She gave a soft little gasp. "Oh. Love you too."

He hung up and held the phone to his forehead for a second. *Look at the mess you've made. Time to unmess it.*

He glanced at the clock and sprang into action. In record time, he took a shower, washed his sweaty hair, and then stared at his reflection in the bathroom mirror, wet locks hanging past his shoulder blades.

Own it. That's what Fred had said. Every action produces a reaction. Even choosing not to act was a decision with consequences. He said he wanted something of his own, but Fred was right. This was all his. He created it, and he could recreate it.

He sat down at the makeup table.

GABE HAD been driving about fifteen minutes when Ellie waved toward a townhouse on the right. "That's Irving's place."

He slowed and pulled over to the curb, but no Tiffany. "Do you think she changed her mind?"

Suddenly, a figure dressed in what looked like pajamas came running from between the two-story units. Ellie said, "That's Mom." She opened her door, but as Tiffany ran toward the truck, the front door of one of the townhouses opened, and Irving staggered out.

"Get back in here, you bitch."

Gabe threw open the driver's door and was on the lawn before Tiffany even made it to the truck. He caught her. "You okay?"

She nodded. "Everything—all my clothes and everything are in th-there."

"Don't worry. We'll get them later. As long as you're safe."

Irving ran across the lawn and stopped a few feet from Gabe. "Let go of her, you slimy pervert."

Gabe raised an eyebrow. "Or what, asshole? I'll go to hell? Get in the truck, Tif."

Irving made a grab for her arm, and Gabe pulled her behind him. Irving snarled, "Tiffany, do as I say. You know you can't leave your precious child with this despicable person, and the courts will see it our way. She belongs in a godly household, being trained in the ways of divine love."

Gabe stepped forward and Irving's eyes widened. Gabe spoke, low and dangerous. "You come anywhere near my daughter and you'll be meeting divine love face-to-face. Clear?" Irving stared at him with hate. Gabe said, "Tomorrow, I'm coming back here to get Tiffany's belongings. If one thing's missing or damaged, I'll have you in court for the rest of your life." He glanced over his shoulder to see Ellie helping Tiffany into the truck.

Irving snarled, "If you come back here, I'll have the cops waiting."

Gabe stared at him. "Be my guest. I'm done caring about people like you." He turned, walked to the truck, and climbed in. "Are we ready to go home?"

Ellie smiled and hugged her mom in the back seat as they drove away.

After a couple of quiet minutes, Tiffany said, "I'm so sorry. I thought Irving was a good man. He seemed so holy and pure. But then I realized it was a mask he wears to hide the hate. I'm sorry I ever let him near you, Ellie."

Ellie hugged her tighter.

Tiffany murmured, "If I wanted to know what a good man was like, all I ever had to do was look at your dad." She dozed on Ellie's shoulder all the way home.

When they pulled into the driveway, Gabe's phone rang. Ellie was still holding it, so she answered as Gabe helped Tiffany out of the car.

"Hey, Jerry." She smiled. "Yep, he managed it like a superhero." Giggling, she said, "Captain America. Right." After listening for a minute, she nodded. "Oh, okay. We'll be watching." She hung up.

Gabe shot her a look, and she shrugged. "He says he has to go be a rock star one last time."

"What?"

She raised her brows. "No clue."

Fifteen minutes later, Tiffany had her head on Ellie's lap on the couch because she refused to go to bed until she saw Jet Gemini. Gabe was sitting on the ratty chair with butterflies the size of eagles soaring through his stomach.

Ellie was holding forth to Tiffany. "You should have seen it, Mom. Here's the biggest rock star in the world singing about how there weren't any birds singing until he met Dad. On TV!"

Tiffany looked at him wide-eyed, and his cheeks heated. Oh for God's sake, he didn't blush.

Tiffany asked, "How do you feel about him, Gabe?"

He cleared his throat. "I like him a lot. He's a good man. But we live in really different worlds."

"Oh, Dad." Ellie frowned at him. "He cares about you, and you feel the same way. The rest is just logistics."

"I do care for him, but I can't picture my life as a rock-star groupie."

On the television, the intro for Bobby Breeson came on. He did his opening monologue, making reference to the TV special, and then promoted Jerry's appearance.

Ellie transferred her mom's head to a pillow and went to the kitchen to get them all oatmeal raisin cookies.

Tiffany sat up and said more seriously, "Those stories about Ellie were pretty awful."

"I know. I'm really sorry—" He stopped and looked at her. "You know what, I'm not sorry. All we did was go for a swim at the home of a nice person who's actually a very good influence on Ellie. He's a great musician, and she has fun with him. The rest was made up in the minds of stupid, small people. My daughter told me something right before we came to get you. You can't spend your life worried about what others will think—"

Ellie balanced a plate of cookies as she said, "Because you may miss out on the best stuff."

Tiffany nodded. "You're right." She wiped the edge of her finger under her eyes. "I've missed out on some good stuff with you, baby, and I'm sorry."

Ellie gave her mom a one-armed hug and grabbed the remote and turned up the volume with the other hand.

Bobby Breeson said, "And now the man of the hour, to answer all our most pressing questions. Here's Jet Gemini."

The curtain opened, and Gabe and Ellie both gasped so loud they could actually hear it over the gasps of the audience on TV. Jet walked onto the stage in a beautiful, perfectly tailored light-gray suit with his hair slicked back from his face. His hair, however, stopped just below his ears. He'd cut the most famous hair in show business.

Tiffany said, "Oh my God, he's so handsome."

Ellie crowed, "Told ya."

Bobby stood and shook Jerry's hand. "You saw it here first, folks. Jet Gemini has cut his hair." Bobby gestured for Jerry to sit on the couch. "So we can't ask one thing until we know why you decided to take this drastic step."

Jerry smiled. "Do you remember that old Melanie Griffith movie called *Working Girl*?"

"Yeah. Kind of."

"She says to her friend—" He adopted a perfect, breathy Melanie voice, and Gabe and Ellie repeated it with him. "—if you want to be taken seriously, you've got to have serious hair."

Gabe and Ellie looked at each other and laughed. Ellie said, "I can't believe he cut it."

Bobby leaned across his desk. "So you want to be taken seriously? I'd think a closetful of Grammys and an Oscar or two would be pretty damned serious, Jet."

"I appreciate every one of those awards, but I have things I want to do in my life that I haven't done, and I need to get on with them."

"Okay, this is news. Tell us what?"

He looked out at the audience with a shy smile that was way more Jerry than Jet. "I'd like to extend my skills as a classical pianist, and I'd like to teach music." The audience burst into applause.

"That is news. But then you really gave us a preview in your concert tonight. How will you fit these new enterprises in?"

"By quitting touring."

The audience buzzed. Gabe swallowed hard and looked at Ellie.

Jerry said, "I plan to write music and record if people still want to hear me, but no more time on the road."

"Your fans will be disappointed."

He nodded. "Other stars will take my place."

Ellie covered her mouth for a moment, then said, "He's giving it up, Dad."

"What?"

"No star ever wants another to replace them."

Jerry leaned back in his seat. "I've been a performer since I was fourteen, and the fans have been kind to me, but now I want to have a home and family." He grinned. "A real home. Not a rock-star home."

Ellie whispered, "Daddy."

Gabe moved from the chair and sat beside Ellie as she clutched his arm.

Bobby was looking around like he'd scored the interview of the century. "Uh, does the person you dedicated your song to at the concert have something to do with this?"

That soft smile came over his face again. "Yes." Then he got serious. "For a long time, there have been rumors that I'm gay. I've never denied them, but I also didn't confirm. I didn't have a reason. But now I'm in love and want to get married, if he'll have me. I guess I should say *they*, because his daughter also has to want to be my daughter."

Ellie bounced in her seat but said nothing. Gabe couldn't say anything. There wasn't room in his throat for his heart *and* his words.

Jerry went on, "If they do want me, I plan to settle down and write and teach and watch my husband build the world's most beautiful furniture."

Tiffany gawked. "Oh my God, Gabe."

Bobby said, "Did you just come out, Jet?"

"If you don't know, you weren't paying attention." He grinned.

"And did we just hear your marriage proposal?"

"Yes." He looked at the camera. "I don't want any more rumors or crap flying around about me and the people I love. I'm gay. I'm in love with a man. His beautiful daughter is, I hope, going to be *my daughter*. I intend that this be the last piece of newsworthy controversy my personal life ever generates."

"You're stealing the thunder from the gossip rags?"

"Yes." His beautiful face got stern. "I realized that as long as I give people cause for rumors and gossip, then it's my fault, not theirs, if they spread it. But I'm out of the gossip business. I plan to live a boring, happy life."

"I've got to ask, Jet. What if people say you quit touring because fans won't come see a gay rock star?"

Before their eyes, Jerry transformed into Jet. He tossed his head and waved a graceful hand. "Don't be silly, darling. They've been coming to see a gay rock star for twelve years."

This time, the audience went totally apeshit. Ellie was jumping up and down beside him, but Gabe was way back there, stuck on *I'm in love and want to get married, if he'll have me.*

On the TV, Bobby said, "Jet, if he'll have you, where are you going to have your wedding?"

"At a place that has great meaning for both of us."

GABE PRESSED the circular saw across the piece of lumber, breathing in the sweet scent of cut wood. *Soothing.* He wore safety goggles and earplugs, plus he was hiding out in the back corner of the store. There were a few reporters wandering around the place, but apparently knowing he was the one Jet Gemini wanted to marry, rather than an underage girl, and the fact that nobody was trying to hide anything made the story a lot less juicy and the photographers more polite. Just as Jerry thought.

Jerry had called after the show, but he'd been surrounded by reporters and his own entourage. He said he had a lot of 'splainin' to do.

Gabe, of course, had Ellie and Tiffany gazing at him as he spoke to Jerry, which didn't encourage candor. Still, when Jerry closed the call by saying, "I love you," Gabe about hyperventilated and managed to say, "Me too."

The saw vibrated comfortably in his hand as he got to the end of the two-by. He flipped off the machine, and Harry waved a hand to get his attention.

"Hey, my man, are you supposed to be here?"

Gabe glanced around. "I told Alejandro I'd do lumber today."

"I don't mean that."

"It's Tuesday. Why wouldn't I be here?"

"Because, uh, you're marrying a rock star?" He threw his hands up toward the ceiling.

Gabe cocked a half smile. "Chop wood, carry water, my friend. Jerry may be a rock star. I work at ImproveMart."

"Can I quote you on that, Gabe?" It was the female reporter who'd confronted him with the story two days before. She was standing a few feet away, phone in hand.

Gabe stared at her and then smiled. "Sure."

"So how do you feel about getting the world's most romantic marriage proposal?"

Gabe gave her a sideways look. "If I can quote my daughter, 'Duh.'"

Her voice took on a little edge. "And how about getting the world's biggest rock star to lay down his stardom and his life for you?"

The sweet voice came from behind her. "I didn't lay down my stardom for Gabe, dear. I laid down my stardom for me, and I'm hoping Gabe will share my life."

Gabe spun to see Jerry, with his new hair better cut than it had been the night before, wearing slim jeans but a pretty baggy sweatshirt. It was his Jerry. No cap, but also no bodyguards. Heat flooded Gabe's chest until it invaded his head and pressed against the back of his eyes. Was it worth it to give up his carefully structured and planned life to be with Jerry? *Oh hell yes.*

He walked slowly toward the most beautiful man he'd ever seen—weird and wonderful. "Excuse me, sir, can I help you find some drawer pulls?"

Jerry smiled. "Yes, please. And will you bring them to my house and make a home with me and stay with me forever and ever?"

Gabe cocked his head. "Do you think we can make it work?"

"Darling, we already do."

Gabe didn't even care how many pictures were taken of them kissing.

CHAPTER TWENTY-THREE

Six months later—

"GABE, TIME to get ready."

Gabe looked up from the fine sanding he was doing on the new credenza for the Massachusetts order. He smiled at Jerry and waved at Alex, one of his two apprentices, to take over the work he was doing.

Alex walked over and gave him a grin. "See you in a couple hours, boss."

Gabe sucked in a breath, and it was shaky. "Yeah, you will. Unless I get cold feet and decide to elope."

Alex patted his shoulder, laughing, and Gabe strolled over to Jerry, his soon-to-be husband, and gave him a soft, short kiss.

Jerry said, "You ready?"

"As I'll ever be."

Jerry chuckled. "Come on, we've got to get you in practice for the Grammys."

"At the Grammys I won't be half the center of attention. You'll be all of it." He kissed his nose. "Where's Ellie?"

"She's over at her mom's. I guess they wanted to dress together. More of a surprise."

Gabe had given Tiffany his house in Talent when he and Ellie moved to Ashland with Jerry.

They walked out of the big building beside the driveway that had been turned into Gabe's furniture studio and business. They wandered in through the garage past Jerry's music studio that now occupied the room in the house they still called the "new space."

Up in their bedroom with all the light flowing in from three walls and the breathtaking view of the mountains, Jerry pulled Gabe into the huge new tub that had been built in the expanded master bath. Jerry leaned back against Gabe's chest, and they quietly caressed each other.

Gabe said, "I think we should enjoy this peace and quiet, because the house may not be this empty ever again until we're ninety."

Jerry laughed.

"Great idea not having the wedding here."

Jerry kissed his hand. "This house is ours. I didn't want to share with quite that many people."

They kissed until the preparation time got extended a little longer than planned.

An hour later, they arrived in the garage fully dressed in tuxedos. Jerry adjusted Gabe's tie. "Are you okay that we didn't get married in jeans and flannel shirts?"

Gabe gave an exaggerated sigh. "Ellie would have disowned me as a father."

"Come on, you gorgeous hunk. Let's do this and get on with being boring."

They drove in Jerry's Prius until they saw the huge banner over the entrance to the parking lot. *Closed today for special event.*

They pulled into the parking space reserved for them near the huge tents that had been set up for the reception. Music was already coming from behind the canvas, and people were milling about—an amalgam of Gabe's friends, Jerry's friends and colleagues, and people neither of them knew who'd been invited by Theoni—like the governor and half the world's entertainment press. By inviting everyone, Theoni had posited that the reporters would mostly leave the house alone. So far, so good.

As they got out of the car, Ellie walked up in a long yellow gown. Jerry raised a hand to his forehead. "I'm dying. You're gorgeous."

"You too, there, rock god." They hugged, and Gabe smiled. If he'd picked from the whole world, he couldn't have found a better stepdad for Ellie than Jerry.

She said, "They're ready for us."

"Okay. Let's do this thing." Jerry squeezed Gabe's hand, and with Ellie leading them, they marched toward the huge warehouse building. Across the sign that usually said ImproveMart was a banner that read—

Wedding. Aisle Sixteen.

As they walked through the front door of the building, phones clicked, news cameras whirred, and the Jet Gemini band broke into a newly arranged version of "Till There Was You."

Hand in hand, with Ellie leading the way, Gabe and Jerry marched down the aisle.

SEVERAL HOURS later, they pulled the Prius into the driveway at their house on Mountain Avenue. Ellie was spending the night with Tiffany, and they'd managed to convince everyone else that they were leaving for a several-day honeymoon in San Francisco.

The house was quiet.

Gabe said, "I'm going to leave the car here for a little while."

"Are you going back out?"

"No. Just wanted to enjoy the moonlight."

As he helped Jerry out of the car, lights went on behind them. Jerry looked up and pressed a hand to his mouth.

The tall, torii-style gate stood outlined against the glow from the front yard.

Gabe took Jerry's hand, and they walked under it onto the new stone path. Lights in bushes shone on the tall trees and illuminated the colors of the fall flowers nestled around big stones that defined the walk. Defined was the word.

Jerry said it. "For the first time, I know where to walk and it's easy to find the front door. It's amazing and so beautiful. Only you understood how important this is."

Gabe stopped and took Jerry into his arms. "I love you, husband."

"And I love you."

Gabe pointed at the walkway wandering through the trees and shrubs with the sound of a waterfall dripping into a pond ahead of them. Just beyond were the wide, inviting front porch and the new, brilliant red front door. He kissed Jerry gently. "It took both of us to find our way home."

TARA LAIN believes in happy ever afters—and magic. Same thing. In fact, she says, she doesn't believe, she knows. Tara shares this passion in her stories, which star her unique, charismatic heroes and adventurous heroines. Quarterbacks and cops, werewolves and witches, blue collar or billionaires, Tara's characters, readers say, love deeply, resolve seemingly insurmountable differences, and ultimately live their lives authentically. After many years living in southern California, Tara, her soulmate honey, and her soulmate dog decided they wanted fewer cars and more trees, prompting a move to Ashland, Oregon, where Tara's creating new stories and loving living in a small town with big culture. Likely a Gryffindor but possessed of Parseltongue, Tara loves animals of all kinds, diversity, open minds, coconut crunch ice cream from Zooeys, and her readers. She also loves to hear from you.

Email: tara@taralain.com
Website: www.taralain.com
Blog: www.taralain.com/blog
Goodreads: www.goodreads.com/author/show/4541791.Tara_Lain
Pinterest: pinterest.com/taralain/
Twitter: twitter.com/taralain
Facebook: www.facebook.com/taralain
Tara Lain's Beautiful Dream Reader Group: www.facebook.com/groups/255111391312743
Barnes & Noble: www.barnesandnoble.com/s/Tara-Lain?keyword=Tara+Lain&store=book
Amazon: www.amazon.com/Tara-Lain/e/B004U1W5QC/ref=ntt_athr_dp_pel_1

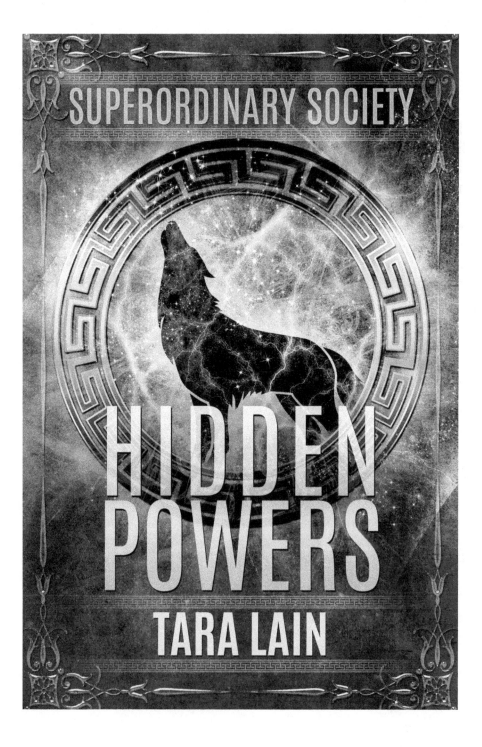

SUPERORDINARY SOCIETY

HIDDEN POWERS

TARA LAIN

Superordinary Society: Book One

Jazz Vanessen is weird—and not just because he's a werewolf. For most of his life, he's felt different from his alpha male brothers and friends. Since he's adopted, he can't even blame it on family.

Now eighteen, Jazz meets his idol, the social activist Lysandra Mason, and her breathtaking nephew, Dash Mercury. When Dash is around, even stranger things start to happen, including Jazz falling hopelessly in lust. Not only is Jazz having visions, making people disappear, and somehow turning invisible, but somebody's following him and threatening to reveal his pack's secrets to the world.

Together with Dash and Jazz's equally amazing friends—Carla, BeBop, Khadija, and Fatima—they discover the danger is even more lethal than they thought, and Jazz's weirdness may save all their lives.

www.dreamspinnerpress.com

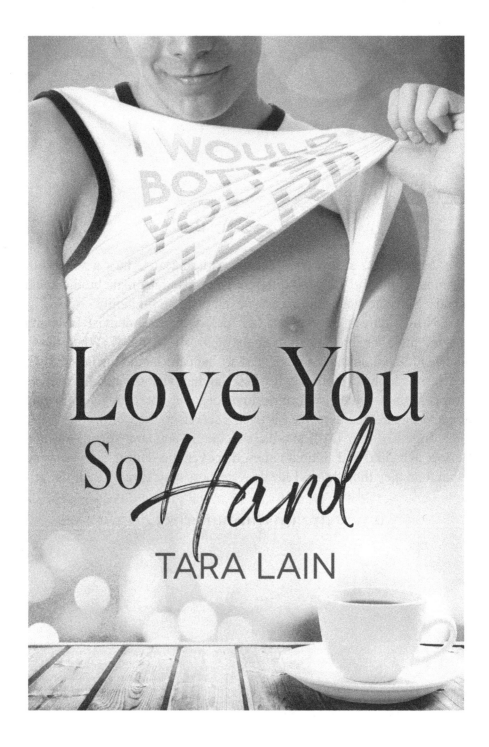

Love You So Hard

TARA LAIN

A Love You So Story

Craig Elson's life has hit rock bottom. Even though he's one of the best strategic planners around, a more confident guy takes credit for his work, and despite being a good-looking man, he suffers insults from the slimiest creep at the bar. Taking care of his beloved mom, who has Alzheimer's, uses all his funds, leaving him in a plain, depressing car... and a plain, depressing life.

Until he sees gorgeous grad student Jesse Randall and his T-shirt that reads "I Would Bottom You So Hard." The message seeps into Craig's soul, and he asks Jesse to teach him to top.

Jesse's had his eye on the quiet hottie who comes into the coffee shop, and he's more than eager to perfect his tutoring. He sets out to get Craig a new job, a new apartment, and a new life so far outside plain and depressing that it's unrecognizable. The problem is, Craig loves his lessons—and his teacher—too much to want to graduate. How can Craig reach the top without losing his sassy bottom?

www.dreamspinnerpress.com

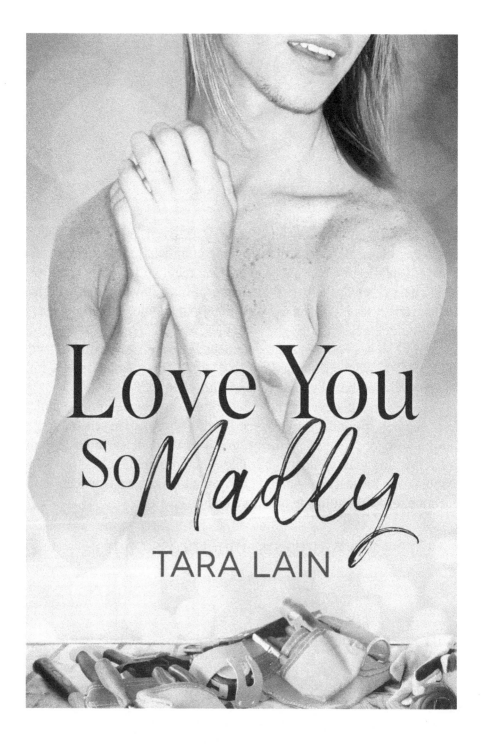

Love You So Madly

TARA LAIN

A Love You So Story

Ben Shane has it all… and he'd like to give some of it back. While he loves his job heading a foundation that funds worthy causes around the world, his engagement to one of America's wealthiest men leaves him feeling more like a trophy wife than a valued partner. The first warning that his relationship might not be designed to last is his irresistible lust for Dusty Kincaid, the golden-haired, bright-eyed handyman for his company.

Though Dusty is odd for a twenty-three-year-old—no liquor, no sugar, and he can't even drive—the more Ben gets to know Dusty, the more he admires him. But is Ben going to give up a guy who drives a Ferrari for one who takes the bus? He must be mad. Dusty knows he and Ben can never work. After all, Ben's perfect… and Dusty isn't. But Ben might surprise everyone with proof that he's only mad in love.

www.dreamspinnerpress.com

TARA
LAIN

THE
CASE OF THE SEXY
SHAKESPEAREAN

A Middlemark Mystery

Dr. Llewellyn Lewis leads a double life, as both an awkward but distinguished history professor and the more flamboyant Ramon Rondell, infamous writer of sensational historical theories. It's Ramon who first sets eyes on a gorgeous young man dancing in a club, but Llewellyn who meets teaching assistant Blaise Arthur formally at an event held for wealthy socialite Anne de Vere, descendant of Edward de Vere, seventeenth Earl of Oxford—who some believe was the real Shakespeare. Anne wants Llewellyn to prove that claim, even though many have tried and failed. And she's willing to offer a hefty donation to the university if he succeeds.

It also means a chance for Llewellyn to get to know Blaise much better.

Not everyone thinks Llewellyn should take the case—or the money. Between feuding siblings, rival patrons, jealous colleagues, and greedy administrators, almost anyone could be trying to thwart his work… and one of them is willing to kill to do it.

When Anne de Vere turns up dead, the police believe Blaise is the murderer. Only the shy, stuttering professor who has won his heart can prove otherwise….

www.dreamspinnerpress.com

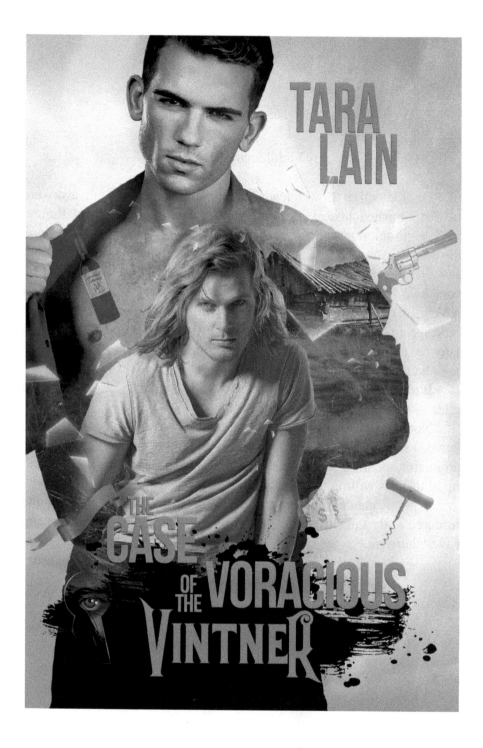

A Middlemark Mystery

Where Bo Marchand comes from, gay men are just confirmed bachelors who never found the right girl. But now Bo's a successful winemaker on the central coast of California, supporting his whole damned Georgia family, and all he really wants is the beautiful, slightly mysterious Jeremy Aames.

Jeremy's vineyard is under threat from Ernest Ottersen, the voracious winemaker who seems to know all Jeremy's blending secrets and manages to grab all his customers. Bo tries to help Jeremy and even provides a phony alibi for Jeremy when Ottersen turns up dead in Jeremy's tasting room. But it's clear Jeremy isn't who he claims, and Bo must decide if it's worth tossing over his established life for a man who doesn't seem to trust anyone. When Jeremy gets kidnapped, some of the conservative winemakers turn out to be kinky sex fiends, and the list of murderers keeps dwindling down to Jeremy. Bo has to choose between hopping on his white horse or climbing back in his peach-pie-lined closet.

www.dreamspinnerpress.com